Robert Graham grew up [...]
Manchester. He teaches [...] writing at Manchester
Metropolitan University, Cheshire. His short stories have
appeared in numerous magazines and anthologies, as well as
featuring on Radio 4's short story slot. He is co-author and
co-editor of *The Road to Somewhere: A Creative Writing
Companion* (Palgrave, 2005) and is currently at work on *How to
Write Fiction (And Think About it)*. He is co-author, with Keith
Baty, of the spoof biography *Elvis – The Novel* (The Do Not
Press, 1997) and over a dozen of his plays have been staged by
youth theatres.

Robert Graham

Holy Joe

Troubador Publishing
9 De Montfort Mews,
Leicester LE1 7FW, UK
Tel: (+44) 116 2555 9311
Email: books@troubador.co.uk
Web: www.troubador.co.uk

ISBN 1 904744 82 6

Cover design: Andy Butler
Photography: Sarah Jones

Typesetting: Troubador Publishing Ltd, Leicester, UK
Printed in the UK by the Cromwell Press Ltd, Trowbridge, Wilts, UK

t² is an imprint of Troubador Publishing Ltd

for Laura Iris Graham

It's 1997
(I May Never Get To Heaven)

I'm not an adult, although my wife is. I know I should be, and I can think of ways in which I haven't been able to avoid it, but for the most part I keep ducking the business of being a grown-up. And when it comes to being venal and immature, my instincts are right on the money.

Take the IRA bomb which blew up our city centre: the Royal Exchange building is out of commission, half the Arndale is destroyed and hundreds, maybe thousands, of jobs have been lost. But what bothers me most about this outrage is that my favourite café has been shut down. There is now nowhere in Manchester where I can go for a near-perfect *cappuccino*.

My name is Joe Porter, I'm thirty-five years old and I'm a freelance IT consultant. I make websites for people and give in-service training courses. My name is Joe Porter, I'm thirty-five years old and although I have been a friend of Jesus for some years, I have a list the length, if not of my arm, then at least of my hand, of things that matter way too much to me. Cafés, yes, because a good cup of coffee is hard to find, but also pretty women, (walking down the street - or sitting still, or speaking, or smiling, and the rest), record shops, cinemas, novels, smoking, achieving, acquiring. All of these and more, and not especially in that order. If I ever get to heaven, I have a feeling that most of the things I care about won't be there. My priorities are askew, I admit. But I suspect other men may be like me.

It's a new year, 1997 (I may never get to heaven).

Nobody but Batman is downstairs when I come back from Safeway with fruit for a fruit salad, single cream and a gift – red spray carnations in cellophane. He looks at me, sends a ripple up his tail and goes, 'Mip.' I can hear Molly's voice upstairs.

'Anybody ready yet?' I call up the stairs.

'Can't hear you,' Sarah shouts back.

'We're *late*,' I boom. 'If we alarm the house and walk out the front door right this minute we'll arrive with Naomi quarter of an hour *late*.'

'Sorry! Can't hear you.'

I notice the stains Molly's greasy fingers have made on the thighs of my favourite chinos: stains that won't wash out. This reminds me that I'm unable to replace them because Gap has not re-opened since the IRA bomb. When I look up again from the trauma of my chinos, my children have appeared. Martha is sitting at the kitchen table, nose-down in her Stanley Bagshaw. Molly is pushing a teddy around the room in her toy buggy.

My kids make me happy, even when they sometimes ruin my clothes or ask me questions nobody could answer, and so I find, a few moments later, I have begun singing 'You Got A Friend In Me', from *Toy Story*. Martha and I often sing it together, a few lines of it anyway.

'What song is that, Daddy?' Molly asks, cutting me off before the punch line.

'Come on, Molly. You know where it comes from.'

Martha giggles enthusiastically. There's nothing she enjoys more than her sister's ignorance or foolishness. 'She's a Silly Billy, isn't she Daddy?' And she joins me as I go into the chorus, so that we are telling one other we've got a friend in each other.

'*Om Beyond!*' Molly shrieks. 'It's *Om Beyond*.'

'Actually, it's "To infinity and beyond", silly,' Martha says. 'And anyway, the film is called *Toy Story*; "To infinity and beyond" is only what Buzz Lightyear says.'

Five Pixar minutes later, Sarah bursts into the room – in which now only Martha and I remain – and says, 'Where's Molly? I thought she came down to you.'

'She did. She was last seen pushing her buggy in the direction of the front room.'

We Indian-file in there, Sarah, me, Martha. Sarah first. Sarah crying, 'Molly! What're you *doing*? Oh for goodness' sake, you pick your moments, don't you?'

Molly is sitting on the floor near the Christmas tree, an open carton of cream in her hands. The contents are spilled over her dress, her tights and, in even greater quantities, over the carpet. It is the cream on the carpet, not the cream on Molly's dress, which Batman and Robin are lapping up.

Molly looks up and laughs, pointing at Batman and Robin. 'Cream!' she says, and makes her cat-noise: 'A-ow!' Behind her on the sofa sit the carnations for Naomi and beside them the Safeway carrier I haven't got round to emptying.

Sarah looks at me and quickly away again. She doesn't say anything. One of the things she doesn't say is that the cream catastrophe is all my fault. 'Look at you,' she says, picking Molly up and carrying her in the direction of the kitchen sink.

'Well,' I say to Batman and Robin, 'you look like the cats that got the cream.'

'Sarah and Joe,' Naomi says. 'How lovely of you to come.' The skin is so tight on her face she appears to talk like a ventriloquist's dummy. She is propped up in bed, inserted beneath her perfect hospital corners. Normally in a neat perm, her white hair is limp and dull. Her physical decline is so great that she isn't raising much of a bump on the smooth, flat surface of her mattress.

'You're looking perky, Naomi,' Sarah says, all shiny and bright, kissing Naomi's cheek and laying our carnations on the bedside cabinet.

I bend and kiss the same papery cheek. My heart is clenching along with the skeletal arm that hooks mine. Her flesh has been disappearing over the last eighteen months. We have grown used to seeing less of her each visit. Even so, I am shocked by how little is left of her and, after first meeting her eyes, look anywhere else.

'Oh, I am, dear, I am,' Naomi tells Sarah. 'They're really looking after me here. I feel terribly blessed by the way this has all worked out. The Lord has seen to everything at just the right time.'

The first place I turn my head, I see that Martha is staring at the figure on the bed, looking alarmed. I smile at her and wink and she looks away.

'Yes,' Naomi says. 'The Lord has been very gracious to me.' I try not to stare at her collar-bones, which are so exposed it looks as if she has had a CD inserted beneath the mushroom skin on either side of her throat. The arm to which I am attached retrieves terms I thought were

3

lost with my (failed) Biology 'O' Level: humerus, radius, ulna – not things I often notice in my friends.

The bed-table, which has been pushed over Naomi's lap, bears a fruit-bowl swollen with Red Delicious, satsumas, big Jaffas, Fyffe bananas and black grapes the size of lychees. Also fluids – hand-sized Ribena cartons, bottles of Lucozade, Tesco apricot-flavoured sparkling water, Orange Barley Water. It's hard not to see this abundance as a taunt to a woman who is disappearing before your eyes.

Molly has approached Naomi's drip. Her eyes follow the tube from its upended bottle down to the point where it enters the back of Naomi's hand.

'Hello,' Naomi says brightly. 'Molly. Aren't you gorgeous! And what about Martha? You're just beautiful, the pair of you.'

Molly inches her head away, and Martha squirms a little under this sudden attention.

'It's great to see you're in such good spirits, Naomi,' Sarah says, moving everyone along.

'Well, the Lord has given me such a tremendous peace about dying. And it's just lovely the way he has allowed me time to take care of all my affairs. I wanted to sort out what would happen to the house and to make it clear where all my belongings should go. The Lord has given me enough time to see to it that no loose ends are left. Everything is nearly in place.'

Martha gets to her feet and drifts over to the window. She climbs up and kneels on a plastic chair. She rests her forearms on the glossed sill and her chin on her forearms. She's studying something down below with such focus that I excuse myself and cross the room to see what's caught her attention. At first, I can't see anything but trees around the tarmac and the roofs of three cars directly beneath us. I slip my hand under her hair and tickle the hollow where her head meets the back of her neck. 'What is it, Marth?'

She doesn't reply and I look into her face for any clues it might hold. She's smiling, a lovely soft smile.

'What?' I whisper over her shoulder and scan the hospice car park a second time. I don't know how I missed it the first time. A man is standing where the grass meets the trees. He's in his fifties, dressed in a pinstriped suit, white shirt and dark tie. His hair is short and black, all neatly in place. Beneath the flaps of his jacket, he has his hands in his trouser pockets. His legs are crossed at the ankles, his black shoes are shining – and he appears to be reclining on fresh air. He holds his head a little to one side and for a moment I think he looks like Leonard Cohen, *I'm Your Man* vintage Leonard Cohen, which is a good thing, but he is looking up at Martha, with a small pleasant tweak on the corners of his mouth, which may not be such a good thing. My eyes swing back to Martha, who is still smiling.

'Do you know that man?'

'I don't think so.'

'Well...' I want to say something adult and protective, I want to express my concern about my daughter smiling at strange men, even if – especially if – they are smiling at her. But nothing more will come out of my mouth. 'What...' I begin, and falter again. What, I suppose I need to say, is a smartly dressed, pleasant looking middle-aged man doing grinning at my infant-school daughter? And in a hospice car park, at that. But when I look back down for further explanation, there's nobody there. He has disappeared, like a magician's white rabbit.

I'm perplexed and turn to the room for help, but the world there goes on as before. Perhaps he's somebody from the hospice – one of the management, to judge by appearances. Or it's possible he's a son taking a thoughtful stroll in the grounds after visiting his dying mother. Wouldn't someone in such a situation, in such a mood, draw comfort from the sight of a little girl looking out a window?

Sarah says, 'It's time we got off. We don't want to tire you out.'

'You're not. It's just lovely to see you. But I would like to pray with you before you go.'

Sarah says that would be nice, if Naomi feels up to it. Naomi waves us nearer. Sarah draws up her chair on one side of the bed and I shuffle and look awkward.

'Here,' Naomi says. She reaches for a hand from each of us and I accept the one I'm offered, which feels like an injured sparrow. There's no way to remain standing without seeming aloof, so I perch on the edge of the mattress.

'Dear Father,' Naomi begins. 'Thank you for Sarah and Joe, and the girls.' Her tone is striking. It makes me think of the way I have spoken to Martha and Molly when they were too young to have understood many words, of how tone says more than words. 'Father, I pray that as time passes you would open their eyes more and more to see how great your love for us in Jesus is.'

Her dry, bony hand is hot in mine; its heat seems to run up my arm and flow right through me.

'And, Lord, I pray that you would lead them into the fullness of your will for their lives. I pray that they might be poured out for you, poured out, as Paul says, like a drink offering. Father, make them living sacrifices for you. Let their lives be poured out for your glory, Lord. In the precious name of our Lord Jesus, amen.'

'Amen,' Sarah says.

Something less emphatic, the hint of a groan perhaps, seeps from my lips. None of my dreams for this brand new year feature me being poured out. Fill me up? Okay, why not. Pour me out? Thanks, maybe some other year.

The girls have gone to bed and Sarah and I are eating cheese, crackers and salad and drinking spring water. I catch sight of the Christmas card I made for Sarah: a painting of a Christmas pudding, with two berried holly leaves on a crown of marzipan: the top lifts open and inside I'd put a voucher for her favourite shop, Monsoon.

'So did you like your Christmas card?'

'What?' She glances blankly at the card and brings it back to mind. 'Yes, of course I did.' She laughs and gives me a warm, indulgent smile. 'Honestly, you're such a needy individual.'

The phone rings and Sarah goes to it.

A few minutes later, as she is relaying the gist of the call to me, Sarah's eyes fill up. 'Poor old girl.'

But I can't help thinking that the timing of Naomi's death earlier this evening puts a seal on what she prayed over us and I spend the rest of the night trying to escape the feeling that her deathbed blessing now seems like a curse.

God knows my priorities are askew, but they're the devil to shake.

People Ain't No Good

It's cold and damp and I feel like the only person in the world: who but a Christian is up and about this early on a Sunday morning?

I let myself into the church building, and pick up the minibus keys. Our early 80s Transit was chocolate brown once, but now the colour is so ghostly the minibus seems like a relic from the days when vehicles weren't really coloured, when everything was a shade of dull.

Soon I am rattling down Hardy Lane and into the Mersey Bank estate, all 1940s council houses and 1990s satellite dishes. The Mersey Bank estate takes its name from the river that runs by it, connecting Chorlton – and me, in some romantic way – to Liverpool, spiritual home of The Fabs, and by extension, all the great guitar bands in the modern world. The Mersey Bank estate is not unlike Burnage, spiritual home of all the completely pants bands in the post-modern world. No Oasis on *The Wang Dang Doodle* this week. No Oasis on *The Wang Dang Doodle* ever.

The Wang Dang Doodle is about the obscure but classy. Blues, jazz, r'n'b, rock'n'roll. A touch of doo-wop. Western swing, bluegrass and cajun. Ska and country.

What they're listening to on
The Wang Dang Doodle this week:
'Oregon Hills'
(Cowboy Junkies)
'The Summer Wind'
(Frank Sinatra)
'Tiny Montgomery'
(Bob Dylan & The Band)

I'm a fool for Bob. If anybody looked at the statistics on my show, the only artist who gets played anywhere near as often is Chuck Berry.

I wind down my window and let a breath of cold air freshen the top of my head for a second or two. I wonder if I could play a Beethoven piano sonata on *The Wang Dang Doodle*. Of course, I can put anything I want on the show's play-list: *The Wang Dang Doodle* is my imaginary radio show.

Here's a thing about my wife and me: I dream of better and better sequences of records on my imaginary show or maybe writing a sitcom with my friend Vince Ford, whom you'll meet. But Sarah pictures herself taking the gospel to the lost in some dramatic scenario – paddling up the Yangtse Kiang with a canoe-load of tracts, or learning Tibetan to witness to a village in the Himalayas.

Lee Hutchinson is my first pick-up, although since the minibus round ends back in Chorlton, he could more practically be my last. But he likes the chat, and I kind of figure half an hour or so of conversation with a real human being, even me, is healthier than the alternative – more couch potato practice.

As usual, I have no more than touched the hand-brake before Lee is opening his flaking, washed-out front door. Most of the kids on this round you have to get out and knock on to raise them, but not Lee. He lifts his hand in a little wave to me and pulls the door softly to. He's wearing hi-top trainers, baggy jeans and a bubble jacket. None of these are items to be ashamed of, but they're never very clean and sometimes Lee smells.

He opens the passenger door and says, 'Iya.'

'Howdy-doody.'

'Okay if I sit up front?'

'It's all yours.'

As traffic permits, I glance across, checking him over for bruising. Sometimes there are cuts – once even a broken arm. His mousy hair is skimpy, not dense enough to carpet his scalp. He has it in a mop with a step. I thought steps had been and gone, but not in Lee's circle, obviously. No bruises.

'Going to Rusholme next, Joe?'

By now, it has become clear that this is one of Lee's smelly mornings. It can be hard not to hold acrid body odour against someone, but Lee has sufficient charm to offset that. Plus I wind the window down a couple more inches, which makes the cab chilly, but, hey, there's something wrong with everything, isn't there?

'Yep. Fancy a curry?'

I say this pretty often. All the same, Lee is prepared to let slip a shy smile as he tells me, 'No.'

'City win yesterday?'

'Nearly.'

I don't know anything about football, but I can busk it. 'Who were they playing then? Stockport County?'

'Cheeky.'

By the time we roll up at Mersey Valley Church, there are thirteen kids in the minibus, all aged 10 or 11, and most of us are singing 'Yellow Submarine'. Taught them myself; just doing my bit.

As long as these kids want to come, this minibus is a lifeboat for them. I hope Lee keeps wanting to come. I hope they all do.

In one of the rooms in Mersey Valley Church's annexe, the kids and I kick off with cups of juice and a plateful of chocolate Hob-Nobs. We play a game of Man The Ship, during which some seem to cling more gratefully to the radiators than others. The business of the day, when we get down to it, is looking at the story of Jesus washing his disciples' feet.

'They didn't have pavements in those days,' I say, 'just dirt paths. And they didn't wear Nike trainers; they would have been in sandals with no socks. Their feet and ankles would have been filthy most of the time. How would you have liked to have washed a pair of feet in that kind of condition?'

Somebody says, 'Not much.'

'Actually,' Tracy says, 'I think it would be a lot, lot worse now than in them days.' Another underfed waif like Lee, Tracy's wearing a cap-sleeved T-shirt and washed-out leggings, not ideal protection from the February cold. 'If you was gonna wash somebody's feet, you'd deffo be better off with no smelly trainers and no stinky socks.'

'What?' Lee says. 'Are we gonna haveta do it?' His bony little face is stiff with terror.

'Maybe another time,' I say. 'Now, time we had another Hob-Nob, eh?'

Many of them want more chocolate biscuits than they are able to get, but there you go, and then it's time for us all to pile back into the minibus. Lee climbs up front on the bench beside the driver's seat and all of the back seats fill up before Tracy can organise herself to get on board.

'Aw-oh, where'm I s'posed to sit?' she whines.

'You can sit there beside Lee,' I say. 'I thought everyone liked sitting up front.'

Her dingy face screws up. 'No way am I sitting beside him. He *stinks.*'

Lee shrivels at this. I mean, it's not that you can see him actually flinch; more a case of his cardboard-coloured skin contracting over his bony little face.

There's plenty I would like to say to Tracy here, but I have to bite my tongue. More pressing is how I extricate us from this tense moment. Even as I contemplate it, I can see that pressing the point with Tracy won't do anyone much good. But what choice am I left? If I ask somebody else to sit up front with Lee, I may easily meet the same response. I'm just experimenting with grinding my teeth, which doesn't improve things much, when one of the other kids chirps up and tells Tracy there's a seat beside her, one I haven't seen.

'Sweet,' Tracy mutters and shoves herself up into the throng of gaping kids.

Sweet isn't the word, really.

Lee, first in, is always last out of the minibus, which today is a good thing. When the last kid but one gets off, he and I are left in a thick silence.

'All right?' I ask.

'Yeah.' He doesn't meet my glance. He looks pale and fragile. He never looks strong. 'I won't be 'ere next week. Me brother's taking us to see City playing away.'

'Really?'

Lee sneaks a glance at me. He knows that I know that this is as likely as Frank Sinatra reading the shipping forecast: his brother uses him as a punch-bag. I could give you a list as long as your arm of the things Lee has to do without: a father, a loving home, a chance. I'd hate to see Kids' Church added to the list.

'Are you gonna let Tracy put you off?'

He looks down and now I see I am tormenting him by even trying to talk about this.

The minibus rattles loosely on.

'Joe?'

'What?'

'D'you think Jesus would've washed my feet?'

By now, we are right outside Lee's house. I pull up the handbrake, and turn to face Lee. Framed in the passenger door window, he looks as bleak and bereft as the pale winter day behind him.

'I *know* he would. He'd be proud to wash them.'

Lee breathes in and lets out a heavy sigh. His hand goes to open the passenger door and hangs there – bird-like, I realise: there's something of the sparrow about Lee. 'Do you think that's true then, what it says about God loving us?'

I would give him a hug to prove it, but it's in the nature of things that I can't. Part of me would like to deliver the most eloquent speech of my life, do everything in my power to convince him of what is available to him.

'What it says about God loving us,' I tell him, 'is the most true thing there is.'

His little Adam's apple moves up and down, and I decide that what is required here is a little white lie.

'Listen, I say. 'I'm doing the minibus round next week.' This is the lie: I shouldn't be on for another month, which Lee will know. But when was there ever a rota that didn't get messed with? 'You'll be coming, won't you?'

He's standing on the pavement, ready to close the door, looking at the seat or the ground or down the road, but then flashing a glimpse my way, just for a second. 'Yeah,' he says. 'See yuh next week, Joe.'

And he's gone.

By the time I get back to Mersey Valley, tiptoe into church and slip in beside Sarah, the second service is beginning. I pat Sarah 'hello' on the leg and look about the place, at this one and that. The conversation with Lee has left me feeling a bit reflective, a bit vulnerable.

'Good morning,' says Geoff Simpson, Senior Pastor, no relation whatsoever to Homer. No resemblance either; if anything, more like a sadder, older Gary Lineker. 'It's always good to come together and worship the Lord, isn't it, brothers and sisters?'

That 'brothers and sisters' gives the game away for Geoff: he is an old-school evangelical. Off duty, he he's been known to sport his John Wesley UK Tour 1756 T-shirt. Wesley '56: a great tour to catch. He still had Scotty and Bill in his worship band, still had three more rocking years before he went into the Army. I made that up. For one thing, Geoff has never been seen in a T-shirt. As far as I know, he wears a shirt and tie when he's asleep. See my trouble being a Christian? This is me in my church, casting my baleful eye over the guy in charge. I don't seem to be able to stop myself.

Part of the problem is, although Geoff Simpson has nothing in common with Homer Simpson, he really is a bit of a cartoon character. For instance, the things his body does when he is addressing the congregation, like now:

'The trees are in bud, the sun is out,' he says. His head is tilted back and his long neck is exposed – it looks, in fact, as if his neck is talking to us. He punctuates what he says with a grimace, a downward turn to the sides of his mouth so that his face resembles an inversion of the Smiley symbol. 'It's a beautiful day –' more neck and the un-Smiley expression (which, if it could speak, would say, 'URGH') '– to worship the Lord, isn't it? Lesley?'

Lesley Moore, the Lesley Geoff is addressing, is tastefully co-ordinated in spring colours, tangerine and custard, which bring out her pale complexion. She approaches the microphone, greets us with a blissed smile, and leads us in some heartfelt singing to God. I look around the room for William, Lesley's husband, but there's no sign of him. We're all in the same home group. William is the church's full-time counsellor and until recently I was meeting with him once a month. This was Sarah's idea. She wanted me to get in touch with my emotions. I sent a few postcards, but they never got back to me.

During a prayerful pause, Dorothy Wood stands up, her silky fair hair in an immaculate bun, every pleat and fold of her clothing just so. She reads from *Isaiah 61*, a familiar passage, which I know sums up the calling of Jesus and anyone who wants to follow in his footsteps – good news for the poor, freedom for the captives, release from darkness. All good things, so why can't I detach the good news from my dim view of the messenger? Maybe it's the way Dorothy speaks. She pronounces each word to the last syllable and sends out her sibilants with a whistling spin.

Maybe it's Dorothy's manner. At most, she's ten years older than me, but she always feels like a scary aunt. Her tone is hectoring – well, it hectors me. Maybe it's the solemn way she savours her short time in the limelight. She lingers a moment to milk any resonance she might have left in the wake of this reading, then folds herself carefully into her seat, next to her husband Roy, who sports a shocking early 80s mullet. I know without being able to see that his cords will be too short and that he will be wearing grey Clark's Polyveldts.

I know these verses from *Isaiah* 61 about as well as I know the songs on *Highway 61 Revisited* – quite well, readers. Good news for the poor and release for the prisoners is what I hope the work we do with our kids from the minibus run is all about. Lee has no father and Tracy has a very bad one. I would like to think that the words Dorothy reads out are dear to my heart. I badly want to live them out. So what's my problem? Maybe it's just that for so many people in church, being at the front seems to be so very important, and for me it's not what they say that counts, it's who they are, and who they are has a tendency to make what they say seem bollocks.

Yep, here I am being acerbic and disillusioned in church again. Clearly I have a lot to learn.

Geoff and his long neck lead us in open prayer, and then he asks Tom Beattie to come forward. As Tom negotiates mic stands and PA cables, I study our new-ish Youth Pastor. He is, we all know, thirty-six, but runs, plays tennis and dresses like a student. Partly because of the wardrobe and partly because of his almost shaved head and pencil goatee, he seems a good many years younger than he is.

Today he is wearing black linen trousers and a grey cotton top that's so loose it's practically playing jazz. He sports lobe-length sideburns, shaved off at a sharp, almost *Star Trek* angle.

I'm still making my mind up about Tom. I reckon most of Mersey Valley is, too. His preach today is a smooth performance. He intrigues early on and takes me with him through some rapid, adroit twists and turns. I look about me to see if the rest of the room is as absorbed by what he's saying as I am. They are. Twenty minutes later, approaching his clincher, Tom stops, shuts everything down – his stalking, his message, his facial expression – and leaves ample silence for us to embrace and absorb all that he has said. When he speaks again, it's in a soft voice, and the inevitability of his closing point is a beautiful thing. This man could sell thermal vests in the Sahara.

After more choruses and hymns, Geoff Simpson rises and addresses the congregation:

'It's been good to worship the Lord together this morning, hasn't it?' (And his neck says, 'URGH.') 'Just an item of business, if I could detain you an extra moment or two.'

People settle to focus on this unexpected coda.

'The elders have been looking at the way we organise our youth and children's ministries. All of the youth and children's work is to continue in its present form for the time being. However, over the coming weeks and months, Tom Beattie and the elders are going to be in discussion with those of you who are giving your time so freely and generously to this area of Mersey Valley's work. And from there, we hope to take things onto a new level. Thanks, everybody. Bless you.'

Around the hall, a murmur of conversation flowers. I'm retrieving my Bible and the church newsletter from beneath the seat in front of me. I'm thinking about what Geoff has just said, trying to decipher the sub-text and Kat Fuller is approaching from the other side of the aisle.

'Hey, Joe,' she says, twinkling. She is petite and her always-platinum hair seems jolly. 'Where you going with that gun in your hand?'

An old joke between us two rock'n'roll fans. Where once we had The Clash and The Velvet Underground in common, more recently it's been doing crèche together or planning Kids' Church rotas. In other words, being grown-up (I wish). We are now people with radios tuned to Melvyn, not Billy Bragg.

I laugh the way I always do with Kat, a small, affectionate sound.

'What did you make of that, then?' she asks.

We're standing in the aisle and she's leaning into me, her eyes gripping mine through her tinted glasses. Before I can reply, Kat is giving her own answer: 'It's only the start. Tom's going to change everything, you know.'

This is news to me. 'He is?'

'Oh yeah. The signs are all there. Scott and I have lived through a church leadership change before. People aren't good at change and move on. It's always a bloody affair.'

The chance to find out more about these signs, which I've obviously missed, is snatched away: Scott appears at her side and whisks her homewards. It's time for the Porters to go home, too. Molly is with Sarah, back from the toddler group, so I set off to find Martha.

I feel tired and ill. I'm weary. Like The Cramps say, people ain't no good. It's inescapable, but always noticing it ain't no better.

I still can't see any sign of Martha. I feel a small tide of worry wash in: Chorlton is not without its dangers. People have been shot, though not so far killed, here. People have had their faces slashed at night.

I spot Martha's pink Barbie anorak. The white fake fur of the collar sits on her narrow shoulders like a stole. She is looking out the French windows. As I watch she turns her head to the right and her lips move. Slowly, I realise she is talking to someone, though because of the throng I'm still in I can't make out who it is.

'Yo, Joe,' a voice I know hails me from the throng. 'You look like a man with a mission,' Tom Beattie is saying, but all I'm thinking is: who's Martha talking to?

'Oh, hi Tom,' I say glancing at him and back at Martha. 'Good sermon. You got me bang to rights.'

'*Ex*-cellent! And the rest of us, including me. Especially me. How d'you think I can talk about it if I haven't been guilty of it?'

Charmingly self-deprecating, but also, let's face it, slicker than a politician on the stump. I crane my neck to get a better view of whomever Martha's with. Between the heads and shoulders that separate me from her, I snatch a glimpse of her companion: somebody squatting by her side.

Realising I might seem not to be paying Tom enough attention, I apologise and explain, 'I'm just trying to keep an eye on what Martha is up to.'

Tom laughs. 'Only another fifteen years of that, eh?'

I haul up a smile and a trickle of a chuckle. I'm peering towards the emergency exit. The size and shape of a hand pointing out the floor-length window by the doors tells me it's an adult with Martha; a rear-view of the head shows that it's a man, a man with tidy black hair.

'Look, you get on over to Martha and I'll see you soon. Yeah?'

I nod and say, 'Yeah, see you.'

'*Ex*-cellent!'

I'm closer and I see their two heads together, in semi-profile. Nothing seems wrong, but all the same I'm worried, anxious that I don't know who this is talking to Martha. He's speaking to her and she's listening, very calm and intent, listening and looking from the man to whatever is outside the window.

Two teenage regulars in bright fleecies impede my view, both of them tall. I see that the man is smartly dressed in a taupe jacket and black polo shirt, which worries me more, since nobody at Mersey Valley ever dresses smartly unless they're getting married. I'm worried, yet now I see that the suave figure is holding a fatherly arm about Martha, his hand settled in the fake fur hood-band. He is squatting and holding my Martha, smiling into her face, talking gently to her and she's laughing. I'm not close enough to hear it, but I know her bubbling laughter well enough to imagine I can.

Martha and the man are swept from view by two roady types humping a hefty keyboard. My heart steps up from a trot to a canter, but breaks into a gallop when, through the crush, the sharp-dressed man's face is revealed. I know him now: the man who leaned back on air in the hospice car park, the one I thought looked like Leonard Cohen.

'Hang on!' I shout, trying to shove through.

From left and right, faces turn to look at me.

'Stop!' I shout and, 'Martha, wait!' and then I am past the fleecies, and I have reached Martha, only Martha, who's looking out the window.

'Where's he gone?' I pant and kneel beside her.

She turns to face me and smiles. 'Daddy, look. Look.'

What she's pointing to, what I see at once, is a bird sitting on the redbrick school wall. Its black body is so black, its orange beak so orange that each seems to make the other luminous. Swaying and bobbing, it gleams in the early spring light.

'A blackbird,' I say, finding it hard to get the words out.

'Mmm.' She looks from the blackbird back to me and her face rises in a contented smile. 'Here,' she says, handing me some folded and crayoned white card. 'I made it for you in Kids' Church.'

'You did? Why? It isn't my birthday, y'know.'

'No! It's for Valentine's Day. Silly!'

And I look at it and make a fuss of the artwork and hug her to me. I squeeze her tight, tight, tickling my nostrils in fur and I wonder what's going on.

Faraway Eyes

'Aw for crying out loud,' I say six days later, when Sarah raises the idea of me taking the girls to Longford Park. 'I was hoping to make a start on this sitcom.'

'I thought you'd given that idea up.'

'What idea? We didn't have one – that was the trouble. But we've got a good idea now. And I was supposed to be working on it this morning.'

'Well, I didn't plan to feel ill.'

'I know. But it's very frustrating.'

'Nobody forced you to get married. Nobody made you have children.'

I must look in need of some sweet-talk, for Sarah asks what the sitcom idea is.

'There are two Poles,' I tell her, 'Boris and Dragon, and they can't get enough of Manchester music. The Smiths, Joy Division, The Fall – if it's Manc, they love it. Something about Manchester music appeals to the melancholy in their Eastern European souls. Well – obviously not Simply Red or M People. A certain kind of Manchester music.'

'Why Poles?'

'That's the trump card, y'see. Loads of the best sitcoms are about outsiders. It helps you to satirise normal society. Look at *The Munsters* or *Third Rock From The Sun*. You can get a lot of laughs if you show things from the perspective of outsiders trying to make sense of the mainstream.'

'Whose idea was it – yours or Vince's?'

'Well – both of us, really. Anyway, they come to Manchester and open a second-hand record shop.' I sigh. 'It'll never get written in any case. I'll be too busy loitering with my kids in public parks.'

In the car on the way to Longford Park, Martha is pretending to read to Molly from a book called *The Miracles of Jesus*. Inventing the contents of

17

books she can't read is a game she likes to play.

'One day,' she says, 'Jesus called all his friends together and said, "I've had a idea about Easter."'

I'm still laughing moments later, when I spot Roy Wood. Or rather, I spot his behind: he's bent over into the engine of a car outside his house on Edge Lane. I pull in and shout him over.

'Well, Joe,' Roy says. His face is smudged, but his mullet would make Michael Bolton proud. 'Hello there, girls.'

'I didn't know you were an amateur mechanic,' I say.

He wipes his hands on the legs of his grey overalls. 'Oh yes. This used to be Naomi's, you know.'

I look at the ancient Datsun Cheesy. 'Oh yeah. I thought it was familiar.'

'She left it to me, so I'm trying to restore it.'

'*Why?*'

Roy looks hurt for a second or so, then smiles. 'Oh ho. The legendary Porter sense of humour.'

'Well – restoring a Jag Mark II I could understand, but –'

Roy smiles his beatific smile and what is there to say?

Underway again, I press on the car radio. Nothing I like is playing. I begin to click through the pre-sets, maybe half of which are for desperate moments like this, when you can't find anything good to listen to. Radio 3, Virgin, Classic FM, Jazz FM – all nothing doing. It's one of those days when you're likely to punch from Simple Minds to Tears For Fears to Cast. But then I hit on Keith West's 'Excerpt From A Teenage Opera', 'Grocer Jack' I used to call it. Driving into the broken tarmac car park at Longford Park, I'm singing along with the children's choir, telling Grocer Jack to get off his back, get in to town and not let them down. Oh no-oh no, definitely not. And Molly is trying to shut me up:

'Sop it, Daddy.'

As we walk from the car, Martha says, out of the blue (everything kids say is out of the blue), 'Which is your favourite Spice Girl, Dad?'

'The one with the dark, straight hair.'

'Oh, Posh.'

'Yeah, Posh.'

'You know Jamie?'

I do know Jamie, who is not yet three. 'Uh huh.'

'Well he said his favourite Spice Girl was the one with the big grubs.'

'So what's her name, that one Jamie likes?'

'Oh, Geri.'

'It was Geri I meant. Geri is my favourite, too.' I'm working hard to keep poker-faced. 'Don't tell your Mum.'

Martha frowns. 'But Daddy – Geri hasn't got dark hair.'

I say, 'No. But she does have big grubs.'

We walk on to the adventure area, where structures made of timber and tyre rubber are crawling with children. A seesaw involving rubber seats hung from a cross on a pole. A thirty foot aerial runway. A log edifice incorporating a climbing frame and a slide, which looks like a third cousin of Fort Apache. You wouldn't be surprised to see John Wayne ride out of it with a small detachment of the U.S. Cavalry.

Molly spends a lot of time with me, sitting on the low log wall, kicking the broken bark ground cover and letting a rivulet of green slime seep down her upper lip.

'Mummy better now?' she asks.

'I don't know. She might be lying down still.'

'Poor Mummy.'

I look up then to check that Martha is okay. I can't see her anywhere on Fort Apache and my chest constricts a little as I get to my feet. 'Can you see Martha, Molly?'

Seconds later, I spot her, standing on the platform at one end of the aerial runway. She's waiting for a turn. It makes me smile all over to think how typical of her it is not to tell me, not to ask me to come and watch. The way she'll do it is to wait until she has succeeded before letting anyone know about it. She is looking over to the left, back in the direction from which we have come. Her hands are tucked in the pockets of her pink Barbie anorak, which looks good with her purple velvet trousers. There's a glancing spring wind that brings a powdery blush to her cheeks and lifts the curtains of her hair off the sides of her face. I wonder what thoughts are going on behind her faraway eyes.

'My don't see her.'

'It's all right, Moll. I've spotted her.'

'My don't see her.'

I pick Molly up by the armpits and shift her on to my right shoulder. 'There. Queuing by the aerial runway. See? D'you want to go on the slide now?'

With heavy concentration, she climbs up the steps to the little wooden corridor that leads to the mouth of the slide. Here she stands and looks solemnly down the stainless steel chute as if it might sprout wings or grow geraniums if she watched it long enough.

I climb up and join her.

'Aren't you going down the slide, Molly?'

'No.'

'I thought you said you were.'

'Change my mind.'

As we're standing there, more children join us and launch down the slide as easy as onions. Molly continues to look expectantly down the chute.

'What do you think can happen to you, Molly?'

'We go back down now, my Daddy?'

Going down the chute myself would be so much easier than accompanying Molly back down the steps, but since she can't retrace her steps alone, I am forced to bend, stretch, wriggle and say 'Excuse us' a lot as we negotiate our way past the queue of bemused kids on their way up. Parenthood is so often humbling, it's a wonder anyone survives it with an iota of pride left.

We're on the way back to the car and Martha still hasn't said anything about managing to do the aerial runway. (I know that she has, because I sneaked a look and saw her sailing down the wire like a Marine.)

As we are approaching the ice-cream van, Molly tweaks my arm.

'No,' I tell her. 'It isn't ice-cream weather.'

'Don't want hi-team. Want a lollipop.'

'What're you going to be when you grow up – a corporate lawyer?'

To my right, Martha wanders off into some rough grass. 'Dad,' she says. 'Look: a football.' She goes behind a tree-trunk and kicks what turns out to be a faded *Flintstones* football. Hollywood merchandising is as good as carbon dating: this will be from the mid 90s – 94 or 95.

'Can we take it home?'

'No. It'll belong to somebody and they might remember to come back for it – if they're lucky.'

Martha says, 'I bet they don't.'

'But if they do, finding it will be a nice surprise for them, won't it?'

We pass a length of tall hedge which meets our path at right angles. When we get maybe ten metres beyond the hedge, I notice that Martha and I are on our own. I look behind us and to the left and right, but there's no sign of Molly.

'Where's Molly?' I ask, although it's a stupid question.

'Don't know,' Martha says in the way children have of acting like nothing can ever go seriously wrong. 'She was here just now.'

'Molly!'

I break into a panicked trot and retrace our route. I only have to go as far as the hedge to find her: she is just behind it.

'Molly, come on. Don't wander off like that.'

'Pingu,' she says and points at a plump pigeon.

'Come on. Give me your hand.'

When we get back on the path, on the other side of the hedge, Martha has vanished, which seems odd. Bemused, I examine the immediate area for a hiding place, but there isn't one. That's strange, I think. It takes a few moments before I begin to worry – hot, stiff worry.

'Martha!' I shout. 'Martha! *Martha*,' I snap, 'stop fooling about.' I keep on resisting what is happening here. Any minute now, she will step out from behind some foliage and giggle at my fretful face. 'Martha!' I cry and shout and scream and Molly bursts into tears. I pick her up and hug her and tell her it's all all right – just Daddy being bad-tempered because Martha is messing around. 'I know,' I murmur close to her hot, wet face, trying to be cheerful. 'I bet she'll have gone to the ice-cream van.'

But none of the children at the ice-cream van is Martha.

I look everywhere I can think to look. We retrace our steps to the aerial runway. I look behind every tree, every hedge. Where possible, we clamber through bushes. After almost an hour, I realise that I will have to do something, something serious.

We are back by the hedge where Martha disappeared and for five minutes or so, I convince myself that this is the place to stay. The last thing I should do is leave this hedge. If I leave it then that's when she will turn up. I have to be there when she returns.

Nothing else to be done: I must contact the police. But we will have to leave the park to find a phone-box. Ever since mobile phones first appeared, I've despised them. Now I would give anything to own one. It's torture to leave the park; but we go and find a phone-box.

When they arrive, the police ask a great many questions, some of which it is hard to understand. They want to know how long we have been in the park. They want to know if Martha has eaten anything. Eventually, they leave me alone.

Plain-clothes people, detectives I suppose, arrive after maybe quarter of an hour. I don't know how long. 'We'll get you a cup of tea shortly,' a young policewoman tells me. I don't know why they think I need tea. The ones in uniform – the bobbies, we used to call them – address me as 'sir'. They can't answer my questions.

'Do children that disappear like this mostly turn up?' I ask a beefy officer with a sardonic turn to his mouth.

'It's difficult to generalise, sir.'

When I protest that I want to be part of the search operation, the WPC who promised me tea says, 'It's better for you to remain here, sir.'

This can't be happening, is what I'm telling myself. I'm praying to God that it couldn't happen, not to Martha, not to us. I'm pleading with Him, please, please, let her turn up. Let her come wandering up to me now. Let her emerge in her Barbie anorak and I will shout at her and hug her and we'll cry together.

'Where's Martha?' Molly asks. We're holding hands.

'I don't know, pet. But we'll find her soon.'

The police want us to wait here by a squad car while they comb the park. There are droves of uniformed police now, spreading over the area all around that fateful hedge. In the American-style blousons, nightsticks and caps of the Greater Manchester Constabulary, they resemble a Hollywood film. This adds to the unreality of what's happening here. None of the police converse. Their faces are solemn, drawn-looking, even though they haven't been at work on this longer than half an hour. The air is crackling with their chest-mounted walkie-talkies.

'Daddy? Martha all right?'

'Yes.' Suddenly I want to cry. I tell myself I can't afford to cry just now. 'She'll be fine.'

None of the police seem to me to be moving fast enough. Don't they realise the urgency? I want to go and shout at them, bully them into more action, faster action, more motivated action. While they are tramping around in their orderly formations, Martha may be straying out to the busy Edge Lane traffic. Is there a pond? I wonder. I can't think straight. I'm not sure whether there's a pond in Longford Park or not. But there might be and she might be drowning in a foot of water by now.

The detectives call me Joe. 'Your wife has been contacted, Joe. She'll be here soon.'

I don't want to see her. What would I say to her? How can I face her having lost Martha?

The police take me through it twice, but in my head I go over and over the final few moments with Martha. I look at it from every angle I can think of, but can't see how she could have disappeared in the time it takes to draw a deep breath. What's more frustrating than the catastrophe that seems impossible?

The WPC who mentioned tea remains with Molly and me throughout. I wonder what the thinking behind that is; do they fear that I might harm myself? It occurs to me that if they don't find Martha I may be a murder suspect. I don't want to think about this. Instead, I speculate that my hypothetical cup of tea has become a delicate issue for this woman. I wonder what makes a woman join the police force. What makes anyone join? The things I find myself thinking amaze me. I wish this policewoman would go away. I really want to be on my own. I want to throw myself on the ground and pummel it.

'What's your name, love?' she says to Molly.

Molly clings to the back of my leg and gives the WPC her shy-girl smile.

'D'you know,' the policewoman coos at Molly, 'that's the most gorgeous smile I've seen all week.'

Molly curls up against me and grins her head off. 'This is Molly,' I explain.

'And I'm Andrea. Andrea Dobson.'

In her quiet manner and open features, she is, I see then, about half my age. Andrea Dobson is a name, I realise, that I will always remember, whatever happens.

Another police Astra appears, incongruously driving along the path normally reserved for pedestrians. I know before I can distinguish the occupants of this car that one of them is Sarah. I can't bring to mind a time when I have actively not wanted to see her, but that's the way I feel now. I would be glad if Sarah would just disappear until Martha is found.

The police car veers onto the grass and bobs across, like a swimmer against the tide, to where Molly and I are standing with Andrea Dobson. In the back of it are Sarah and somebody else, not a police officer. I can't make out whether or not it's someone I know.

My torso feels hollow, but at the same time I feel so heavy I wonder how the earth can bear my weight. My misery hurts.

Sarah gets out of the car and runs toward me. The other person turns out to be Kat Fuller, former Clash fan. Sarah reaches me and bursts into tears as we cling to each other.

'Mumm-ee,' Molly pleads.

'Oh, chicken,' Sarah says and stoops to sweep her up into our arms. She smudges kisses over Molly's face.

'What happened?' she asks, when she lifts her face to mine again, and I start to tell her. I start, but I'm not far into it before my voice breaks up and I am sobbing, then both of us are sobbing together, hugging and weeping. But I eventually get my story out.

'I don't understand,' she says. 'How can she have just disappeared, in so short a time?'

'I don't know. I can't understand it either.'

She looks to the hedge that I have pointed out to her. Her face is hurt and mystified. She looks young and helpless. I squeeze her close into me again. 'She'll turn up soon and there'll be some ridiculous explanation.'

'D'you think so?'

'Yes, of course. She'll have bumped into a friend and wandered off with her.'

As I say this, I'm beginning to convince myself. How can Martha have disappeared into thin air? She can't have. There has to be a mundane explanation and this is an appealing one. She will be with a friend. It's almost convincing, but the tightness in my chest persists.

Andrea Dobson, who throughout this has been within earshot, steps forward. 'We're covering the whole park, Mrs Porter. If Martha is in the park you can be sure we'll find her.'

Sarah says, 'Thanks,' and starts to whimper.

I go into my everything's-going-to-be-all-right spiel, but don't get far before my voice breaks up and I'm crying.

'Excuse me,' somebody says, the beefy officer, who has already questioned me. He checks with Sarah that she is 'the mother'. He shakes hands and introduces himself, a name and a rank that fails to register with me. He says, 'Please rest assured that we will do everything that can be done, Mrs. Porter.'

Sarah seems to be searching his blunt face for anything that might lead her out of her distress.

'We'll fetch you a cup of tea as soon as possible.'

Another plain-clothes man, one I haven't seen before, a blonde-haired young man with fashionable glasses, interrupts. 'Murdock,' he says, and touches the arm of the beefy guy speaking to Sarah. When he smiles at Sarah, the bespectacled detective looks as wily as a bag of weasels. Wily, but too young – just *wrong* – for police work. He should have been a social worker, and he shouldn't be smiling. It angers me and I don't need any more emotions adding to my current palette.

Murdock excuses himself with a brusque nod and he and The Smiling Detective walk away, murmuring.

'I don't know what there is to smile about,' I say to no one in particular.

I tell Sarah what has been happening since the police arrived.

'What about that tea?' I ask Andrea Dobson.

Sarah looks from the policewoman to me, like: Has everyone taken leave of their senses?

'A cup of sweet tea would be good for you now,' I tell her.

'Why are you just standing there?' she snaps at me. 'Can't you *do* something?'

In the evening, with the police still around, home no longer feels like home. We phone the parents of every one of Martha's friends, friends from school, from the neighbourhood, from Mersey Valley. In between times, in one way or another, the police seem not to want to leave us alone.

Andrea Dobson makes several pots of tea and listens to Sarah expressing and expressing herself. When the beefy officer, Murdock, and Clayton, the smiling detective, interview me at greater length, Sarah remains in the room with us. It's as if she can't bear to miss out on anything that might offer a glimmer of hope. The policemen take me through everything that happened in the park again. They dwell on the final few moments with Martha. They ask about the *Flintstones* football.

I wonder if the football wasn't some kind of booby trap. 'I can't actually conceive of any way in which it could be, but–'

'What?' Clayton says.

'It's just that I keep on thinking that picking the ball up triggered something. I know it sounds silly...'

Clayton pushes both of us to come up with something, no matter how unpromising, which might be a lead.

'Wait a minute,' I say to Sarah. 'There was something strange. A man I saw at the hospice when we were visiting Naomi.' I turn to explain Naomi to Clayton: 'A friend of ours from church.'

'When was this?'

'New Year's Day. We were in her room, Naomi's room. Martha was smiling at something out the window – I think that was what made me look out. She was really happy, I remember that. And when I looked out the window, there was a man below, in a pinstriped suit. A man with black hair running to grey, maybe in his fifties.'

Sarah says, 'You never mentioned this! Why didn't you tell me about it?'

'I don't know, it just kind of got swept aside that evening.'

Sarah looks all set to pursue me like a gun dog, but Clayton cuts in: 'Anything else about this man?'

'Well yes, there was another strange thing. He seemed to be leaning back on the air. The perspective looked all wrong. And his feet were crossed at the ankles. It looked as though he was lying down in a relaxed pose. But he wasn't; he was standing up. Either way, the perspective looked wrong.'

Murdock says, 'What do you think might explain that?'

'Nothing I can imagine.'

'And yet you didn't feel the need to mention it to anyone afterwards?'

'Things get swept aside. You know how it is: children, work, the speed of life.'

Nobody says anything. Murdock looks at me, spade-faced. I sigh. On the carpet by the music system, I spot a jewel case, Randy Newman's

Good Ol' Boys, which must have been the last disc I played before normal life ended. I seem to be looking at that CD case down a tunnel. I feel like I should wave at it, at the old world that just passed on.

'I saw him again,' I tell Clayton.

'Was Martha present?'

'I saw him with her, at our church last Sunday morning. He was squatting by her on the other side of the room from me. It was crowded and by the time I reached them, the man had gone. When I was a dozen feet from them, my view was blocked for a moment and when I could see where they were again, he had disappeared. Martha was standing by the window.'

Clayton says, 'And she was all right?'

'She wanted me to look at this blackbird out the window.'

Sarah says, 'I can't believe what I'm hearing.'

'So both times you saw this man, Martha was happy?' Clayton says.

'That's right.'

'Both times she was by a window?'

'I hadn't thought of that, but yes. The first time, Martha and I were looking out the window at this man. The second time, she and the man were beside the window – before he disappeared. In fact, he disappeared outside the hospice, too.'

'What's the *matter* with you?' Sarah shouts at me.

I swallow hard. It feels as though there is a whole plum in my throat which is refusing to go down.

Clayton says, 'Why didn't you do anything about the man on either occasion?'

'I don't know. With hindsight, it's easy to see that I should have done something – but I just thought it was one of those odd coincidences. Not spooky, just mildly puzzling, really.'

Murdock says, 'Didn't it seem a little more than 'puzzling' to you that a stranger should be talking to your little girl? And a stranger at that who you'd recently seen lurking in the grounds of a hospice?'

'It was odd, yes. It felt mysterious, really.'

'But you did nothing at the time?' Clayton again, the smile again.

My head is spinning. I feel like a ball being knocked from one racquet to another. 'Well – no. It's hard to explain. It probably sounds stupid now, but he looked benign to me.'

A couple more plain-clothes people arrive and spend half an hour asking us – and particularly me – questions. Many of them are the same questions Murdock and Clayton have already asked, but they also interrogate me about my relationship with Martha and Molly. After they have gone, I ask Clayton what kind of detectives these two are.

'They're psychologists.'

'Psychologists? Why would they want to –' And the question dies on my lips.

When Clayton and Murdock have gone, Sarah and I put Molly to bed. Maybe we think we need the pair of us to make sure something doesn't happen to her as well. As I feed Molly's limbs into her *Snow White* pyjamas, she asks Sarah again when Martha will come home.

'I don't know, chicken. Maybe she'll be here in the morning.'

Molly looks concerned. 'She'll sleep in her clothes, won't she?'

'God will be looking after her, pet,' Sarah says. 'Don't worry.'

'God takes care of us all, doesn't he?' Molly says. 'Like Noah and his animals.'

'Yeah.'

Mid-evening, Dr Ghosh, our GP, calls with pills for Sarah: Librium to calm her – she laughs at the idea – and something to help her sleep. I wait on the bay window sofa for Martha to walk up the road and open the garden gate. When I'm not staring at the yellow gloom beneath the street lamps, I fix my attention on the phone and will it to ring. At some point, for no particular reason, I go to bed.

'Sarah?' I say in the wee, wee hours. 'You awake?'

'What do you think?'

Three times I try to coax her to take the sleeping pill, but she won't relent.

'I don't care who Martha's with,' she says, deep in the night, 'as long as she's warm and indoors, as long as she's come to no harm.'

We cling to one another and weep and howl. When we fall out of each other's arms, we rotate on the extremities of the bed, spinning and sighing. I remember a line from *Psalm 63*: the watches of the night. I pray. I plead and weep before God. I weep. The skin around my eyes stings with salt. 'I'll do anything you ask in future if you'll just bring her back. I'll do anything, I'll go anywhere for you,' I say, thinking, I suppose, of Sarah's canoe-load of tracts up the Yangtse Kiang.

★

In the morning, the kitchen smells of cat food. Cereal bowls and toast plates litter the table. Packets of Sultana Bran and strawberry-flavour Country Crisp sit on the worktop with their flaps flung open to the heavens. Somewhere down the road an alarm is ringing. If I slept last night, I wasn't aware of it. I look at the mug of tea I made I don't know how long ago. The grey scum on its surface tells me that it will be stone cold. The *Jurassic Park* dinosaur image on the mug seems suddenly grizzly. I lift my gaze to take in the view from the bottom kitchen window. The back garden isn't large, but this morning it feels more cramped and poky than usual. The house, too, seems to have shrunk around me. The ceilings are too low, the walls too close. Molly is pounding along the landing above me, shrieking and laughing.

Postcards and mini-posters are clip-framed on the kitchen walls: Popeye, Dennis The Menace, Tintin, Felix The Cat, The Bash Street Kids. I look at them and decide that I will take every last one down. I want to throw the mug of cold tea through the window, but I know it won't make me feel better, so I don't, which makes me feel worse. I haven't cried since getting out of bed.

Derek, Sarah's father, is to come during the course of today. He will talk about road numbers and be incapable of talking about feelings. He will need extra attention, for which I have no energy. I wish Sarah had asked him to stay at home. In the kitchen, I study the mug of tea again. In the next room I can hear the sound of a tape Molly is playing: *The wheels on the bus go round and round, round and round.* It sounds too normal, too much like a child's ordinary, happy domestic life.

The doorbell rings and I prepare myself for Derek, Sarah's father.

'William and Lesley are here,' Sarah says, ushering them into the kitchen.

Lesley Moore is as colour co-ordinated as ever, though tastefully muted for these unhappy circumstances in a pewter suit and blue-charcoal lambswool top. Her husband William, with his big, dark beard and forceful belly, looks like a serious fell-walker, which, as far as I know he isn't. Maybe it's because he tends to wear thick, ribbed sweaters and weatherproof coats with hoods, zips, pockets all over the show and layers of linings – what the Land's End catalogue would probably describe as a *squall jacket.*

'Sarah,' William says. 'This is desperate. I don't know what to say to you.'

He embraces her and then me: shampoo and the sharpness of his after-shave. A man with a beard who uses after-shave. It's odd what you notice. When he was my counsellor, he and I spent hours discussing my buried emotions.

'There's no news?' he asks and I shake my head.

Lesley hugs Sarah. 'My heart is breaking for you,' she says.

Surely, I can't help thinking, Sarah's heart, not Lesley's, is the one that's breaking.

I consider offering them tea or coffee. First I think I should, then I think I shouldn't. My thoughts bang around inside me like a reluctant cat in a cat-box.

'We wanted to come round and pray with you,' William says. 'We'll all be praying for you in the morning service. Everyone's just devastated by this. Just devastated.'

I don't know what to say. I glance at Sarah, hoping she might.

'Please, sit down,' she says, and everybody does, William looming over the table, a big, burly man who dwarfs his petite wife.

And then, who knows from where, words start pouring out of Sarah, fast: 'They're still searching Longford Park. They searched until dark last night. I think they might've searched through the night, in fact. They've been good about keeping us up to date, but so far there's no trace of her. I think it's an unhinged woman that's done it – you know, someone that can't have a baby or something. I don't think Martha will be hurt.'

Lesley asks Sarah if she has eaten anything.

'I haven't felt hungry.'

'Let me make you something. Have you eggs and bacon?'

'I'd be sick,' she says. 'The smell alone would make me vomit.'

It's raining. At first, I thought the sound of it was whispering and it startled me. I look out of the bottom window and see the rain falling, slanting freely across the window frame. I think of Martha somewhere outside, somewhere cold and wet, a place where I can't reach her.

William says, 'Shall we pray, then?'

Sarah says, 'There was a little girl who survived a night in some woods after being abandoned, wasn't there? A night when it froze.'

Before William has advanced very far with his prayer, Lesley bursts into tears, choking, hiccuping and making little moans. William puts his arm around her. 'I'm sorry. Job's comforters, eh?'

When Sarah's father arrives, I lead him into the kitchen. He approaches her across the room with his right arm extended, ready to embrace her. He wears his empathising expression – head to one side like a terrier. She hugs him. When the introductions are over, she tells her Dad he has made good time.

'Ah yes, well, normally I would break the journey at some National Trust property or other. There are various places to choose from between home and here. However, I just drove straight through. Only made a quick stop at services on the M6 – or was it the M1? M6 or M1, one or the other.'

'Good,' Sarah tells her Dad.

'Brought a flask with me and had a coffee in the car. Very nice it was too.'

'Are you going to sit down, Dad?'

He pushes his knuckles against the back of his pelvis. 'No thanks. I'm ready for a bit of standing up, as it happens. Heh heh.' He notices Lesley daubing her eyes, cuts his chortling short and begins looking all around him. 'And where's my favourite two-year-old?' he asks.

'In the front room, Derek,' I say. 'She mustn't have heard you come in.'

'Concentrating on something she's doing, I expect. Something important, no doubt. Mm.' He turns to the Moores. 'Tremendous powers of concentration that girl has. Quite amazing. Martha's the same, of course, just' – the wind drops from his sails – 'the same.' He ducks his head and marches out of the room.

At lunchtime, a squad car takes us to police headquarters in Stretford, where we are to go before television cameras and make an appeal to the public. When we get to speak, much sooner than I have been imagining we would, it is without any priming from the police.

'Just say what you feel,' Clayton says. 'I couldn't suggest anything better than what you would naturally say.'

When we step forward with Clayton, Molly stands to one side, hand in hand with Andrea Dobson.

After it's all over, I won't remember what I said. How unimaginable it is to be on this side of a public appeal. So many flashguns going off, it feels like we have just won Wimbledon.

Sarah addresses the abductor directly: 'Please give us back our little girl. Nobody need ever know who you are. Just drop her off somewhere and get her to ask for help. She's a clever girl. She'll know what to do.'

'You were amazingly composed,' I say to her afterwards.

She gives a small, bitter laugh. 'Librium.'

The police drive us home, and when the door is pushed to, I am standing side by side with Sarah and, if only for a few seconds, we are alone together. Our eyes meet briefly. I could reach out and touch her. She could hold my glance. Either action might make it easier for both of us, but we can manage neither. She walks away from me and back to the kitchen. Seconds later, she storms through the hall, tearing her coat off its hook on her way past me, launches herself out of the front door and disappears hell for leather down the road.

The Keeper of Sweetness

Sarah and I place flyers indiscriminately in Chorlton, Stretford and the city centre. Each one has a photograph of Martha that was chosen because it reproduced well in black and white. *Martha Porter,* they say. *Have You Seen Our 5-Year-Old Little Girl?*

At first, we try to be strategic about where the flyers go. Libraries, medical practices, leisure centres, newsagents' windows all seem priorities. But soon we cover other places where flyers go: café bars, health food shops, arts centres.

While I'm at work, Sarah and Molly regularly take the tram into town, where they tour around looking for Martha. They cover Market Street and St Anne's Square, the Arndale and King Street. Victoria and Piccadilly and Deansgate and Oxford Road railway stations, also Chorlton Street bus station. The Northern Quarter. Whitworth Street. Sackville Street, where rent boys and young girls solicit on the pavements.

Sarah places adverts in free-sheets, local and national newspapers. These other approaches – the adverts, the flyers – I can see the point. When the police stage a television reconstruction of the events leading up to Martha's disappearance I can see the point of that, too. But trawling through the city centre in the hope of bumping into Martha – well, no.

Weeks pass, weeks in which that Saturday in Longford Park flips up each morning like 'I Got You Babe' in *Groundhog Day,* and then it's bright, hot May.

Sarah has been going to home group on Wednesday evenings, regular as clockwork, as if nothing has happened, whereas I've been missing as many weeks as I've been attending. People desperate to help just keep missing the mark or actively putting their foot in it. I mean, how comforting is it to be told, as we were by one home group member, that God will be looking after Martha? *So,* I wanted to snarl, *what was He up to during the Holocaust then?* But you can't, can you?

One evening when I do make it along to home group, though, Kat Fuller leads a Bible meditation on *Psalm 103*, which concerns the love and compassion of God. Even though Sarah and I are obviously not involved in Kids' Church at the moment, I can't help relating aspects of this psalm to the kids – Lee, Tracy and company – from the minibus run: the bit about God working justice for the oppressed.

'What about Lee Hutchinson?' I ask, cutting across whatever was being said. 'How's Lee getting on at Kids' Church?'

William looks at me a moment. 'Haven't seen him.'

Kat inclines her platinum blonde head. 'He hasn't been for weeks. Don't know what's happened there.'

A response dies on my lips and I fall back out of the conversation, for I know with sudden certainty exactly what has happened to Lee. The Sunday before I lost Martha, I promised him I would pick him up for Kids' Church the following week and of course by then I had other things on my mind. Nothing to be done about it, but realising what must have happened, I can feel my heart sink and sour in my chest.

When everyone who wants to has shared what he or she feels God was saying to them in the meditation, Dorothy pipes up, with characteristic seriousness and import. 'I believe there's a verse here which is especially for you, Joe.'

Inside, I cringe. I wonder how I will get through the next few moments without biting her righteous head off. I nod in a neutral fashion, regarding the sharp lines of Dorothy's features, and try to show willing.

'Yes, it's verse 17: "But from everlasting to everlasting the Lord's love is with those who fear him, and his righteousness with their children's children." I believe the Lord wants to reassure you, Joe. I know this is difficult for you to hear just now, but he knows how faithful you've been to him in your life over many years, and the Lord is no one's debtor.'

I'm concentrating on maintaining an impassive expression, which, if she so wishes, Dorothy can read as grateful interest in what she's saying. In my heart, it's wintertime, nuclear wintertime.

'So I feel the Lord wants to reassure you that whatever the outcome of this, he will bring good out of it.'

Dorothy stands and approaches me. *Don't, please don't touch me.* If anyone touches me, I think my heart of stone will turn to frozen titanium.

But Dorothy kneels and takes both of my hands in hers. 'What I feel the Lord is saying is the devil intends to harm you through what has happened to Martha, but the Lord intends to bring good out of it. None of us can see that now, but I think the Lord wants to encourage you.'

In the petrified ghost town inside of me, cold, cold winds blow tumbleweed down the deserted, dusty streets. Whatever Dorothy may feel the Lord is saying, I go home not encouraged, but thinking of Lee waiting for his lift the week I didn't show, that and thinking how when it rains it really does pour.

A family outing, the three of us Sunday-driving to friends in Bolton. Sarah sitting over the wheel the way she does, Molly behind me in her car seat looking at a Little Mermaid picture book

'Where are you going?' I ask Sarah.

'To the motorway, where else?'

'Why are you taking this route, though? What's wrong with the way we normally go?'

She snorts, takes a firmer grip on the wheel. 'Look, who's driving? Just give over, will you?'

Molly distracts me. She has dropped her book onto the floor; with a degree of groaning, I have to unfasten my seat belt, twist round and sit on my knees to reach it for her.

Belted in again, I say to Sarah, 'This is dumb. If you'd taken the normal route, we'd be halfway to Bolton by now.'

Silence. Tearful silence, it turns out.

There have been so many silences and so many tears. 'What is it?' I say.

'You're the one who's dumb. Wouldn't it ever occur to you that I am unable to drive past Martha's school?' Her face flashes red, full-on at me, and then she looks back at the road ahead. 'Eh??'

'Here's Daddy, Molly,' Sarah says one evening when I get in from work.

Even though her tone is bright, I can tell as soon as I see her face that the brightness is false. Something bitter around her mouth and in her eyes, something I've grown fed up with seeing, just as I'm fed up with Barber's *Adagio* and Mozart's *Requiem* being on the hi-fi and tears, tears, tears.

'Hey, girls,' I say, for I can affect a false tone, too.

Sarah says, 'Well, Daddy.'

'Any chance of a hug, Molls?' I ask, and get one. 'How's my cuddle-bunny?' I enfold her sturdy little torso and pat her back. I resist the urge to ask Sarah what she has been doing today; I realise I know the answer.

'We ran into Clayton.'

'Smiler. Did you?'

'He was working on an attempted murder case.'

'So?'

'What?'

'What about Clayton?'

She turned her head away, glum. 'Oh, nothing really.'

'You just thought he would be spending all his time looking for Martha?'

She turns to face me again. 'What's wrong with that?'

'Nothing. Nothing at all. What about a hug?'

I ask this even though I'd as soon hug a porcupine with PMT as Sarah. Tonight I am giving my fight-back campaign a relaunch. Lately, the fight-back campaign has been in the doldrums.

'I suppose I could rise to that,' she says and surrenders to a slight, withholding embrace.

I say, 'Let's go out somewhere and try and enjoy ourselves.'

Sarah steps away. 'Doesn't sound very likely to me.'

Despite growing weary of playing The Keeper of Sweetness, I bite my tongue. 'When was the last time we set out to have a good time?'

She sighs. It sometimes feels to me that she has been sighing for years now. I don't blame her exactly; but it can get tedious.

Sarah hesitates further. 'I think we should be looking for Martha.'

'We *are*. There's never a day goes by that we aren't looking for Martha.'

'So, what? Are you saying we're looking for her too much?'

'No. But it wouldn't do any harm to try and have a brief distraction.'

She continues to study the top of the table.

'Well?' I say to her back.

'All right.'

'That's good,' I say, 'because I'd hate to have bought flowers for nothing.'

She steps back, surprised. 'You've bought me flowers?'

'Uh huh. In the hall.'

'That's nice.'

I won't try to generalise about women as a sex, but Sarah in particular is definitely a sucker for flowers. It works every time, like pressing a button.

She brings them in, mellowing. 'Yellow lilies! They're lovely.'

'And you'd better get dressed up – we're going out to eat.'

'What?'

'Kat Fuller is baby-sitting and we're going out.'

'Oh, so you've already planned it.'

'So what's wrong with that?'

'Nothing. It's just Friday night isn't the best time to go out. Everybody's tired and past their best on a Friday night.'

I'm on a mission here and I exercise fabulous self-control. 'I'm just trying to inject some enjoyment into our lives,' I say in as even a tone as I can manage. 'Some much-needed enjoyment.'

'I know, I know.' She punctuates her remark by touching my arm with the flat of her hand. 'It'll be okay, I'm sure.'

'Come on, Sarah. It's only until half-ten or so. If we flag, we can take some drugs to keep us going.'

Sarah doesn't respond to my attempts at humour as often as I would like her to. However, I remind myself that this is, after all, a campaign. It's not a one-off skirmish where I risk losing everything at once; it's a series of battles, and I don't have to win them all.

'Where are we going?'

'Wait and see.'

'But I hate surprises.'

'I know.'

'*I* do it,' Molly says, as I wrestle her into her pyjamas.

'But you couldn't do it the night before last! You've never been able to do it!'

'I want to do my *poppers!*'

'But you can't! I know you want to, but you've never flipping been able to. D'you see?'

'*I* do it.'

'Okay. Do it then. Prove me wrong.'

She climbs down from her bed and shambles across the room, her all-in-one pyjamas flapping loosely around her.

'I do it over here,' she tells me. Over where I can't possibly interfere.

'Okay. Best of luck. Give me a shout when you've finished.'

She sits on the floor, her legs splayed out before her, and starts to fumble with her pyjama poppers. Moments pass, and I am rigid with frustration.

'Daddy help me?'

When the poppers have all been pressed, I say, 'What about your slippers? You'll need slippers if you're going to go downstairs and play with Kat.'

'No.'

I wait until I have found a patient tone. 'Why not?'

'It's too hot. I want to walk on my feet, Daddy.'

In West Didsbury, we stop off at the Chelsea wine bar for an aperitif - Martini for Sarah, Amstel for me – which to some extent achieves the conjuring trick of putting a little fizz in the dry, dead air between us.

Half an hour later, when a tall, self-contained waitress leads us to our table in Gorky's restaurant, Sarah looks pretty good for somebody who was reluctant to come out, for somebody I have been married to for close to a decade, for somebody whose child is missing. The festive air of a room crowded with diners and the slight lift of our toot in the Chelsea makes me feel a little positive about the outcome of tonight. Maybe booze and ambience have affected her in the same way, because she says to me, 'This is nice.'

And I say, 'Yes, it is,' thinking that maybe if she says it's nice, it will become so.

'I'm sorry for being in a bad mood earlier.'

I feign ignorance.

'Sorry for not being very enthusiastic about going out to eat.'

'That's all right.'

'Really, it's a lovely idea. And I think you're right: I think we should try harder to have a good time together.'

'Did I say that?'

'Not in so many words. But that's what you meant, isn't it?

'Well – no criticism implied,' I lie.

'That's all right.' She smiles and raises her menu. I've always liked Sarah's eyebrows and I think as much again just now as she lifts them in an optimistic way and says, 'So, what are you going to have, Joe?'

I love the language of menus in restaurants where some trouble has been taken over it. *Mushroom gratin; polenta dusted risotto cakes; noisettes of lamb; saffron pavlova with cream and caramel sauce; cranberry frangipan tart*. It's a racket, of course, just as much as concepts like 'fruits of the forest' or 'ploughman's lunch'. It's somebody somewhere – not necessarily in an advertising agency, perhaps it's somebody in a back room over there – somebody somewhere using language to seduce you. I like that.

'I don't know. All of it sounds good to me. What do you fancy?'

'No starter anyway.'

'Why not? When was the last time we were in a restaurant?'

'I'd only get fat.'

'Sarah, take a starter. It's not going to be much fun for you sitting watching me fill my face with *guacamole*, is it?'

'Look, I'm just going to have a main course – this monkfish, which will be pretty rich.'

'What, a piece of fish on a lettuce leaf?'

'What's wrong with you? You're being very awkward tonight.'

'I'm being awkward?' I prod my chest with a couple of fingers and lean closer to give her a better view of my presumably aghast expression. '*I'm* being awkward?'

She blinks, like I am imagining conflict which simply isn't there. 'I'm going to have a sweet, if it makes you feel better.'

'Fine. I'm going to have a cigar,' I add, to annoy her. The evening is turning out to be a bit of a challenge for The Keeper of Sweetness.

'Okay.'

My attempt at being annoying hasn't worked. 'You won't mind?'

She looks away and looks back. Takes a breath. And says, 'I'd like it if we could have a talk.'

'But we talk all the time, Sarah.'

'Not the kind of talking I mean.'

'What kind of talking *do* you mean?' I ask, although I know the answer.

'Your trouble is you just can't handle anything emotional.'

'It is?'

She stares at me, her face slumped. 'You know, we can discuss Martha without you having to lacerate yourself for what happened. I *need* to talk about it, Joe.'

'We have talked about it. We talk about it on a very regular basis.'

'See? You're doing it again. You're making out that I'm over the top about Martha's disappearance.'

'Well maybe it isn't healthy to think of nothing else. I can't talk about it all the time, that's all.'

'Oh!' she shouts. 'How much time could we devote to the subject and remain healthy?'

'All right, all right,' I say.

'You just think that if you keep busy enough, the problem will go away.'

'All right. I will try harder to talk as much about this as you want to.'

'As I need to.'

'Need to.'

The way she looks, I can tell there is more, but she has judged it best not to go on.

The waitress who greeted us takes our drinks order. She's wearing a well-ironed, white WOMAD T-shirt, which looks cool in the heat of this evening. She has the air of someone who is having a good time inside her skin, and I kind of wish I was her, or she was sitting opposite me, smoking French cigarettes, ordering something basted in fat, something drooling sugar. We would be drinking high-octane beers with tequila slammers, giving it some collective 'Nyick-nyick', *Easy Rider* Jack style. I know all the words to 'Tangled Up In Blue'; she might be impressed.

The waitress returns promptly with our drinks. She smiles at us. I like it here. Everything is sharp and merry. I like it here and, considering the cloud that surrounds my life outside these walls, I'd like to ask the waitress if I could stay. But I don't and I don't recite 'Tangled Up In Blue' and I feel appropriate and competent for doing no more than making my requests from the menu after Sarah has made hers. How's that for grown-up? I want to shout after the waitress.

All of which brings me to what they're listening to on *The Wang Dang Doodle* this week:

'Going Steady With The Blues'
(Skeets McDonald)
'Understand Your Man'
(Johnny Cash)
'Therapy'
(Loudon Wainwright III)

Sarah says, 'Somebody was telling me at Mums and Toddlers that there are fifty children under five in the church at the moment.'

'That's one way of increasing numbers.'

Silence, in which I know Sarah is trying to say something.

'What?' I ask.

'Nothing.'

'I hate it when you say nothing when it's obviously something.'

'Well – it just seems unfair that there are fifty children in our church who are fine and...'

'And Martha isn't?'

'Yes.' The sound stalls in her throat.

I say nothing.

'Look,' Sarah tells me, 'I know you don't want to talk about Martha. But there are issues we need to discuss.'

These counselling terms: *issues, role, coping, process.* They put me in touch with my inner redneck. 'I know you want to talk about it,' I say.

'Why don't you want to talk about Martha?'

'All I want to do is put as much distance as I can between me and what happened in Longford Park. I want to be at the other end of the earth from that day.'

'But losing Martha –'

'Do you have to keep spelling it out for me?' I shout. 'I know I lost her. There isn't a second when I can forget it.'

For a moment, it is as if we are in a freeze-frame.

'I wasn't trying to berate you about it, Joe. All I was going to say is that losing Martha is the worst thing that's ever happened to either of us.'

'And that's why I want to get as far away as possible from it.'

She begins to pick at the torn skin around her fingernails. I take advantage of the break to lift my glass and take a mouthful of wine. It feels too pale, too weak for my needs this moment. I scarcely notice the waitress when she brings my *guacamole*. Stabbing it with a pitta-bread finger, I feel even more annoyed with Sarah for not having a starter with me. I'm not looking at her.

'What's your *guacamole* like?'

'It's like something ruined by the mood you've put me in.'

'Oh for goodness' sake.' She picks some more at the skin on her finger. She chews a rag of it.

'You should've ordered a starter.'

She snatches her finger from her mouth and grimaces. 'But don't you see? Your response and my response are mutually, mutually –'

'Exclusive?'

'Yes!' She nods in agitation. 'I want to talk about it, but you don't. You don't want to talk about it, so –'

'Sarah, I know what 'mutually exclusive' means.' We're waist-deep in muddy water. The only way out is to try and make up. 'All right – let's be helpful. Anything else to report from town today?'

'Okay,' she says, and inhales like this is going to cost her all her patience. 'I've been to the Disney Store. I thought that if she had any kind of freedom, if she had any say in her life with whoever has abducted her, maybe she would ask to be brought there. I made a pilgrimage to the cuddly toy mountain. I scanned every small face both below and above the height I think Martha might be now. And then I went to the Early Learning Centre and the Warner Brothers Store. At one point, I found myself standing in front of Dillon's, staring at a display for a novel called *Laura*. You know, Laura, one word, just like Martha in the newspapers. "Police stage Martha reconstruction". "Police hunt for Martha continues". And next to the *Laura* display was another, for a book about child abduction cases. So I decided to go in and torture myself with it. I picked up a copy, read the blurb on the back and flicked through the pages, stopping at a long list of the ways in which children are taken from life. And I soaked up each item in that list: run over, accidentally poisoned, drowning in the bath, falling thorough ice, fatal diseases, murder. I read that page until I choked and then I ran out of there. Apart from that, nothing else to report from town today, Joe. But thank you for asking.'

She looks forlorn. How could I expect her to look otherwise? Did I think she would put her feelings in the wardrobe and have a night off from being torn apart? I'd like to offer her a soft word, an acknowledgement of what she's going through, but I can't find anything adequate to say.

Something moving at the edge of my vision makes me turn and look. I'm expecting the waitress – and once again feeling like I would be having a better time if she were to dine with me and Sarah were to wait on tables – but the mildly shocking truth is that it is Roy Wood. I look him over, from grey Clark's Polyveldts to giant snow-crystal patterned sweater. It's warm – why is he wearing a sweater? Seeing Roy here is a surprise. I wouldn't have thought of Gorky's as Roy's kind of place. He raises a flat palm, like Michael Rennie in *The Day The Earth Stood Still* and the surprise isn't over yet, for in his wake comes not Gort the robot, but Dorothy.

'Ah, Joe,' Roy says. 'And Sarah.' Like it was unusual to find the two of us together. 'Fancy seeing you here.'

And ditto squared, Roy. We all say hello and smile – even Sarah and I are smiling now.

'Having a romantic evening together?'

'I tried having one on my own,' I say, 'but it just didn't work out.'

Roy chuckles. Dorothy beams blankly.

'Have you eaten?' Sarah asks.

'No. Actually, we just called in on spec, so to speak, but there isn't a table available until ten, so it seems.'

We're having such a medium time, I could offer them ours – but I manage to resist the urge.

Sarah says, 'That's a shame.'

Dorothy says, 'What about you two? How are things?' And she raises her eyebrows expectantly.

'Not bad,' I say.

'Up and down,' Sarah says.

'You're very brave.'

Roy nods in agreement.

'We do pray for you,' Dorothy says. 'And I know a lot of other folk are praying for you, too.'

'I know,' Sarah says. 'And we appreciate it.'

Roy says, 'I wish there was a real way we could all help you.' His eyes glisten and he mashes his lips against each other. 'I don't know how anybody gets over something like this.'

I don't either, but I couldn't say as much to a likeable soul like Roy. 'So how's it going with that Datsun, Roy?' I ask.

'Oh, slowly, slowly.'

'They'll be restoring Protons next.'

Roy takes the kidology in good part. 'You wait. I think you'll be surprised, you know.'

'Maybe,' I say. 'Anyway, sorry you haven't been able to get a table.'

'Worse things happen at sea, ha-ha-ha,' Roy says, but then realises that worse things also happen to the people he is talking to and chokes on his laughter. 'We can always call in for a carry-out and get home in time for, ahm –' He has been making a good recovery, but now he's suddenly run aground.

'*Frasier?*'

'No, no – not that one. Although he's very good, too. Very funny, Frasier. No, the fellow in the police. Ohhh, wait a minute now – he's not really in the police. He's more of a, well, what is he?' Roy turns to Dorothy for help.

'I don't watch it, do I?' Dorothy says and adds that they must be going, and then, with more prevaricating and squirming from Roy, they are gone.

'I felt guilty not asking them to stay.'

'Don't be ridiculous. There isn't that much room for us as it is.'

'Don't call me ridiculous, please.'

'I'm not.' I turn to look around for the waitress, who is nowhere in sight. 'Where're our main courses? And I want a beer, dammit. I want a lot of beer and I want it now.'

Sarah laughs. She doesn't laugh when I make jokes, I'm thinking, she just laughs when I'm being entirely serious. And it makes me mad. She looks fondly at me. 'Can I just ask you one more serious thing?'

I draw in breath.

'No, just a quick question – that man in the pin-stripe suit? You don't think that he abducted her?'

'I don't know what to think about him. But my gut feeling is that he meant her no harm.'

Sarah is studying my face.

'Okay?' I ask.

'Okay.'

'Are you having a nice time, dear?' I say, and though my tone is ironic, I really mean what I say.

'Not so far. But the night is yet young, Napoleon,' she says, and smiles broadly.

'Cha-cha-boom.'

Where her smile has come from is anybody's guess, but of no interest to me just now, for calling me Napoleon is Sarah's invitation to rumpy-pumpy and what I'm thinking is that a cigar and a spot of kettling might just salvage the evening for me.

It's quite a happy Joe Porter who stands in the shower attending to the details, who not only brushes his teeth, but also swigs and swills with Plax.

'Hello,' I say when I am under the duvet beside Sarah.

'Hello.'

'Looking for a good time?'

'Possibly. How late is it?'

A question like this doesn't exactly enflame me with desire, but things have been going well for a little while now, after not going so well for longer than that. So, I am determined, like Bing Crosby and The Andrews Sisters, to ac-cent-tchu-ate the positive and e-lim-i-nate the negative.

'Not late.'

'How not late?'

'Not eleven. Not even close to eleven.'

'Hm.'

I begin to massage Sarah's back, kneading the soft flesh beneath her shoulder blades.

'That's nice,' she says, although she could sound more certain about it.

'Good,' I say and rub my lips against the back of her neck. Some time later, I'm still doing much the same.

'Joe?' Sarah says out of the dark.

'Yeah?'

'Do you resent me for feeling differently from you? About Martha, I mean.'

'No.' Not the whole truth and nothing but – just a reasonable response, given the circumstances. More pecking and kneading. A long silence. I know what's coming, but I soldier on, expecting the worst, hoping for the best. Eventually, in the face of such passive resistance, even I have to give up.

'But you do?' I say. 'You resent me feeling differently from you.'

'Yes.'

I roll onto my back and sigh.

'I'm sorry,' she says. 'I just can't be romantic when there's something between us.'

'Then why suggest going to bed in the first place?'

'Did I?'

Bloody woman, I'm thinking. I'm observing to myself that you don't eat the same meal every night, you don't listen to the one disc all the time, you aren't stuck with the same car for life.

'I'm sorry,' she says, 'I have to feel close to you, Joe.'

As it happens, The Keeper has just exceeded his overdraft limit in the First National Bank of Sweetness. 'Forget it then.'

Minutes later, I am sitting on the sofa by the hi-fi. The window is wide open and the air it admits is baked, even now. In the headphones, Steve Earle is giving it maximum twang on 'Guitar Town' and I am sipping San Miguel from the fridge and pulling on my Villiger and the plumes of smoke take me back to when I used to smoke Gauloises.

Bonanza

Not long after I became a Christian – ten or eleven years ago – I went to a party in the country. This was before I got married, before I met Sarah. I was twenty-five. At this time, I was still fairly new-fangled with reading my Bible every day, going to home group mid-week and church on Sundays. Only a year before, I had spent a fortnight breaking into involuntary fits of weeping tears of joy at the discovery of God.

I got a lift with Kat Fuller – Kat Armstrong as she was back then. She always has had style and her 1970s Porsche (a Porsche Rooty-Tooty, you would have to say) complemented her 3-D personality. Most of the way out, she was enthusing about one aspect or another of Christian living – Kat hadn't been a convert much longer than me – and most of the time I was enthusing right there with her. Some of the time, though, I was thinking how exciting it was to be going to a party in a Porsche. I don't generally have friends with Porsches. My friends tend to drive Toyota Dullards or Rover Sheepskins.

'Listen,' Kat said as we drew up outside the house where the party was. 'Can we not leave too late? I have to work in the morning.'

'Fine by me.'

'About midnight then.'

Nothing was the way I thought it would be. I had pictured a farmhouse, but Ellen, whose party it was, lived in a tiny limestone terrace. I had imagined the place would be full of fell-walkers, types in lumberjack shirts and plaited leather bracelets. The way it turned out, there were all kinds of people present – in suits and little black dresses as well as jeans and T-shirts. I planted myself in the kitchen. Kat and I were talking to Ellen; Kat was gone to dance and I was talking to Ellen and some other people; I was drinking beer and smoking. Ellen, or one of her friends, had made up good party tapes. There was Nina Simone, Lyle Lovett, Warren Zevon – good music you wouldn't necessarily have to dance to

– and plenty of stuff you could scarcely not dance to: Prince, The Stray Cats, Wilson Pickett.

The thing with standing in the kitchen at parties is that the party you're having can change out of all recognition in the space of five minutes. Everyone has to visit the kitchen to top up their drinks, and so the population of the kitchen is always shifting. You can be in an interesting conversation about teenage love or the end of the world, asking yourself, *Where have these fascinating people been all my life?* and then seventeen revellers invade for new drinks. When they've gone, you find the cast-list in your conversation has changed, and worse, the conversation has changed, too. Suddenly, beefy men in V-necked sweaters are extemporising about some sporting event you have never heard of: the FA Cup or Wimbledon.

We were discussing how someone as bland as Paul Simon can be such a great lyricist – was it a corollary of Magritte dressing like a bank manager to paint? – when there was a drinks stampede. After it was over, somebody near me was saying:

'The thing is, everyone will have a personal pension before long.'

'Yes, everybody ought to have a personal pension,' somebody else was saying, 'just as everybody ought to have a fixed-rate mortgage.'

I peeled myself away from them and was clicking open a can of Boddingtons when this dark, nutty voice next to me murmured, 'You'll be straight down to your building society in the morning, won't you?'

I looked to my left and connected the voice to a tall, dark-haired woman. 'Well, I would,' I said, 'but I don't have a building society.'

She was wearing a fuchsia pink dress, a proper party dress, velvet and sculpted, and she was beautiful – a firm-jawed, Glenn Close kind of beauty.

'Poor you. You wouldn't have a cigarette, though, would you?' Her voice was like a Radio 3 presenter's: you could imagine it purring words like *Bach, serenade* and *viola.*

I handed her my Gauloises.

'Oh my hero,' she said.

She flicked her thumb against the bottom of the soft package, a white cigarette jumped in the air and she caught it between finger and thumb. Like a majorette with a baton, she rotated the cigarette until it was poised between her first two fingers. She propped the elbow of that arm on her other hand, waiting.

'I suppose you've got a Zippo as well.'

I produced it, said, 'Bingo-zingo,' and handed it to her. I was inter-ested to see what she might do with it. What she did wasn't as close to juggling as the trick with the cigarette, but you couldn't help noticing that she was very dextrous. Her fingers were short and all more or less the same length – monkey fingers. She drew on the Gauloise. 'Aren't you having one?'

'I'll just watch you smoke.' Her skin was pale and cream. With the dark hair and black eyes, she looked oriental.

She exhaled politely to one side of my head. 'Are you trying to charm me?'

'I'm not trying. It must be natural.'

She shivered. 'Oh, I can't *bear* anything natural. It's so false.'

'What happened to the cigarettes and lighter?' I asked.

'They're in your pocket.'

I patted my pocket. 'But I don't remember you giving them back to me.'

'I didn't. I just put them in your pocket.'

'You did?'

'Uh huh.'

'What do you do for a living? Pick pockets?'

With a deft tap of her finger, she knocked ash off the cigarette into a willow-pattern saucer.

'I've enjoyed watching you smoke,' I told her.

'Oh well. I'm giving up. Do you dance at all?'

'Only like Hoss from *Bonanza*.'

'I'll look forward to that,' she said, taking my hand and setting off. 'Hoss – big hat, easy in the saddle – quite appealing, really. Although I always had a soft spot for Adam. All that manly seriousness.'

'How do you know so much about *Bonanza*?' I asked. 'I'd have thought you were too young. I mean *I'm* too young to know about *Bonanza*.'

'I'm a big fan of old TV westerns. Ask me about Rowdy Yates.'

I was impressed. 'Clint Eastwood?'

She dragged me by the wrist towards the music. 'Ask me afterwards.'

The dancing was in the front room. Maybe a dozen people shaking about to The Beach Boys' 'I Get Around'. We began to move, too. I was looking to one side or the other, taking in bookshelves, table-lamps – anything but her. When I did allow myself to look her way, she was looking straight back at me – a frank, bare-faced stare. The next record was 'Louie Louie'. I took in her strong cheekbones, her firm, straight neck. She was poised, upright. She had a supple smile. I leaned across to speak into her ear. 'I'm glad you didn't go for Ben.'

'Ben who?'

'Ben Cartwright. You know: leather waistcoat, silver wig.'

'Oh yes. What is it with Americans and wigs? Don't they realise that everybody knows?'

'Who's your favourite star in a toupé then?'

'William Shatner?'

'Early or late Shatner? TV or movies *Star Trek*?'

'Oh movies, I think.' She looked up at me. 'Who's your favourite?'

'For artistry, it's hard to whack Steve Martin.'

'Steve Martin doesn't wear a wig.'

'That's the level of artistry I'm talking about.'

She was a good dancer. She did the twist and the mashed potato in a mannered way that was appealing. I had the feeling she would know the watusi and the lambada, too. When my unformed bopping brought me into her orbit, I caught her scent, something musky and festive; she smelt like a carnival.

I asked, 'Do you live out here?'

'Yes, yes I do. Quite nearby. So, do you live...in there?'

'That's right. As far in there as I can get.'

'You don't like it out here?'

'Well...cows and sheep: I don't mind eating them, but I draw the line at socialising with them.'

She shoved my shoulder. 'How rude! This is where I live.'

'It's not rudeness, exactly – the country's just not me. I mean, you rural types like to walk everywhere, even when it's raining, and some-times up hills. And where are the café bars, where are the cinemas?'

She laughed, pulling a face.

'I suppose you're a fell-runner,' I said, 'or -hopper?'

'Oh no. I've been known to walk in the hills, but that's about the height of it, ha-ha.'

The room was warm and the dancing had reached the stage where you keep bumping into other people. I hadn't had much to drink, but my head felt in a spin. I said, 'So who are you, then?'

'I'm Gill. Gill Forsythe.'

'Gill Forsythe,' I echoed, turning the syllables this way and that, watching her smile broadly without parting her lips, watching her crow's feet squeeze up like concertinas. And then I remembered that I was Cinderella and that if I weren't careful, Buttons would soon be whisking me off in her Porsche. 'What's the time?' I asked.

She looked at her watch. 'Five to twelve.'

'Riders On The Storm' played and we danced close. I held the soft, sturdy flare of her hips from her waist. She gripped my upper arms and swayed beneath me, looking off over my shoulder. Some strands of her dark hair were damp and clung to her smooth neck. I drew in that carnival odour again, sharp and sweet, but not too sweet, and wished I wasn't dependent on Kat for a lift. 'I'll have to go,' I told Gill. 'I turn into a toad at midnight.'

She laughed. 'You're already a toad!'

On cue, I spotted Kat's platinum hair-do coming out of the kitchen.

'Here comes my lift now.' I tilted my head to indicate Kat, who, being a gung ho Born Again, I knew would be wondering what I was doing canoodling with somebody who wasn't.

Gill didn't even turn to look. 'Just tell 'em you're not ready yet.'

Kat, from the edge of the room, held up two polite fingers. I nodded.

'Two minutes,' I said to Gill.

'Oh, but you mustn't go now!' She scoffed as though I were suggesting something awful and ridiculous – going off to the war, maybe.

I shrugged. 'What can I do?'

'*Stay*, for heaven's sake. There's bound to be somebody else driving back to Manchester later.'

And then Kat was beside us. 'I'm sorry, Joe, but I've really got to go now.'

'Okay, just coming.'

To prove her seriousness, Kat was making straight for the door.

'You can't leave now. We were just getting acquainted.' But Gill began to concede the situation, borrowed my pen and wrote down her number. She kissed me quickly as I was leaving. 'Spoil-sport,' she said.

I shrugged.

Outside, the Porsche was ticking over. Its headlights, a white, blinding flare, shone into me as I left the party. When I regained the use of my eyes, I saw that Kat had shoved the passenger door open. I squatted by it and looked in.

She glanced my way. 'Are we right?'

'I think I'm going to stay on for a bit, Kat. I can get a lift back with somebody later on.'

Her face was half-lit in the glow from the dashboard lights and I could clearly make out a frown on it.

'I'm only dancing, Kat!' I laughed, shrugging this off. 'Thanks for the lift out. I'll see you at church on Sunday, okay?'

Gill Forsythe's bra was black, shiny like Lycra, her panties white with a satin panel. Without any discernible self-consciousness, she threw off the lingerie, flipped back the duvet and flung herself beneath it. By the time I was in beside her, she was doing a crossword.

'I'm sorry. I can't go to sleep unless I've done this.'

It didn't inspire much confidence in a potential lover. 'That's all right,' I said.

'It's only *The Guardian* quick: I won't take long.'

'Okay.'

I turned to examine the paperbacks on her bedside table. A collection of short stories by André Dubus. *Midnight's Children. Aunt Julia And The Scriptwriter.* Something by Alice Hoffman.

I looked about the room, too. A nice, battered, pitch-pine wardrobe with clothes hanging on as well as in it. One hanger on the outside held black Lurex stirrup-trousers and a brightly-patterned, sequinned bolero jacket.

She flung the newspaper to the carpet. 'Finished.'

'That sequinned outfit on the wardrobe,' I said. 'What does a person wear that for?'

'I use it for work.'

'Really? What's your work?'

'Never mind.'

'Go on.'

'It's a secret.'

'I won't tell you what *I* do.'

She laughed. 'Oh, I know what you do already.'

'You do?'

'Ellen told me.'

'*When?*'

'Just before I came over to blag a cigarette from you.' She wriggled closer to me. 'Are you going to sleep now?'

'Not sure.'

'Come here, then,' she said, and kissed me with her muscular mouth and twisting tongue. She swung astride me and pulled the duvet up over us like the wings of a giant bird. I broke my mouth from hers to catch my breath.

I said, 'I won't take long.'

'Oh ha–ha.'

It turned out she did know the watusi and the lambada. The monkey, the jerk and the merenge, too. At one time, in the dark and in my passion, I moaned, 'Oh Gill.'

'What?' she asked, flat.

In the morning, I stared at the ceiling for hours, waiting for her to wake up, thinking about Kat Fuller's warning. For months now, like it or lump it, I had been an Evangelical and Evangelicals were supposed to avoid marrying non-Christians, so recreational rumpy-pumpy was going to be right out of the question. Sexual intimacy was meant to be something sacred, something to be kept within the bounds of marriage. Before Jesus found me, I had slept with two women, and it had been love both times, long-term relationships. This was different. I had never fallen straight into bed before. I couldn't tell how much of my uneasiness I should attribute to having become a Christian, but I was never going to do this kind of thing again, ever. And next time I saw Kat Fuller, I was just going to have to act my little cotton socks off.

Somewhere around mid-morning, I watched Gill tuck her breasts into the pockets of that black bra and snick her supple legs into those white panties.

'I enjoyed that,' she said. It was as if she were talking about a game of badminton. 'We could do this again sometime, if you want.'

'I'd love to.'

Downstairs, I saw she was good with colour: her kitchen was honey yellow with ivory skirting boards and architraves. The small dining table seemed to be hundreds of years old. I ran my fingertips over the ribbed grain of the wood.

'Any special dietary requirements?' she asked. She was opening cupboards and arranging food and utensils on the worktop by her gas cooker. She said, 'I'm a partial vegetarian.'

'Oh yes?'

'I eat vegetables, but I find they go very well with meat.'

She seemed incapable of doing anything – smoking a cigarette, sliding the grill-pan out – without a skilful flourish. And things fell from her hands into inadvertent display. I watched her frying eggs, the way she handled the spatula as if it were a paintbrush and the frying pan her palette. When the eggs were done on one side, she flipped the pan and they somersaulted and landed reversed, without breaking.

'That's impossible!' I said.

'Yes, it is.'

We would meet in Manchester and maybe see a film at the Odeon or the Cornerhouse. Or we would go for a walk in the countryside, have a pub lunch. We always ended up in bed, which is where we were one day when Gill said, 'Ellen says you're a born-again Christian.'

'Does she?' My breath caught, stuck.

'I thought Christians didn't do this kind of thing?'

'They're not supposed to.'

She curled around me. 'Oh, but why not? It's such *fun*.' And she purred in my neck. It never took us long to get going. Presently, I did something for her and when I'd finished, Gill said, 'Mm, that was nice.'

'Well, you know, it's better to give than receive, isn't it?'

She made a thoughtful *moue*. 'No, on the whole I think it's better to receive than give.'

Later, we were drinking red wine while James Brown was telling us that he felt good and Gill said, 'Really: why are Christians not meant to go in for it?'

'We're supposed to save *it* for marriage.'

'That's ridiculous. I don't even save it for love.'

'I know,' I said. And I did. Being with Gill was always fun, and exciting, but you couldn't call it romantic, or emotional.

'Go on: tell me what goes on between Christians and God. I'm curious, honestly.'

'Let's change the subject.'

'Am I troubling you, Joe?'

'Why don't you tell me what your work is?'

She studied me a little longer than was comfortable. 'Give me a cigarette, then.'

I pointed to the heap of clothes on the floor. 'In my jacket pocket. Do you never *buy* any cigarettes?'

'No. I told you,' she said, and lit one. 'I'm giving up.' She inhaled and laughed her rugged laugh. She gripped the Gauloise in the corner of her mouth, screwing up her eyes to keep the smoke out, and pulled another one from the package. 'Get me three mugs from the kitchen.' With the flat of her arm, she swept her bedside table clear. Books and ear-plugs crashed to the floor.

I did as I was told.

She up-ended the three mugs and, breaking the second cigarette in two, put one piece beneath a mug.

'Okay,' she said. 'Slide the mugs around as much as you like. Just remember where the ciggy is.'

I did my best, but no matter how many times Gill tried this on me, I was never able to guess which mug had the half-cigarette beneath it.

'Good trick.'

'Transposition: what I do.'

'You do "transposition"?'

'It's one of the things I do. And production and vanish. And transition, and levitation.'

'You're a magician.'

'A children's magician. You win the *Crackerjack* pencil.'

I asked her how a person got to be a magician and Gill explained that she had done half a degree in Philosophy. 'Which is about right,' she said, 'since I've half an idea of what's going on.' And she went to Florence to busk. 'I wasn't very successful. Tourists only have a limited tolerance for Captain Beefheart and Frank Zappa strummed on a Spanish guitar. By the time autumn was coming and it was beginning to grow too chilly for busking, I was ready for home, and I was nearly there. Got as far as the railway station, looking into the price of a ticket to England – and then I met a magician.'

'And became his assistant?'

'Only in the sense that I'm your assistant: I assisted him with his cock.'

'And in return he showed you magic?'

She nodded. She was all the way back there. I could almost see her on the Ponte Vecchio, all hair-braids and ankle bracelets.

'Okay, I said, breaking the spell. 'How about a transformation? How about turning this, whatever we've got here, into a love affair?'

The reverie dissolved on her face. She gave me another of her fixed stares. 'How about filling me in on the deal between you and God?' She held her eyes on mine. 'Ha!' she said when I didn't respond. 'Turned the tables on you now, haven't I?'

'No. I'll talk about it. What do you want to know?'

'What I'd really like to know is how somebody intelligent comes to believe in God.'

'What, like the existence of God is too good to be true?'

The air between us was thickening, her face hardening. 'You're not answering my question. What I don't get is what makes somebody who's not a fool and, well, not *inadequate* – not in obvious need of a prop – throw in the towel and turn to religion.'

I look at her and put on my best twinkle. 'I thought it would make me the envy of all my friends.'

She practically splutters. 'What? What? *No*body envies Christians.'

'I was misinformed.'

I could have come clean and told Gill of how broken-hearted I had been, how long I had lived in Heartbreak Hotel after The Former Girlfriend. I could have told her what the former girlfriend did, how my life became a war zone. I should have come clean and told her how I fell to my knees one night in my bedroom and said, 'If you're really there, Jesus, please help me.' I should have told her that Jesus came in like, I don't know, like a hurricane, and next morning, in the bath, I was a new person. Chin tucked into my chest, I looked through the soapy bath water at my body. It appeared new to me. I had to tell myself that it couldn't in reality be new, but that's the way it seemed to me. I knew it must be the inside of me which had been made new, yet the outside appeared shimmeringly fresh.

And I was staring incredulously at the square of blue sky framed in the bathroom window, leaking tears of joy and bubbling over with an ecstatic peace. And it felt unbelievable, unbelievable and inexpressible.

Two or three days after I ducked out of telling Gill about my conversion, the pair of us came back to my place after seeing, appropriately enough, a film called *Flirting*. Two or three days isn't long, but these were days in which the ground seemed to have shifted beneath my feet. The leaves had turned and most of them had fallen. She gripped my fingers in her monkey hand and tugged me towards my front door.

'Come on,' she said, laughing, 'I'm feeling frisky.'

Inside, we hung our coats over the newel post. She climbed up a step on the staircase, turned, enfolded me in her arms and kissed me breathily. I surprised myself a little by pulling free.

'What's wrong?'

'I can't.'

'What do you mean you can't?'

'I have a great time with you – you know I do. But what you said about Christians and sex outside of marriage – it seems to be true. Since I've been sleeping with you, God just seems to have run a mile.'

'Really.'

'And I miss him.'

'Oh well. Naturally, it's hard for me to understand somebody who thinks I'm less important than God – but, y'know...'

'I'm really sorry.' What Kat Fuller had said about getting hurt came back to me. 'It's just that I feel more and more guilty every time we sleep together.'

'Well, you know how I feel about it.'

'I just don't seem to be that casual, though.' I searched her eyes, which sparkled back at me. 'I really like seeing you.'

'I know you do.' She smiled. She put her coat back on. 'Listen, you have a nice time with God.'

She kissed me. At the door, she turned to face me a moment. She said, 'And finally today, boys and girls, watch this: a vanish.'

The Steve Earle album has long since finished playing, the San Miguel is gone and, with a final plume of Villiger smoke, I blow the memory of Gill Forsythe away into the fog of the room.

What Do You Think Is The Matter With Me?

Some days later, the phone rings, I answer it and it's Georgia, the mother of one of Martha's school friends. She struggles to get out some sympathetic remarks before asking for Sarah. I tell her Sarah is out, with Molly at the Wacky Warehouse. Georgia asks if Sarah could ring her back. 'I thought it would be nice if we could meet up.'

When they return, I deliver Georgia's message.

'Hmn,' Sarah goes, not looking up as she wrestles with Molly's anorak.

'What?'

'Look, will you just bend your arm a bit?' she asks Molly.

'I thought it was good of Georgia to get in touch.'

'Ha. You must be kidding.'

I have no idea what she's in a strop about. 'No, I'm not. I thought you and Georgia got on well together.'

The anorak comes off, finally, and Sarah straightens and heads for the coat-hooks in the hall. 'How stupid can you get?' she snarls over her shoulder.

'What have *I* done?'

She turns to give it to me with both barrels. 'Can't you understand? How could I be friends with Georgia, who hasn't lost her daughter when I have lost mine? Tell me how and I'll give it a go. But otherwise shut up with the stupid ideas, okay?'

'*Okay.*'

Disparate things happen, pushing me this way, pulling me the other.

I'm sitting in the study one night, in my dressing gown, my Bible before me, looking at a passage from *James* about persevering. This is

months after I lost Martha. I look at the words, which suggest that blessing comes out of perseverance, which reiterate that the Lord is full of
compassion and mercy, but even though I have known him for years,
even though the most exalted moments of my life have been with him, I
have trouble with God's mercy and compassion, all the trouble in the
world. I try to be patient, and nothing happens, no sense of encourage-
ment, no smidgeon of comfort.

I wake next morning to find it's only five. On a whim, I throw
some clothes on, get in the car and drive, without meaning to, to
Fletcher Moss Park.

Going through the park gates, I'm thinking, This is stupid, this is
going to rake me up: Fletcher Moss has been a regular haunt for us from
about the time of Martha's birth onwards. Down at the pond, I follow the
mud path in as close to the water as I can get, so that my beige desert boots
are stained wet. Giant leaves on stalks hang over the water – rhubarb trees,
Sarah and I always call them. I stroke the yellow head of a bearded iris.

'Martha,' I say, quietly. It's as though I believe that she may answer if
I call her name softly enough. I turn through 360°. Pale morning sky, fir
trees; the alpine rockeries on the other side of the water swirling around
me. I step slowly through the circle again, murmuring, 'Martha? Marth?'
Tears fall, and before the circle is complete, I see a figure walking on the
middle path through the rockeries, a man in a green, waxed Barbour
jacket. An 'Oh' pops out of me.

The man carries a walking stick made of briar. He doesn't look
towards me and I can't make out his face. I follow his progress across my
line of vision until he disappears behind some tall rhododendrons. The
path, I know, will bring him round and down and when he comes into
view again he will be facing me, near me.

I retrace my steps to the pond and set off in the opposite direction
from the man in the Barbour jacket. I walk briskly. I shouldn't have
come here. Apart from Longford Park, I can think of no worse place to
have chosen – and I have been to Longford Park and should have learned
enough from the experience not to inflict this morning's foolishness on
myself. I am tripping over memories wherever I turn in Fletcher Moss. I
ought to have tried harder to go back to sleep. I'm too tired to handle
anything this morning. Everything is falling apart. I'm beginning to think
that this is something I won't get through. I'm –

The man in the Barbour jacket stands across the water directly ahead of me. He has gone from one side of the pond to the other without my seeing him. The only possible path was visible – if he used it, I would have seen him walking along it. I'm stopped in my tracks.

The man holds his briar stick in one hand and slowly raises the other until it rests, palm up, facing me. His hair is short, neat, black. He looks about fifty. He lifts both hands – the hand that holds the walking stick and the hand of greeting – up in the air. With this posture and the effect of the sheet of water between us, he looks like a statue. But his face moves, composing itself into a gentle smile.

I take off, running hard in my previous direction, racing to join the man on the other side. I pass behind three large acers which cut him from view. When I come into the open again, there is no sign of him. I run up to the rockeries, along all of the paths. I run until I'm worn out, desperate for a glimpse of that Barbour jacket.

When I've resigned myself to giving up and going home, I make my way to the park gates again. I pass the drinking fountain and, realising I'm dry, I stop and depress the chrome handle. Water shoots up from the stainless steel basin and I gulp from the fountain for a long time.

D.I. Clayton comes round in the afternoon, faster than I expected.

I offer him tea or coffee, which he doesn't want, and I'm about to guide him into the front room, but he makes a beeline for the kitchen, where he declines my offer of a seat, too.

'Have a seat, Joe,' he tells me, the involuntary smile compromised by his authoritarian tone. 'And tell me again what you saw this morning.'

Familiar now with some sort of approach to giving the police a full and clear account of things, I sketch out what I saw in Fletcher Moss, filling the picture in at the corners with some reference to how I felt about the experience.

'You think this man may be Martha's abductor?' Clayton says.

I can almost sense myself shrivelling under what now feels like his weary stare. 'I don't know what to think. It'll sound stupid, but –'

'Go on.'

'He disappeared. Before my eyes. And before that, what I saw of him, there was something reassuring about his presence.'

Clayton digs his hands into the pockets of his car-coat and his smile expands. 'You seem to have a bit of a habit of seeing characters who vanish on you. The man at the hospice car park – you said he disappeared suddenly, too.'

I had forgotten that: Pinstripe was there, leaning on the air, and then he was gone.

'Okay,' Clayton says. 'We'll be in touch.'

At the front door, I say, 'You do believe me, don't you?'

'Look, Joe.' The lenses on his granny glasses flash in the sunlight. He pulls a solemn face. 'Put it this way: I don't in any way regard you as a suspect. Right? All I would say is that trauma does strange things to the mind.'

He nods and makes for our gate.

'I didn't imagine either of these men,' I call after him.

He regards me kindly or patronisingly, depending on how you want to read it. 'Nobody's saying that. You take care now, Joe.'

And he's off back to his Ford Mundane.

Somewhere in this same period, when I am growing used to the idea that things will never get better, when I am starting to ask myself if there is a way that grinding my teeth together might be made to seem agreeable, my old friend Vince Ford phones.

– Agent Smart!

'Uncle Fester!' I say, glad to hear a cheery voice.

– How's it going?

'Fair to Middleton.' You're the reader; you know this is a lie.

– Fancy getting on with this sitcom?

'I would. I really would.'

– I think it has potential. I mean, where is the good Brit sitcom, eh?

The tone of voice Vince uses – energetic, enthusiastic – shows he has no idea of where I am up to with my so-called life. But no doubt he is trying to brighten my day, trying to offer distraction from what won't go away. It's clear he doesn't realise that energy and enthusiasm are beyond my mustering. 'Yeah,' I tell him. 'Have you had any further thoughts?'

– Well, so far our boys are from Eastern Europe. Let's say they are Serbian – topical, and with roughly the same standing internationally as white South Africans or Ulster Loyalists.

I used to know what we had in mind with this sitcom idea. I used to care. 'Yeah, Boris and...'

– Dragon, who is big, beefy and stupid. He's not only inarticulate, he's sometimes downright incomprehensible.

'Can't go wrong with a stupid character.'

– Boris is nervy and insecure. He's paranoid and prone to going into adrenaline-driven rants.

I'm getting a bit bored with character sketches now. 'What about writing one series and then just knocking it on the head? I always liked the way Cleese only made a few *Fawltys*.'

– Could do. *Fawlty Towers* is crap, though.

Part of the thing with Vince is that he takes a dim view of 98% of all culture. The rest of the thing with Vince is that the 2% of culture he likes, nobody else does. Some of Vince's favourite films? *Waterworld*, anything John Carpenter made after he stopped having hits, and *Ishtar*. The prosecution rests.

'What about making it one plot over the entire run?' I ask.

– We would need a strong story line.

'A quest plot – Dragon & Boris are after something. Maybe a rare record.'

– Such as?

'Dylan's original *Freewheelin'* had a different track listing. Only a few hundred copies were pressed up.'

– Yeah but he's crap.

'It could be a road-movie – a road sitcom – as they chase this rare record around the UK. That way, they needn't be tied down by owning a record shop.'

– Nick Hornby's done the record shop.

'I *know*. So anyway, their car would be a Trabant.

– What's a Trabant?

When Vince wants you to explain things, you never do. It's invariably a trap of some kind. 'So what else is new?'

– Having a Billy Fury phase at the moment.

'Not again.'

– 'Long Live Rock' on the *That'll Be The Day* soundtrack: triffic!

Vince lives for the rock'n'roll of the years just before and just after he was born. Even though *That'll Be The Day* was in cinemas while Vince was in primary school, I wouldn't be surprised if it and *American Graffiti* were his all-time favourite films. Given a choice in life, he'd have been an English teenager in 1962, when The Beatles broke, or an American one in 1956, when Elvis rose out of Memphis like a rocket.

– So you're all right?

It's clear to me that Vince and I are never going to talk about anything as painful as how a person in my shoes might feel. He doesn't want to hear it and I don't want to tell him about it. 'All right.'

– If there's anything we can do to help, we're here, you know.

What? (Most of the things you need to say to people you can never say.) What? What is there you can do to help? If I knew anyone who could help, I would have made a beeline for them. I can feel the air being drawn up my nostrils. I can feel my chest rise to breathe. Your body is reluctant to let you die. This helps. Having this thought, that your body won't want to let you give up the ghost – it helps.

– Becky thinks you probably want to be left alone.

'It seems like a good idea to keep busy. So the sitcom thing is appealing.'

– Here's something to think about: if Stevie Wonder dresses the way he does because he's blind, why is Ray Charles so natty?

Sarah catches my eye. 'Are you in a mood with me?'

'No. Why should I be?'

We are driving into town on a Saturday afternoon: retail therapy. Molly is with the Fullers, playing. A tape is playing on the radio-cassette – The Pixies' *Doolittle* – and ahead of us, Manchester looks fresh. Slipping through the traffic, I smell garlic and something else – some kind of sauce cooking? – from the restaurants on the Deansgate edge of Castlefield.

'Aren't you looking forward to this?' Sarah asks. 'I thought you were the one who was keen on getting on with our lives.'

'What do you mean?'

'I don't know. You seem to have been trying to put on a brave face and, I don't know, go jolly-chasing.'

'Jolly-chasing?' My strongest urge is to go on the attack again, even though I'm aware that it may not be helpful. I get weary of always being in the wrong. Because I want to run from Martha's disappearance, probably the whole world thinks I'm not feeling this. But it's feeling it that makes me want to run. I keep *shtum*.

Black Francis is just telling us again that our man is coming when Sarah ejects the tape and starts stabbing her way through the radio presets. *What are you looking for?* I would like to ask, but don't. *Mahler FM? Or maybe a station that only plays the tragic bits from Italian operas?*

'You know,' I say after a while, 'in Longford Park that Saturday I was distracted for seconds, Sarah. It could have happened to you just the same way.'

I'm looking straight ahead, trying to pass my remark off as casual – just a thought I happened to have.

'I'm not thinking about that.' She looks even more fed up than she usually does, which is surprising, because I thought she had reached her operational ceiling on that score. 'All I think about is finding her.'

'But you can understand me thinking about when I lost her?'

'I don't care what you think.'

'What's the matter with you?'

'What do you mean, what's the matter with me? What do you *think* is the matter with me?'

'That's not what I mean. I just wondered why you are so down on me all the time. Y'know?'

'You don't want to talk about Martha. And when I'm talking about her, or when I'm crying, you make me feel that I'm being over-the-top. It's *ridiculous*. You act like it's a case of 'pick yourself up, dust yourself off and start all over again'. Well, it's just *not*.'

'It's the worst thing that's ever happened to me.'

'But you don't even want to talk about it.'

'I can't help it, Sarah.' I let out constricted air with what feels like physical pain. 'I've no more control over the way I react to this than you do.'

Through the car's wound-up windows, I can smell the escape people on the streets are out looking for and I want a share of it, like water in the desert. It doesn't matter that discord sits like a toad between us. I want my escape, I want my getting clear of it all.

'Ah, for crying out loud!' I stab my foot on the brake-pedal as a car shoots out of a side street right in front of us. 'Turkey-brains!' I shake my hand in the direction of the offending motorist.

Moments pass, and then Sarah speaks to me in a more conciliatory tone. 'Clayton said that all Martha's details are with every police station in the country.'

'I know. You told me.'

'He said that her details are in every police-station and that they're posted on the Internet, with links to support groups in this country and in Europe.'

'Good.'

'They've had a lot of crank calls, but he said that often genuine calls can come in quite a long time after disappearances, months and years afterwards.'

But I can't be thinking of months and years. I can't be thinking of hours and days. And what I can think of, I daren't admit, even to myself.

We separate for an hour, then meet in the San Marco, an Italian café in a basement. She has bought a dress from Next and a scarf from Accessorise, which seems to bring a moment's pleasure. I tell her that I have bought Los Lobos' *Kiko*, which I know won't interest her much. As I talk, she begins to focus on something at the top of the stairs which lead to street level.

I turn to see what she may be looking at, then see a Barbie anorak up on the street, right outside the plate-glass door. The pink is the same, the fake-fur edged hood is the same. The little figure is the right height.

Sarah gets up and climbs the stairs toward the child, slowly, as though she is wading waist-deep in the sea. Shuffling after Sarah like a man hypnotised, I know it can't be Martha, but it looks like her hair, as well as her anorak. She is walking with a man my age.

'Martha?' Sarah says gingerly when she draws near to her target. And then again, louder, 'Martha?'

The man glances over his shoulder, but the girl doesn't turn. I feel like we might be seeing a ghost. Sarah reaches out to touch her, but hesitates; withdraws her hand; reaches out again.

'Martha?' She touches the elbow of the Barbie anorak.

The little girl who turns and looks up, chubby-faced and sullen, is nothing like my Martha. I wonder if I can really get through this.

The Astonishing Ant-Man

Disparate things, desperate times. I don't have a survival plan. I just get up in the morning hoping that the situation won't worsen before bedtime.

I come down for a break from the computer, mid-afternoon. While the kettle boils, I hear Sarah pressing out a number on the phone in the hall.

'D.I. Clayton,' she says. 'Thank you.'

I click the kettle off.

Sarah calls out, 'Molly? What are you doing?'

'My watching Penguin.'

'That's what I wanted to ask you,' Sarah says, in a different tone – presumably to Clayton.

She listens as Clayton makes a brief reply, then tells him, 'I've had no word for a couple of weeks, that's all.'

More indecipherable sounds from the receiver. I am desperate to get as far away as possible from this phone conversation. At the same time, I'm compelled by it.

'Look – just what are the police doing at this stage in – something like this? I mean, early on it was all over the papers and the TV, so I could see that the police were seriously trying to find Martha –'

Clayton interrupts her.

'Well it feels that way.'

This time, he responds at some length.

'Just what is it that's snowballed? You haven't made any progress so far as I can see.'

At this point, I surmise, Clayton defends his efforts.

Sarah scoffs. 'You've eliminated the immediate family as suspects. Big deal. Very big deal. Look, weeks ago you said you were "very hopeful". What happened to that?'

Whatever Clayton's comeback, she isn't satisfied with it. 'None of you are capable of saying anything direct,' she shouts. 'It's like an uninhibited statement on anything – how many sugars you like in your tea, the weather – would bring the Greater Manchester Constabulary to its knees.'

I imagine Clayton is reaching new heights of conciliation here.

'No,' Sarah snaps, 'you definitely cannot afford to string me along.' And she hangs up.

She comes into the kitchen. Seeing me, she bristles – no, bristles isn't the right word. She looks set to explode. Instead, she turns on her heel and seconds later is stamping up the stairs. *I* wanted to run up the stairs.

At this stage, I don't know how far we are through this nightmare journey. Is it halfway over or just beginning? It occurs to me that Martha's disappearance may only have brought things between Sarah and me to a head. Maybe we were always wrong for each other.

On the kitchen shelf in front of me is Martha's favourite Wallace and Gromit beaker. I reach out and touch it and a memory of Martha comes to mind.

One day, instead of the uniform trousers, Sarah let her wear a pair of flares to school, flares with flowers embroidered round the shin. Martha came home full of it: 'A big girl came up to me at lunchtime and said, "I like your trousers".'

And then I bolt – into the car and down to Ivy Green Road, where I slam and lock the door before plunging myself into Chorlton Water Park. I pound along the gravel paths, panting and grimacing at the big heavy sky, across to the river. The Mersey is swollen and moving fast and hard. I climb an embankment and steam along in the direction of Jackson's Boat, a pub where an iron bridge crosses the river, a handy place to turn around for home, should I ever feel that way inclined. How I feel, though, is like Jake La Motta in *Raging Bull*: on the run from my demons.

Before I reach Jackson's Boat, I cut down the embankment away from the Mersey and through a field to Sale Water Park. When I emerge from a gap in some tall hedging, I'm faced with a lone wind-surfer on the water ahead of me and goose-shit on bare, slimy earth beneath my feet. It's slippery enough to risk losing my footing, so I move gingerly to the right, clear the slime and hobble over some stones to the water's edge. I can't articulate everything that is surging through me. Would it make any difference if I could? I weep my leathered-over heart red-raw, so that I'm breathless, gasping and hiccuping. I can feel cold air pass through my lungs, or is it the shock of my wounded heart opening up?

I don't know how much time passes before I'm at the sniffling stage and a voice beside me says, 'Iya, Joe.'

Lee.

'Hey!' I go, mopping my face and mustering my best Paliachi impression. 'Howdy doody.'

'Iya.' He's gripping the handlebar of a mountain bike and staring at me like I'm a road accident.

I blow my nose. 'So – didn't know you were into wind-surfing, Lee.'

'Yeah,' he says, then a smile dawns on his wizened little face. 'I was North of England champion, couple of years back. But I had to give it up. Too much pressure.'

We both laugh, more than the joke warrants.

'So what're you doing in the water park?' One of the things he's doing, I know, is wagging school.

'I come here a lot.'

'Mountain-biking?'

'Yeah, and looking for things. You can find a lot of things round here.'

The lone wind-surfer distracts me for a moment. He's on the other side of the water, but facing us and advancing towards us. I suddenly see that he is a figure separated from me by an expanse of water – like the man in the Barbour jacket at Fletcher Moss – and, for the umpteenth time I wonder what that was all about. I play back his upraised hands and his gentle smile – and then I'm looking again at Lee Hutchinson's woe-begone features.

'D'you want to walk along with me for a bit?' I ask him. 'There's some sort of observing thing the other side of that embankment.'

'The hide, you mean? Where you can watch birds?'

'You took the words right out of my mouth.'

We see a heron, taking off from the water, before we even reach the hide. We stop to watch as it lifts into the air with all the grace of a Ray Harryhausen pterodactyl. When we move on again, I can't help noticing that Lee's mountain-bike looks very shiny and new, can't help wondering if it's been half-inched. Admittedly I don't know much about Lee's family circumstances, but what I do know wouldn't lead me to think that his Mum would shell out a hundred quid for a new bike. For one thing, Lee's appearance never suggests that anyone has spent so much as 50p on his wardrobe.

A plaque in the timber hide shows us the other kinds of bird we may see: seagull, magpie, snipe, kestrel. I look at Lee's shrimpish form and for the second time in five minutes I study the expression on his face. The way his face looks when it isn't doing anything else. What it says is: It's a crap life, anyway.

'You interested in birds then?' I ask.

'Nah.'

For some moments we scan the place where the birds ought to be.

'But I like having a place to hide meself away sometimes.' He fidgets with his bony little fingers. 'If there's people here, I can hide in them trees behind.' He jerks his head back to indicate.

No sign that he resents me for failing to show when I said I would. Kids get used to being let down; kids learn fast that they have to forgive adults. Besides, there's no reason Lee would think he was missing out by not getting to Kids' Church; it's me who thinks that. I wonder whether he knows about Martha. Even if nobody buys a newspaper in Lee's house, it's been in all the free papers that get delivered in Chorlton. But who's to know if Lee reads newspapers? He might have seen something on the local news, if he watches news.

'I hear you knocked Sunday mornings at Mersey Valley on the head,' I say.

In response, Lee's head turns but he doesn't meet my eye. 'Yeah. Me Mam takes us out on trips on Sundays.'

'I'm sorry I let you down. Last time you went, I said I would pick you up the following Sunday – remember?'

A tinny buzzing causes us to look around and what we see, maybe a quarter mile away, is a little red remote control plane buffeting the air. The person controlling it is nowhere in sight.

'Yeah.' He fidgets with the zipper of his coat.

'I felt bad about letting you down, Lee, but there was nothing I could do –' I'm not sure how to go on. I don't want to bring up Martha. I don't want Lee thinking I'm looking for his sympathy.

'Don't matter.' He shapes up to make a move.

The little plane fizzes along, circling high above the meadows. It looks too puny to stay up there under its own power, but it makes its descent, back to its invisible owner.

'There was nothing I could do about it,' I tell him as he heads on, and I start after him, lost here.

We're standing by my car, about to go our separate ways, when a sporty 1980s Honda with alloys and dark-tinted glass shoots by us, brakes and reverses to where we are standing. The passenger window winds down to reveal a diminutive skally in sunglasses and a baseball cap.

'All right, Lee,' he says. He tilts his chin at me, not precisely friendly. The driver leans across and leers at Lee and me. This one is a fat boy, has the obligatory baseball cap – it probably says I ♥ HANNIBAL LECTER above the peak – and what look like expensive sunglasses: aluminium frames that hug the eye sockets.

'Iya Waz.' Lee doesn't seem wildly pleased to see these two.

'See yaw in the precinct café later, a-right?'

Lee's face is carrying a practised, neutral expression. 'Sorted.'

'Sweet,' the five-foot skally says, and the Honda rockets off, low profile tyres shrieking as it disappears around the corner of King's Hill Road.

I look at Lee, but say nothing.

'Anyway,' he says, 'better get on.'

'Sure.'

He nods, meeting my eyes and looking away again. 'See you.'

As he throws a leg over the crossbar, I wonder again what the story is with this handsome mountain-bike. Like Lee's wagging school, it's something that, for whatever reason, I don't broach. Lee has his problems and Tracy has hers, but I've got enough of my own to be going on with, thanks. I don't want more aggravations; I want distractions, I want relief, and any kind will do.

'Joe,' Lee says, surprising me, for I have gone off somewhere in my head. 'It was your little girl, wan't it? That Sunday when you never showed; your little girl...'

It's all over his face now. I don't know what it is he can't say, but I'm glad that he can't say it. Another second or two and at least one of us would be in tears.

I nod and try to muster an encouraging smile.

'That were well bad.'

'Yeah, it was.' I blow out heavy air. 'But anyway: how about I try again this Sunday? Eh? If you'd like to go to the class at Mersey Valley, I could give you a lift on Sunday.'

The offer of an agreement between us seems to open an escape route from the awkwardness of the past few moments. 'Okay,' Lee says.

I arrange to call for him at what used to be the usual time, but when I do, nobody answers. For a long moment, my eyes bore a hole through the front door's chipped paint, paint worn dull over many years. Looking down at the dilapidated mat, I see a flattened, rain-washed milk carton which I stare at for a further moment or two before kicking it away. Not a lot of point in me inviting Lee to church, really. How much of an advocate for it am I at the moment?

Me setting the kitchen table for tea. Sarah is cooking, spaghetti *bolognese*, it's almost ready. The windows are steamed over and it's dark outside. Molly is arranging her bobbles on one end of the table – according to size, she tells me. Sarah is draining the pasta. I'm pulling the cork from the bottle, but wait – Sarah is staring at the table. I look at it, too, but I don't get what is drawing her attention.

'What?' I say.

Sarah makes no reply. She dumps the colander on the draining board, goes to the table and lifts one of the place settings.

'What?' I repeat.

'There are only three of us," she murmurs.

Sarah is always going off for little prayer meetings with Leslie Moore, or Kat Fuller, or Dorothy Wood. I'll be working at home, and Leslie will call and take Sarah out for an intense cup of coffee. Or Dorothy will walk Molly round the park for a couple of hours while Kat and Sarah get in a holy huddle, praying their way into the despair like Jack Hawkins and Richard Todd hacking their way through the Burmese jungle with machetes in some old war film. One part of me admires them for supporting Sarah so well, but another part is irked each time the post brings Sarah another pastel notelet with an encouraging Bible verse and some loving words from, more often than not, Leslie. I can see it's something Sarah needs, but the very presence of these ministering angels in my airspace suggests I might need whatever it is they bear – therapy? A listening ear? – too, and I don't. Talking about it or praying about it is the least appealing thing I can think of. My strongest impulse is to put a thousand miles between me and all this...*trauma.*

So: Sarah's spiritual needs are being met outside of Sunday services and I just don't want mine met. All the same, the two of us are persevering with attending on Sunday mornings. Maybe we're just stubborn.

One Sunday, a couple of items of church business are tacked onto the end of Mersey Valley's second service. Our treasurer is on his feet and sauntering into a financial update.

'This time last year,' he explains and slides a transparency onto the OHP, 'the picture looked like this. I don't wish to bore you –'

You're too late!

' – but let me take just a few moments to explain why.'

Don't let him!

And before he's got beyond staffing costs, my mind, like Elvis, has left the building. I am free-associating. Cat-Man, I begin. Gene Vincent's Cat-Man. The Beatles' Nowhere Man. *Rain Man. Repo Man.* Iron Man. Elastic Man. Ant-Man. I love Ant-Man. I have never understood why the world took Spider-Man and not Ant-Man to its bosom. They were both, after all, half-man, half-insect. But you only have to look at the covers of their respective comic-books: Spider-Man stars in *The Amazing Spider-Man* – so convenient to find in a comic-shop rack – but Ant-Man was located in something called *Tales To Astonish*, which gives the game away. All the second-rate superheroes featured in generic titles: Aquaman in *The Brave & The Bold* and the Legion Of Superheroes in *Adventure Comics*.

And you can sort of understand why these weren't Premier Division superheroes. Aquaman: he can hold his breath underwater. Good trick, but it has its limits. And what about Ant-Man himself? All he can do is shrink to the size of an ant. Although he does turn out to have to have plenty of character development: as Hank Pym, his scientist alter ego, he finds a way to do the opposite of the shrinking process and evolves from Ant-Man into Goliath (and later, if you want to be pedantic, to Yellowjacket). And Hank is a *great* name. Plus, as Goliath, he picks up the nickname High-Pockets, which is pretty cool, too. Best of all, he has his own personal Tinkerbell, Janet Van Dyne, a.k.a. The Wasp, who – apart from being able to shrink to the size of a wasp, grow insect-wings and antennae, apart from being adventurer, fashion designer and independently wealthy socialite – is one curvaceous bug. She can zap me with her bio-electric sting anytime.

And then I notice the church treasurer has gone (did somebody lassoo him and drag him out of town behind a broncing stallion?) and Geoff Simpson is on his feet again and his neck is talking. 'The organisation of our children's work,' he says. 'As you know, this has been a matter under discussion for some time. But can I just state very categorically here that we don't propose to discuss it at this time. This is for information only, if you understand me.'

I look around and make eye contact with Kat Fuller, who drops her white-haired head forward and pulls a face at me, a kind of lobotomised face – half Boris Karloff's Frankenstein monster, half Steve Bell's Margaret Thatcher.

'From the end of this month,' Geoff says, 'we have decided that our children's work be put *on hold* for a period of time.'

Everyone in the room does a synchronised flinch, and then begins to murmur.

For crying out loud. What's the point of me going out of my way to get Lee Hutchinson back to Kids' Church if there's going to be none when I get him there? I can't begin to imagine what putting it 'on hold' might amount to. A flash of Lee pedalling up King's Hill Road after his skally friends – the alloys, the baseball caps. The small-scale crime and low-life abuse his skally pals are leading him into. I wonder if the skallies are willing to put all of *that* on hold while Geoff Simpson and our elders dick about.

'So, firstly: from the end of the month, and for a short time thereafter, all of the Kids' Church classes will meet as one large, er, assembly. Secondly, for reasons which I'm not prepared to discuss from the front, we're going to stop our practice of bussing in, as it were, un-churched kids from around South Manchester. So, ahm, having made both of these two points about the matter can we postpone any discussion until later?'

That linguistically challenged shit-wit. I thought the church was the only organisation in the world that existed primarily for its non-members. What am I supposed to do now? Call round on Lee and tell him that we're too busy with church politics to bother with him at the moment, but can we get back to him in a year or two's time, when we've sorted ourselves out? What a bunch of tossers. I think of Lee and his handy brother, and Tracy with her dodgy Dad. And then I think of

Martha and a long dark tunnel opens before me, but I refuse to let myself go down it. Instead, I fix my gaze ahead. Which makes it easy for me to spot Roy Wood rising to his feet, a lamb with his hand in the air.

'Yes, Roy, I'm afraid I have to repeat that this is not an item for discussion,' Geoff says. 'The elders want to postpone any airing of views until we have more concrete plans for –'

'But why should we abandon the children we bring in from outside the church?' Roy says in his gentle, reasonable way.

The whole room shifts position to join me in staring at Roy, an unlikely rebel.

'Please, please,' Geoff cries. 'Roy – please. Can I ask you to sit down? Please?'

Roy looks to his left and to his right, but stands his ground. 'Really, Geoff, I can't see that this is a valid way for you to proceed.'

Voices rumble around the room. Geoff looks all at sea. He has both arms raised from the elbow so that he resembles a police cadet who wants to direct traffic, but suddenly can't remember any of the signals. 'Ah,' he says, his neck thrusting up and out, his mouth going into one of its *URGH* expressions. He looks upset and seems to be scanning the congregation for other elders to support him. If he is, none of them picks up the signal. 'I don't know whether we can go on with this.'

I'm not sure I can either. I keep coming back to how I let Lee down once and I thought I was going to be able to make amends. I can feel my blood pressure going up by the second.

Tom Beattie is on his feet now – the cavalry! – and holding his hand out for Geoff's lapel mic. Geoff doesn't hesitate to unclip it, unfasten the transmitter pack from the back of his belt and pass them over.

'Guys, guys,' Tom oozes, 'I'm sure none of us here thinks this is the kind of leadership which would drive through new policy without adequate discussion. That just isn't the Mersey Valley way, now is it?' He leaves a brief silence for his words to sink in and some of the tension is already defusing. He runs a hand over his stubbled skull and flashes a sanctified smile to the east and west of the room. 'Good. Good. Now perhaps I can I make a proposal to the whole church body?' I don't know if he expects an answer or not, but he leaves space for one anyway. 'Can I?' It seems he can. 'Will people be content not to debate this point this morning if we come back to you in a month's time and try to put our case for the future of Kids' Church in clearer terms?'

This has a settling effect and everyone's attention is now focused on Tom, who nods thoughtfully. 'Okay, Roy?' Roy Wood takes his seat again. 'Sorted.' Tom practically wags his head as he registers his own new high on the charm-o-meter. *Ex*-cellent!'

But then William Moore, his W. G. Grace beard bristling, rises up like Neptune from the waves. 'I'm not sure what you're saying. Is the minibus run going to be discontinued or not?'

The two hundred and odd people in church this morning could not be more attentive now, could not be closer to the edges of their seats.

'Please,' Geoff says. 'We don't want anyone to get the wrong end of the, of the – stick. There are reasons for re-thinking the use of the minibus, and we will return to them at the meeting in a month's time that Tom has just suggested. But can I just make one thing clear –'

'If only!' I say, loud enough to carry. Way down inside, my nuclear reactor is about to blow.

'– we're not actually talking about closing anything down here. We're talking about opening up new possibilities.'

And I am on my feet and there's a clatter. The clatter, I realise was my chair hitting the wooden floor tiles. I am on my feet and I am on my way out of the building and what I'm muttering in my wake is: 'Bloody amateurs.'

As I make my way to the exit, people are staring at me, much the way the 1966 crowd at the Free Trade Hall might have stared at the guy who shouted *Judas* at Bob Dylan, but I don't care about being a pariah; I just don't want to know.

'Look, please understand –' Geoff is appealing to the crowd. 'Clearly, quite clearly, the elders have the highest regard for what has been achieved in Kids' Church –'

I don't give a shit. I'm through to the foyer, in every sense I'm outta here. Lee will grow up a petty criminal, but it was always going to be that way. Whatever sordid things may have been done to Tracy in dark corners of her so-called home will condemn her to a lifetime of abuse from men like her father. And Martha is probably lying in a shallow grave.

Picture the closing frame in the comic book you have been reading: as the ant he rides gallops out of church, The Astonishing Ant-Man is shouting over his shoulder, 'And I ain't coming back!'

The MBWM

From my window in the tram, I see that leaves are turning and falling. Each season of 1997 seems to have lasted a year.

I reach the Cornerhouse bar and here is Vince, approaching.

'Charles!' (As in Hawtrey, not Prince.)

'Herman!' (As in Munster, not Goering.)

He removes his parka. Underneath, he wears the Vince uniform of T-shirt, V-neck and blue jeans.

'Blinking dreadful place,' he says and sits down.

While I'm waiting at the bar to order our drinks, Vince is tilting his head back, eyes languorously half-closed, and stroking the hair at the back of his head in a parody of narcissism. I laugh, but also hope none of the people at whom this is directed, the fashionable drinkers around me at the bar, see what he's up to.

When I re-light my cigar to accompany the fresh drink, Vince says, 'Feeling suicidal again?'

I say, 'You're ideally situated for a spot of secondary smoking,' and send a column of smoke flying over his head.

Vince says, 'Let's talk turkey, then.'

We both pinch our wattles and go, 'Gobble, gobble, gobble.'

I'm thinking that there is quite a bit of turkey I would like to be talking just now that, with Vince, I can't. The ominous feeling I have had about Sarah and me just about forever, it seems like. And then there's the journey I've been on since I last saw Martha, which I wouldn't want to discuss even if Vince were able to bring it up.

Vince says, 'I think we should get on with *Boris & Dragon*. I think we're onto a winner here, so we may as well set off on the road to sitcom heaven. There's so much crap out there.'

'I know,' I say. '*Seinfeld, Frasier, Third Rock From The Sun*. Never more than one laugh every three minutes.'

'British crap, I mean. You know what I mean.'

'We'd be doing well, though, if we could write something half as good as *Seinfeld*. Look at it: all you need are four great central characters and the best team of comedy writers at work in television today. Should be a piece of piss.'

'Fine. Let's do it.'

Neither of us says anything.

'Off we go then,' I encourage.

Vince says, 'We've got the situation: Eastern Bloc music anoraks on a quest in the West.'

'Hey! Good title: *Quest in the West*.'

'Nah.' He pauses for a couple of seconds' contemplation. 'Nah. Doesn't have the cultural resonance of *Boris & Dragon's Capitalist Trip*. So, as I say, we've got the situation. Now all we need to do is develop the characters a bit.'

'All we need to do is to develop everything.'

Ignoring me, Vince leans forward, his face all lit up with enthusiasm. I move my smoking cigar further away from him and fan the air clear.

'I've got it!' he says, 'Fantastic character quirk. Tell me: what's the most popular sport in this country? By far.'

'I don't know. Football?'

Vince slaps the table. 'Wrong. Everybody says that. But it's *fishing*. Ha!'

'Why is a sitcom character who likes fishing going to be funnier than one who doesn't?'

'It's not the funniness that's significant here. It's the extra dimension of characterisation. You could have Boris and Dragon as world-class fishermen who fund their quest for the holy grail of the original *Freewheelin'* by working their way through fishing competitions round the British Isles. They're *fly* fishermen. Fly fishermen on the hoof: a unique road movie sitcom. I love it!'

'Okay,' I say. 'What do we know about fly fishing?'

'Nothing.'

While Vince is at the toilet, I glance to the right and see something that causes my heart to rocket up my neck: Gill Forsythe, not twenty feet away. My eyes lock on her and I follow her every gesture as if my life depended on it. She's talking to another woman in the cinema con-course. She looks a little different: coiffured, expensively turned out. My chest is thumping.

Presently, Vince is across the table again from me, with a Diet Pepsi and a Budvar. He is telling me how easy it would be, how little time it would take, to research fishing sufficiently to be able to bluff your way in writing a fishing sitcom. I have to interrupt him because out of the window that separates the bar from the concourse, Gill Forsythe is crossing from the ticket desk to the stairs which lead to the galleries.

'See the woman with the dark hair near the staircase? Hair in a bob?'

He stops talking and turns his head. 'Uh huh.'

'Probably The Most Beautiful Woman in Manchester.'

'That's a fact?'

'That's a certifiable fact.'

He looks at me, non-plussed. 'And?'

And a kaleidoscope of emotions. And my heart goes this way, that way and the other, dancing in heavenly places with The MBWM. And nothing I can say.

Vince goes, 'Hello?'

I look from Gill back to him. 'I used to know her.'

'Cue the Bruckner.'

'Cue the cement-mixer in my guts.'

Vince looks at his watch. 'We're going to miss *Johnny Suede*.'

I am starting to come over all *temps perdu*. Part of me really wishes I were the sort of person who could be unfaithful to his wife and see it as no more than what I have coming to me, the bonus that is due on life as a result of the many wrongs it has done me.

I am giving lip service to my conversation with Vince, but I keep expecting to come face to face with Gill. The High Anxiety Tympani Orchestra in my heart is playing 'The Ride of the Valkyries'.

As we go through the swing doors that lead to Cinemas 2 and 3, Vince laughs. 'You're incredible, y'know. Look at you: you're happily married. God knows how it happened but you've become a perfectly respectable family man and here you're acting like you were seventeen.'

'Help me. I'm coming straight out of adolescence into mid-life crisis.'

Being a perennial fantasist, what I'm thinking as Vince and I enter tonight's cinema of choice, is how much I would like to see Gill again.

By the time Vince and I have taken our seats, I am thinking how much seeing her would be like surfacing from the deep, breathing again. And then I stop thinking about her. The theatre is darkened, the images are playing on the screen, a Pavlovian crackling sound comes from the speakers and I put Gill Forsythe out of my mind.

On the screen, Brad Pitt, before he was a big name, is starring in *Johnny Suede*. This is the third time I have seen it, the second time Vince has. We are big fans of poker-faced irony. We love to recount the choice moments – Brad Pitt's singing voice, the dry-as-straw humour, Nick Cave's performance – the way people do with *This Is Spinal Tap*.

My thoughts keep turning to Gill. I am a man who has lost his daughter. I am a man who just walked out of his church, with no plans to return. I am a man who has been living on the edge for long enough to make jumping seem like an attractive option. But then, I love my wife and I like being married. And I suppose that, on my best days, I plan to stay that way. Even if Sarah hasn't been very loveable just lately – or very loving – I plan to stay that way. I look at those who break their marriage vows and see the inevitable reward: broken homes, economic suicide, long-term unhappiness, eternal guilt. No thanks.

But the scent of imagined *amour* lingers there in the dark. Poetry of the heart, some romantic mechanism has been triggered and the part of me that does more than just pump blood is off somewhere, flying, flying.

Catherine Keener plays the girl Johnny Suede ends up living with. Her character is fantastically sympathetic and she looks, I realise now for the first time, enough like Gill Forsythe to count. Maybe, without realising it, that's part of the reason I like *Johnny Suede*. But there are enough reasons besides that to love this film, reasons which I tell myself I would do well to concentrate on just this moment.

Maybe the most memorable scene is where Johnny's decorating partner, who is much sharper than our hero, helps him weigh up the pros and cons of moving in with his lovely – and enough-like-Gill Forsythe-to-count – girlfriend. The partner nails a paper bag to the wall of the apartment they are decorating and, with a marker-pen, uses it as a chart to collate Johnny's responses to his questions about moving in with the gorgeous woman.

Thus we get something along these lines:

For	Against
• Has her own colour TV	• Prison similarities: with
• He could have a private	her 24 hrs a day
room there	• Limits the things a guy
• She always keeps snacks	does (e.g. farting)
around	• Her shoe-throwing tendencies
	• They are opposite types

But the film's private resonance for me, which I've just become aware of, has me snared. I want not to think about Gill, but *Johnny Suede* makes that impossible.

Outside the Cornerhouse, the Crusty with collie and tin whistle hits us for change. Oxford Road is its usual night-time mix of the young and well heeled with the worn and penniless. We're turning up Whitworth Street, where a queue of coaches is parked adjacent to the Palace Theatre. We are walking along the side of the theatre, where posters reveal that this week Sir Cliff Richard is starring in a musical.

'Have I ever played you my *Cliff Live in Japan* LP?' Vince asks.

'No.'

'Between songs, the audience shouts out, "Creef! Creef!"'

Faster than I can at first keep up with, he is back onto What's Wrong With Life Today, Section 3B: Management. 'The world is really screwed up when they pay people who don't know what they're doing pots of extra money to manage people who do know what they're doing.'

Our conversations are usually a litany of protest about the imperfect state of the world. One of the reasons that Vince and I have remained friends over a lengthy period of time is that we both like to talk as if there were a better world waiting for us somewhere.

'Have you ever thought that the reason I am Vince Ford, primary school teacher, and not, say, Jerry Lee Lewis is that I just don't have the talent?'

'Well, not about you, but I've often thought similar things about myself.'

'Still – look at Colonel Saunders: failed at everything and came up with Kentucky Fried Chicken in his sixties.'

We're in Piccadilly Station. Our pace slows to meet the rhythm of our conversation, to meet the level of enthusiasm this conversation has reached. We've been talking to each other this way for so long, it feels like assembling a jigsaw puzzle that's been done so many times it's become too easy.

The railway station is nothing but a string of closed outlets, including, frustratingly, the only tempting spot, Costa's coffee bar. Not many people are around and those who are appear sad. In a railway station at night, everyone looks sad.

We try to put a positive spin on the evening by setting a deadline for producing half each of the opening episode of *Boris & Dragon's Etc.*

Vince says, 'Good to see you.'

'You too.'

'You seem in better shape than I expected.'

In the chill of the railway platform, the seriousness of my situation returns to me, more painful than ever. I look him in the eye. 'The truth is, the guilt is killing me,' I say. 'If you had a daughter that disappeared while you were supposed to be looking after her, you'd feel the same.'

'I can't imagine what it must feel like.'

'Well – I can't stand myself.'

Vince's return ticket will take him to his one loving wife and two devoted heifers in the cold, dark and damp of the Peak District. Meanwhile, I escalate down to the Metrolink station. I stand on the platform in the stark light waiting with one Rasta and two lesbians.

A tram glides into the station and stops, leaving a doorway right in front of where I'm standing. I go to press the release button and see, on the other side of the glass, Gill Forsythe. Gill clocks me right way, never bats an eyelid, and, from her side, opens the doors. As they slide apart, it dawns on me that she must be on her way home, she will have been going for the Hayfield train, the train which has just left with Vince on it. So, for at least the next half hour, she will have time on her hands. As the wheels in my head turn through these deductions, the shock of the conclusion almost takes the platform from beneath me.

'Gill,' I say, weakly. 'Hello.'

She smiles like a panther.

A Nice Little National Front Tea Room

Derek is coming to stay, and we are driving out to meet him. Sarah twists the volume down.

'I can't hear it,' I say, inching the car stereo up and reaching for a Liquorice Allsort from the bag on my lap.

Sarah turns the knob back down. 'It's too loud.'

'I can't hear it.'

'You'll wake her.'

'How can she hear it in the back if I can't hear it in the front?'

The M56 is jammed solid three lanes wide. We are in the fast lane, going slow. A white Ford Fiasco passes us on the inside.

Sarah says, 'That's the third time that white car has passed us.'

'So?'

'We're in the fast lane, allegedly.'

The Vauxhall Viagra ahead of us dogs the car in front of it like a greyhound after a racetrack rabbit – in slow-motion.

Sarah winds the window down, admitting wind and engine-noise. 'What is this we're listening to?'

'Tom Waits.' I inch the volume up again, and take a sip from my Ribena carton. Jockey full of bourbon, Joey full of lukewarm blackcurrant squash. I see Wilmslow signed and wonder how long it may take at this rate to cover the handful of miles from here to the Knutsford junction.

Sarah waggles a finger at the stereo. 'Do you really like this?'

'Yes! Why not?'

'Noise,' she says and adds, 'Go in there.'

'Sarah, it's illegal to overtake on the inside. How many times do I have to tell you?'

'I'm only suggesting what everyone else is doing. See that thing?' She indicates a Japanese jeep – looks like it's been on steroids – zipping by on her left. 'We overtook it back on Princess Parkway.'

I turn to her with what I hope is an aghast expression. 'I'm not even in any hurry to get there!'

'I know you're not. But this is what people do with their in-laws – entertain them.'

'Not my idea of entertainment.'

'It's not about entertaining yourself. It's putting yourself out for your parents the way they put themselves out for you when you were a child.'

'I didn't know your Dad when I was a child.'

'Oh shut up.'

I turn Tom Waits up a further millimetre.

She takes a final potshot. 'You've just got no concept of the responsibilities of being married, have you?'

And I wish, I wish, I wish that were true.

When Derek finally troops into the National Trust Gift Shop at Tatton Park, I have done a full fifteen minutes amongst the racks of heritage tack, the shelves of reproduction Victorian children's games, overpriced ginger marmalade and milk chocolate bars which, strangely, have been packaged like cooking chocolate.

When he has finished kissing Sarah and fussing over Molly, he spots the box of notelets ('English Cottage Garden') which I have been examining with horror.

'Lovely. Quite lovely,' he tells me. 'I've often thought about trying to design my front garden in that style. Pure Englishness, isn't it?'

I deposit the box on the nearest shelf, resisting the urge to go 'Isn't it? Mh? Isn't it?' like the football pundit on *The Fast Show*. 'Yes.'

'Marvellous.'

We traipse round the house and study the messy opulence in which the aristocracy liked to live, the barn-sized rooms that must have been impossible to heat and the stretch-limo-length tables around which it must have been difficult to dine in any relaxed way.

My upbringing featured years and years of visiting relatives, of day-trips and family holidays in which I had no choice. How would the eighteen-year-old I used to be cope with knowing that he wasn't going to escape from all that powerlessness for more than a few short years? How would he ever be able to put one foot in front of the other if he knew that the future would find him standing on a dusty Axminster making responsive-sounding responses to his father-in-law's National Trust observations?

'Look at the condition of that brocade! My word, that's a durable fabric.'

And we don't neglect to spend a strained half-hour in the National Trust tea-room, nose-down in our broccoli & Stilton soup, Earl Grey and poppy seed cake.

'Smashing!' Derek says. 'Good, wholesome food in an attractive setting. Couldn't be better. You can't beat a nice little National Trust tea-room. Hn hn.'

A nice little National Front tea-room, the eighteen-year-old inside me thinks.

Of course, there will be plenty of other developments in that young man's later life that would set him back on his heels were he able to look ahead – and I don't just mean tragic developments. Some day he could look forward to discussing top-up pension schemes, genetically modified crops and the number of togs in a duvet. Some day he would find going to IKEA moderately entertaining. Some day he would discover that most of the things he thinks are important just aren't and that a lot of the pointless things older people do aren't just sad, they're inevitable.

'Ah, agapanthus,' Derek is saying. 'Glorious. But very difficult to cultivate.'

We're nosing the end of October here and the hay-day of the agapanthus is long past. We are still making our tour of the grounds, snuffling our shoes through dry copper and yellow leaves. There is supposed to be a large fountain somewhere, but we're making heavy work of finding it. When we paid on the way into the car park, they did give us a guide, but we seem to have left it in the car. All these paths look the same to me. We need a landmark – such as the large fountain that we cannot find.

'You've come across agapanthus before, Joe?'

'Wasn't he something to do with Helen of Troy?'

'Eh?'

'Only joking, Derek.'

'Oh, I see.'

'I've probably heard the name.'

'It's from Africa, originally, which is why it's difficult to grow in our climate. It's a lily, really. The name comes from the Greek: love flower is what it means. Very romantic. It'd be just the thing for a young couple like you and Sarah to have in their garden. Mmm?'

I look at Sarah just as she is looking at me. I think we understand each other's facial expression here. I say, 'It's a nice idea, but there isn't much room in our garden at the moment.' And I can't help thinking that soon there may well be less.

Sarah says, 'It'd have a much better chance of surviving further south with you, Dad.'

'Ho! It's much too late for love flowers in my garden. Ho ho.'

For about five minutes, we have been following a path through pine woods. Derek thinks there is a large fountain somewhere. I couldn't care whether there is or not. Either way, there's no sign of it and all these paths look the same to me.

Molly asks, 'What is a fountain?'

'It's a big tower of water,' Sarah explains.

'A big, elusive tower of water,' I say.

Molly looks puzzled. 'What's it look like?'

'You know the way water looks coming out of a tap?' I say. 'Well it's like that, only upside down and hundreds of times bigger.'

'It's a upside down tap, Daddy?'

'Sort of.'

'Just a minute,' Sarah says. 'Isn't there a big fountain at Chatsworth?'

'Is there?' Derek says. 'Goodness. I think you're right. Ho ho. We're looking in the wrong stately home. Ho ho ho.'

We trudge back.

Derek says, 'Sarah tells me you may have something on television.'

'Oh I doubt it'll ever get that far.'

'But a television company is interested?'

'I'm going down to see them at the end of the month. It's a very small production company. If they take the sitcom on, there's no guarantee that they can persuade any of the networks to fund it.'

Sarah says, 'But you don't think the production company people seem very good, do you?'

I hate it when she gives me conversational feeds like this. Also, I prefer not to discuss things that are still only tentative. Which Sarah knows, perfectly well.

'It'll probably all come to nothing,' I say. 'That's mostly what happens.'

Sarah says, 'But you thought they didn't seem to know what they were doing, didn't you?'

I can feel my ears pinching back against the side of my head. I want to shout at Sarah, *For crying out loud! Don't you get the message?* In the circumstances, though, I have to restrain myself.

'Still,' Derek says, 'it's jolly good that somebody is interested in your script, isn't it? You must find that encouraging, surely?'

'Well – yes. Nobody likes getting rejection slips all the time.'

'I think it sounds very promising.' He stoops to pick up Molly and carries her along on his hip. 'Your Daddy is going to make lots of people laugh on the television. Oh yes. Isn't that marvellous?'

It's meant well, but of course I don't believe any of it. Derek doesn't know anything about our script, sitcoms or the way TV works. And besides, I'm unable to concentrate on what he's saying; all I can think about is what I would like to be saying to Sarah, and none of it is marvellous.

When our visit to Tatton is finally over, we decide to go to our car and transport Derek from there to his, which is parked over by the lake. It seems to take us about an hour and a half to reach the spot where we're parked. That's how long it feels to me, anyway.

Sarah wants to drive back, which means moving Molly's car seat behind the driver's seat, because when I sit in front of Molly, she hasn't enough legroom.

'What are you doing?' Sarah says, when I've completed the move.

'Swapping Molly's car-seat to the other side.'

'No need. Dad needs to sit in front on the way to his car.'

Derek has wandered off with Molly and is, I can see, playing catch with her, as well as talking; I know he will be explaining something to her in fastidious detail. 'He does? Nobody told me.'

'He said he felt a bit car-sick driving up this morning, and he doesn't want to risk anything starting it all over again.'

'What? He's going to get carsick if he sits in the back for half a mile?'

'It's not worth the risk.'

'For half a mile, at fifteen miles an hour.'

'You don't mind sitting in the back, do you?'

'No. I just mind moving Molly's car seat for no reason.'

'Oh. Well, I thought you knew. I thought you were there when he was telling us about the carsickness.'

'I may just have tuned out of the conversation for a fraction of a second.' I glance back at Derek, who is still blathering at Molly. 'Why didn't you say something when you saw me doing it?'

'Sorry,' she says.

'Forget it.' My magnanimity probably doesn't sound very convincing. It's the National Trust experience, not Sarah, which has put me in a bad mood: all this traipsing and trudging, all this frittered time.

'*Okay*,' Sarah says and starts the engine. 'Everybody's happy, so let's head for *Grandpa's car!*'

'Leck's go, Mummy!' Molly shrieks, laughing.

Sarah revs the engine hard, lurches up the hill a few feet and stalls. All too heart-stoppingly quickly, we are freewheeling back in the direction of the car parked behind us.

'Sarah!' I shout, just as she jams the brake pedal towards the floor.

We jerk to a halt. Somehow we have failed to collide with the car behind us. Looking out the back window, there doesn't seem to be any space between us and this car, a new, red Alfa Romeo - I doubt the owner would appreciate any damage to it.

'For crying out *loud*, Sarah,' I say. 'What are you playing at?'

She clenches her teeth and ignores me.

'Can you be a bit more careful?' I demand, as she starts the engine again.

My words are scarcely out when Sarah accelerates back up the hill, straight towards a large shrub of some kind.

'*Sarah!*'

She veers suddenly, but not quite quickly enough, to the right and the offside of the car trawls through the outer branches of the unidentified shrub.

'What are you trying to *do*?' My voice is high and constricted now, not at it's most attractive.

'We're all right,' Sarah says. 'We didn't drive into it.'

Derek says, gently, 'It was only leaves, really.'

'Look, just stop, will you? Stop the car.'

She does and I get out and stomp round to the other side. I'm certain that the paintwork will be damaged. It isn't, but in the entanglement the front numberplate has been knocked off.

'Amazing,' I say and slide the numberplate onto the dashboard. 'You've got all the space in the world to get out of this car park and you decide to submerge the car in a shrub.'

We follow the driveway round to Derek's Ford Frankenstein in solid silence. We don't make eye contact all the way home. Along the M56, she clicks on the car hi-fi. When Tom Waits comes out of the speakers, she snaps it back off.

What they're listening to on
The Wang Dang Doodle this week:
'(I Can't Get No) Satisfaction' (Devo)
'Another Girl, Another Planet' (The Only Ones)
'Dixie Chicken' (Little Feat)

It's late afternoon on the third and final day of Derek's stay. Also the third day since the incident in the car park at Tatton, since which time Sarah has said no more than two or three words to me. Derek and I are loading the boot of his car. I don't understand why he carries some of these things with him – a shooting stick, Wellington boots, a folding picnic table – and I'm not about to ask. I've never seen him use any of them, but, every time he comes to visit, I help him tote them into the house, where they remain until we tote them back out again.

Derek packs his boot with military skill. It looks like the open boot in a new car brochure.

'There we are!' he says. 'That ought to take care of it.'

He pushes the boot-lid down and it shuts with a gentle thump. He leans close to look at some imagined smirch his hand may have left on the paintwork, then buffs it with the forearm of his lambswool cardigan.

'That's better.'

All of the Porters stand on the pavement by the open driver's side window, waiting to wave Derek off. All of us have already hugged. He is putting on his calf leather driving gloves.

'It's been lovely,' he says.

'It's been nice having you,' Sarah says. 'Drive carefully.'

The gloves donned, Derek has turned his attention to the position of seat and rear-view mirror. Nobody but him ever drives his car, so it's difficult to understand why anything should need adjusting. And then, waving as he rounds the corner, he is gone.

Sarah turns from Molly and me and goes back into the house. When we follow her, she is already up the stairs and heading into the spare room.

Molly and I go into the front room, where Batman and Robin are stretched out on the arms of the Chesterfield. Molly takes out her Lego box and sits down with it at her little pine table.

'Did you have a nice time with Grandpa?'

'Uh huh. I'm going to make a bungalow. A bungalow like Grandpa's.'

'I see.'

'Only bigger. A big, big bungalow.'

Never mind the big, big bungalow; I am finding it hard to think of anything but the big, big mountain that has been sitting between Sarah and me for the past three days. I know I should go up to the spare room and try to clear the air. I should, but it isn't very appealing. A more appealing alternative exists, one I've been trying to ignore. It's getting harder to ignore.

Soon the bungalow is big, a high-rise bungalow.

'That's very good, honey-pie.'

I have an idea: taking the Hoover up would be a conciliatory act. I prevaricate a moment or two, but finally I do it.

When I reach the landing, I find myself remaining there. I wait and wait. Maybe a dozen feet from me, my wife is in the spare room, tidying and even from this distance I can feel the hurt silence. The spare room door is ajar and as she goes about her task, I catch the odd glimpse of her. Either she genuinely doesn't see me, or she's choosing to ignore me. I know she is angry with me for shouting at her in the Tatton car park, but then she is angry with me for worse things than that.

I wait and wait on the landing with my peace offering beside me, like I'm on guard at Buckingham Palace and the Hoover is my rifle. I fidget with its neatly wrapped cable. I hate apologizing, especially when I'm not completely in the wrong: after all, she did nearly crash the car twice and the numberplate is still sitting on the dashboard. The air between us is so muggy I can't imagine a storm big enough to clear it. Being single would be so much easier. Easier in the morning, easier at night. Very quiet at weekends.

I soldier on towards the spare room. I push the door open wide. Sarah's back is towards me when I carry the Hoover into the room. It looks like a human back, but it seems like a porcupine's.

'I've brought the Hoover up,' I say.

Seconds, quite a lot of slow-moving seconds, pass without either of us saying anything.

'I'll Hoover in here when you've finished.'

She thanks me without looking round.

I wait a little longer. I would like to say how much I miss Martha and how I would do anything to get her back. I would like to say that my failure as a parent in Longford Park is more than I think I can bear. I would like to hide myself under the duvet on the spare bed and stay there forever.

For what I want to do I do not do, but what I hate to do.

Disley Girls

It's coming up to 10.15. I'm Trevor Howard today and Celia Johnson is due to join me for our brief encounter at 10.30. Rachmaninov's second piano concerto should be playing. Far from feeling bad, 'gleeful' is the term that comes to mind. Part of what I feel like is the Woody Allen character in *Shadows & Fog* when he is confronted with a torch-lit vigilante mob. Accused of a series of murders, he is asked how he pleads.

'Not guilty,' he announces. 'In fact, I deserve a bonus.'

Story of my life, and never more so than this past year. Picture me caught by *paparazzi* fighting my way out of 1997, and the blurb beneath *The Mirror*'s page 5 photograph reads:

'Let me out of here,' Porter snapped.

What did I do to deserve 1997? In 1996, I was happily married with two lovely girls and I thought I knew where I stood and where I was going.

Apart from me and the waitress, John Coltrane, Art Blakey and Dexter Gordon are the only ones in the Impulse café bar in Disley. The jazzers are in black and white and the waitress and I are in full, living colour. The waitress is dark, with sallow skin, and kind of squat. For maybe the first five years or so that I was aware of Disley, I used to think 'Disley Girls', because of the Beach Boys song, 'Disney Girls', and be tickled by the notion of blue-eyed, bikini-ed surfing babes in damp, grey Disley, tanned, blonde honeys running out of the dismal terraced houses into the Derbyshire drizzle and shouting 'Surf's up, everybody!'

Because a *cappuccino* in the heart of the country is too risky, I order a *latte*. As I'm checking my watch over and over, I can't help noticing that the *latte* takes eleven minutes to arrive (and I am the only customer). Ben Webster, Charlie Mingus and Sarah Vaughan get me through 10.27, 10.35, 10.38, and 10.43. Between-times, I wonder what the *cappuccino* might have been like.

Just after quarter to, the rickety café door opens, ringing the old-fashioned bell dangling above it, and a Disley postman – can there be more than one? – shoves some letters at the waitress: utility bills, something from Britannia Music and a magazine in a plastic envelope. *Surfin' UK,* probably.

By 10.50 I'm pretty sure I have been stood up, but at what time do I abandon hope? If something has come up and she can't make it, if she has been delayed, she has no way of letting me know, has she?

'Excuse me?' I call to Bar-bar-bar-bar-bar-bar-Ann. 'Could I have a *cappuccino*, please?'

Nothing to stop her phoning the Impulse café bar, though.

As the big hand climbs to the top, Billie Holiday is telling me she'll never be the same again and the *latte* is, as they so often are, a watery *expresso* drowned in foamless milk. If I thought they sold Gauloises in Disley, I'd take up smoking cigarettes again.

Maybe it would have been better if Peggy Lee had been singing 'Happiness Is A Guy Called Joe' when the bell above the door jingles and Gill Forsythe walks in. In reality, Peggy is purring her way through 'The Folks On The Hill', which is good enough.

'Hello Joe.' Small words that feel large.

I get up and fail to decide on a kiss and she laughs – at me, I assume – and, to be agreeable, so do I. 'It's great to see you,' I say and regret saying – bland, and not cool enough.

She laughs again with her big, easy mouth.

We sit down across the narrow table from each other. 'This is nice,' I say. From bland to gormless, I have it taped.

'Yes.' She's not exactly accepting my observation. 'A lot has happened in the last ten years, hasn't it?'

Marriage, children, a lost child – I don't want to go with my side of this. 'What about you?' I ask. 'Married? Kids?'

'Uh-uh. The men I've been with, who needs kids?'

'What about the magic?'

'Poof!' she holds up her hand and flicks all her fingers open like a starburst, eyes twinkling. Short, useful, monkey fingers, crow's feet fanned round the dark eyes. 'All gone.'

The waitress sets Gill's camomile tea between us.

'What? You just gave up being a magician?'

She nods, opens the little hand-thrown teapot and tugs the teabag string repeatedly.

'That's too bad.' I know she isn't going to volunteer any further information because now I am with her again I remember some of what she used to be like. And I'm determined not to let her manoeuvre me into asking any more direct questions. But again, as at the Cornerhouse, she has a well-heeled look about her, which she never had before. A river of pearls sets off her upright mien, and going by her Napa leather jacket and nicely tailored suede trousers, the pearls are probably real. Some change. She used to be Affleck's Palace; now she's King Street.

She plops the lid back on her teapot and pours. 'I have a little business that developed out of the magic.'

'I see.'

Her eyes lock on mine. 'What about you?'

'Bit of this, bit of that.' Touché.

'And what have you grown out of?' She takes a sip of the camomile.

'Nothing! But I've been forcibly weaned from almost everything that once seemed vital.'

'What? By Jesus?'

I flinch a little. In the present situation, I don't want my faith broached. 'Some of it. Mostly by children.'

Gill nods and, for a moment, regards me more openly – a soft look. 'I wouldn't mind getting back to some of those frivolous pleasures, though.'

She raises her eyebrows. 'I bet.'

The implication of this, though not the kind of frivolous pleasure I meant, is more like it. I laugh, because her innuendo is preferable to bringing up God. 'No. Pleasures like sleeping in, having spare dollars, going out on the town.'

'And that would be enough?' Her folded arms are resting on the table and she leans towards me to punctuate the question. 'Hmm?'

What's rippling up my chest is none of Rachmaninov's second piano concerto. More like one of those awesome peaks early in Elgar's cello concerto. Flushed with anticipation, I imagine myself giving it some Austin Powers: *Yeah, baby, yeah, yeah, yeah!* Instead, I say, 'I don't know. I'd like some kind of reward for being up against it too long. Compensation.'

Amused, Gill pats my upper arm – too companionable by half, and what did I say that was funny? 'It's good to see you, Joe.'

'Well – me, too.' I'm trying to keep pace with her in the game of giving nothing away.

'You haven't changed a bit.' She retrieves her slim purse from the table and stands up. 'C'mon, let's go.'

Go where? I'm meant to say, but won't. Nor will I ask about these shamefully inadequate men she's had to put up with – nor ask if there's one of them on the scene at the moment.

'You suffer from impossibly great expectations,' she murmurs as we step through the jingle-jangle doorway. She holds her arm out in the Disley drizzle and plips the alarm off on a bright red Audi Aspirant that I hadn't noticed. 'Get in,' she says, moving swiftly towards the far side of the car. 'It's wet.'

Inside, I catch her musky perfume at the same time as I'm struck by the absence of family debris.

'"Compensation",' she says, like the idea was ridiculous.

We're accelerating through drizzly Disley before my door has thunked shut. The LED on her car hi-fi reads 'RADIO 3' and a woman's gentle voice is speaking too quietly. Gill switches it off and asks, 'How did you manage to wangle the time for this?'

'I'm largely freelance.'

She has taken a left by the railway station and we are ascending a steep hill with sleeping policemen too fast. 'How did *you* manage it?'

'Thursday is my day off. I work Saturdays.'

When either of us speaks, our natural cadences are broken by tremors as we bump over the sleeping policemen.

'You can swim, can't you?' she asks.

'Sure. But I haven't brought any trunks.'

'We're not going swimming.'

I sigh, but bite my tongue.

The road takes us to a peak where it seems we can see half the hills in Derbyshire, and drops us back down into a built-up area I don't recognize. 'Where does this come out?' I ask, bored with the game.

'Round the side of Whaley Bridge. I come here most Thursdays.'

We veer sharply right, shoot up a narrow road where the remaining leaves on the trees are yellow and brown, and swerve left up a gravel path. Bizarrely, fifteen or twenty yachts moored on trolleys are beside us. Gill drives towards them, brakes and reverses in an arc before scrunching to a halt beneath a slate wall.

I shoot a look at her; we are at least a hundred miles from the sea. 'A yacht club?'

'I like it when the little boy in you shines out.'

I don't think I do, but before I can respond, she is through the door and round to the hatchback. When I join her, she is halfway out of her suede trousers and I am looking at the goose bumps on the sallow-blonde flesh of her thighs.

'Are you all right in those clothes? You can have this –' she throws me an orange lifejacket '– but I've only the one wetsuit.'

'Fine. Are we sailing in any water at all?'

Resting on the rim of the boot to pull on her wetsuit trousers, she indicates the slate wall with a jerk of her head.

I stand on a small ridge in the wall and step up to see a reservoir full of choppy, dark water. Wet-looking water. Wet-looking, October water. When I step down, I'm looking at Gill's bare back and lacy white bra-straps, which gift-wrap her shoulders. She drags one arm followed by the other into the wetsuit jacket sleeves, fastens the bottom at the front and the zip is already shooting over her bust as she turns to face me again.

'Put this on.' She hands me the lifejacket. 'It'll be cold out there.'

Cold is not the word, and the temperature not my only problem. The alleged yacht is a glorified windsurfing board, something Gill calls 'a Laser'. Getting me on this flying toothpick involves slapstick contortions.

'See?' She grins as we scud away from dry land. 'I told you there was plenty of room.'

It's all right for her in her little hollow, guiding the rudder as she leans against the back of the boat. I'm perched on top of the Laser's white plastic body next to the boom. The boat's surface has been designed with aerodynamics, not passengers in mind. It feels like sitting on Molly's tricycle.

'Joe? If you find yourself slipping around when I tack, don't grab the boom, okay?'

'Okay.'

'Just slide under it.'

What I'm beginning to think is that she must really not like me and the only reason I can see for this is that she still feels pissed off from all those years ago. The ride gets rougher as we approach the middle of the reservoir.

'How come nobody else is sailing?' I shout above the wind noise, the flapping sailcloth and the clinking of a range of metal bits and pieces on the mast.

'It's a small club, and nobody sails much this time of year, especially midweek.' She laughs, a bit too raucously for my liking. 'Don't look so worried. I'm a dab hand at pulling people out when they fall in.'

For some extra jocularity, she rams the rudder away from her, shouting, 'Look out!' a split-second before the boom clips the top of my head and comes close to knocking me into the deeply uninviting waves.

We are crashing over the sleeping policemen on our descent back into Disley. Gill reaches her gear-change hand across and places it on my leg, close to the knee. 'I think about your situation a lot, y'know.'

'What?'

'About your little girl.'

'Oh.'

'I can't imagine anything worse.'

I don't want to talk about this with Gill now any more than I wanted to talk about God with her earlier.

She withdraws her hand from my knee and changes gear. We're approaching the big pub on the corner of the main road through Disley.

'Especially for Sarah,' she adds, tapping another nail into the coffin of my unreasonably high expectations.

We are at a T-junction and the road ahead is clear, but Gill is looking at me, not the traffic. A car-horn parps behind us.

'You'd better drive on,' I say.

'Where do you want to go?'

'I'm parked round the corner. I need to get back really.'

She heads right and pulls over at the junction I've pointed out.

'Were you and Sarah close before this happened?'

I must look blank.

'Why are you here?'

I unfasten my seat-belt, which slithers across my chest. 'She wants to talk about it all the time, and I want to talk about it as little as possible.'

'You never think about it?'

'I think about Martha all the time.'

'Well, it's no wonder, is it?' she says.

'I miss her like an arm or a leg.'

She wraps her monkey fingers around my right hand, which shocks me with a warm surge.

'The worst of it – well, there is no worst of it. It's all the worst. But what I find so hard is not being able to do anything about her disappearance. I couldn't do anything about it in Longford Park when it happened, and I can't do anything about it now. And that – frust*ration* – is like having your feet immersed in cement. I can't do it justice to anyone, the infinite *impotence*.'

I turn my head and search Gill's face, hungry for a morsel of empathy. As soon as our eyes meet, she enfolds me in a strong, snug embrace and I soak up the perfume and shampoo and lambswool until, with a couple of pats to my shoulder, she signals the end of it. I withdraw and run my eyes, all that's available to me on this present grievous note, along her dry lips. I'm looking across to that shore at the end of *The Great Gatsby,* the soft breast of the new world, full of promise. Couldn't I just run away from it all? Couldn't I have a new start? Couldn't the world begin over for me, away from all that I have spoiled? A fresh start with Gill a thousand miles away from Longford Park. Couldn't I?

Wherever I have been in my thoughts, Gill has been somewhere else. She says, 'There was one man amongst the let-downs, you know.'

'Oh yes?'

'He was married, too.' She keeps looking straight ahead. She nods once. 'A lot of pain, a lot of disappointment.' She twinkles her crow's feet again. 'How about something gentler next week? I find you – calming.'

'What do you need calming from?'

'You'd be surprised.' She filches a business card from the glove box. 'Here. Call me.'

I pull the latch and the heavy door opens a little. 'I'll definitely give it some thought.'

I turn and find myself eye to eye with the waitress in the window of the Impulse café bar. She averts her gaze and swabs a table with a Jeye-cloth.

'Wax that woody,' I mutter – my only Beach Boys surfing jargon – and head back to 1997 as I have known it.

Joe's and Vince's Capitalist Trip

A spotty youth is bent into the sale dump-bin where CDs and tapes are piled up higgledy-piggledy. He's wearing a miserable check shirt, not tucked in. Even so, he looks nothing like Neil Young. He's trawling through the unruly stacks with both hands, hell for leather, flipping the jewel cases one over another, clack-clack-clack, like finding a bargain is going to save his life.

I don't like Woolworth's much. They sell many things I don't want: socket spanners, dahlia bulbs, Platignum pens, brown teapots and, in season, unappealing Christmas cards and giftwrap. The aisles are too narrow. Everything feels plastic. But worst of all, Vince *always* finds incredible bargains in Woolies and I never do.

This goes back to when I first knew him, fifteen years ago: I remember him smugly explaining to me that his copy of *Twenty Golden Greats* by Frank Sinatra had cost 99p from Woolworth's. Of course, when I went to investigate, the only copies they had were £5.99. Woolworth's, it has to be said, is Vince's spiritual home.

Miserable Check Shirt has moved on from the sale bin, so I step up and take his place. Why not? There's always that one in a million chance that my hands will fall on *Sweetheart of the Rodeo* or *The Queen Is Dead* wrongly priced at £3.99.

I have to stoop to riffle the plastic, which adds to the ignominy of the activity. I have to stoop like some ugly predator and, flipping, all I find is dross: Michael Bolton, Right Says Fred, *The Best Bagpipe Album In The World Ever*.

I give it up for a bad job and scan the store for Vince. No sign, so I go for a wander. I walk through the gardening bit, the area where they keep tools, the sorry selection of stationery.

What I'm thinking about and trying not to think about is the state of play between Sarah and me. I suppose I could just have apologised for shouting at her in front of her Dad, but to be honest, I'm tired of being conciliatory, I'm fed up of pussyfooting around her. None of what we are going through is easy for either of us, but she shows no sign of realising that.

When I tune in to my surroundings again, I find I'm in the Pick'n'Mix part of confectionery, which stops me in my tracks. From when Martha was two onwards, I used to bring her, and later Molly too, to Woolworth's to buy loose sweets. She loved it, so much that I used to try not to walk by Woolies with her. To her, it was always 'the sweetie shop'.

This is why I stand at the Pick'n'Mix and strain to find breath. This is why I stand stuck there in the confectionery, like a robot waiting to be activated. I don't know how long I'm like that: thinking of Martha's sweetie shop, and felled by it.

'Go for it,' a voice, a familiar voice says, 'buy some liquorice torpedoes. You can do it.'

I turn and say 'Hi' to Vince.

'Are you all right?' he says.

'Yeah. All right. Can we get going, though?'

'Sure. But I need coffee badly.'

'Let's stop on the motorway. You've got the script?'

'If you want – but it'll cost twice as much. In my rucksack.' He mimes patting it over his shoulder. 'Just give me a minute to check the CD sale-bin.'

He makes his way to it, as if guided by some special bargain-seeking radar, and I follow him, and watch him peer into the collage of tapes and discs. It's like watching Alfred Brendel poised before a Steinway. He neither riffles nor flips. He just studies the contents of the bin for a moment before dipping his fingers in and pulling out a jewel case.

I move closer and say, 'What is it?'

'Nothing special. You've probably got it.' He holds the front of the album out for me to see: Elvis Costello, *King Of America*.

'No, I haven't, funnily enough.' His thumb is over the price sticker. 'How much?'

'£2.99,' he says, and turns to pay the lugubrious assistant behind him.

As we make our way to the doors, Vince is extracting his disc from the blue Woolies bag. He is fondling it. He scans the track listing.

He says, 'This is Costello's finest hour, y'know.'

'Of course I know.'

'Wrongly priced, eh?'

'I would think so,' I say and let the door swing free in my wake. Elvis has left the building, me too, and I promise myself not to return – to the Pick'n'Mix, or the CD sale-bin.

```
[ EXT: MOTORWAY. BORIS & DRAGON'S TRABANT STRUG-
GLES OVER THE PENNINES. CUT TO INT. CAR. DRAGON
IS AT THE WHEEL.]
     DRAGON: D' you know, I don't care if we never
find this record. I'm having so much fun in
England. Land of freedom, homeward, brave - eh?
     BORIS: No, no. You are speaking of United
States. Here, land of hope and glory.
     DRAGON (WITH DREAMY EXPRESSION): 'Land of
hope and glory'. Yes! I like that! 'Land of hope
and glory'. What is it mean though?
```

On the way to Birmingham, Vince asks, 'What were Lineham & Matthews doing before they sold *Father Ted*?'

'Watching sitcoms all day, I would say.'

I look across at Vince fidgeting with his rucksack on the floor between his legs. From it, he extracts another Karrimor-type bag, which he unzips. Inside that is a plastic carrier, inside which is another carrier, inside which is a Tupperware box. Vince is mad for wrapping.

'Sandwich?' he says, holding out a rectangle of bread and cheddar.

'I'm okay, thanks.'

He feeds the floppy morsel into his mouth like a dead fish.

'Good?' I ask.

'Bout as good as two pieces of bread with cheese between them can be,' he says, chewing noisily.

On the M6, we pass a Services sign, and Vince says, 'What about that coffee?'

'Okay.' I signal and head up the slip road. 'There's no use

entertaining fantasies about *Father Ted*-style success. If we ever even get *Boris & Dragon* made, you can bet it'll be one of those Tuesday night, 8.30 sitcoms that nobody can ever remember the name of.'

```
[INT:  MOTORWAY  SERVICES.  BORIS  &  DRAGON  IN
RESTAURANT QUEUE.]
     BORIS: Safe to believe that we can afford
only one cup of coffee between -
     DRAGON: LOOK!!
     BORIS: What is it? A cheaper place to buy
coffee?
     DRAGON: No. It is original drummer from
Human League.
     BORIS: Hm, interesting.
     DRAGON: This is why I come to the West.
     BORIS: Yes indeed - no, wait: in Human
League, drummer is drum machine.
```

The services we've stopped at is brand, spanking new, with an interior rich in chrome and limed oak veneer. In the style of an airport, it has a variety of food outlets, one of which is an American diner. I like the look of the fittings, chromed table trim, maroon leatherette seats, sugar pourers. It's empty, though, not a soul in sight. We take a seat. There's no lack of choice. One other table is occupied, by Thora Hird's body double, with a cat-basket on the floor beside her. It seems like nobody on the M6 is aware yet that these services have opened.

'What sort of name is Willie for a woman?' Vince asks when we are sitting with our coffees.

'Wilhemina, I don't know. Americans have strange Christian names: Randy, JoBeth, Rubella. The English have odd surnames: Spinks, Arbuthnot, Crapper. It's just the way of these things.'

'Think she's a babe?'

'I haven't thought about it.'

'I'm expecting him to be a plank. All Julians are.'

'Well be nice to them. We're not going to blow this deal just because you don't like the name 'Julian'. Right?'

'Or women called Willie.'

'Whatever. Be tactful.'

Some staff are gathering in the American diner now – nine or ten waiters and waitresses in matching uniforms. They assemble in three rows.

'Look,' I go. 'Showtime.'

The intro of 'Greased Lightning' from *Grease* blares from a PA somewhere close and suddenly the waiters and waitresses are doing a pretty respectable bit of rock & roll dancing. When they have finished, they bow, smiling, and Vince, Thora Hird and I applaud demurely.

I notice my Birmingham-approaching landmark, the RAC headquarters. I feel weary just going over all my troubles again and I'm beginning to relish getting off this motorway and on to our appointment. 'I reckon I probably just don't have the emotional reserves for what we're going through. I'm up for shallow pleasures and cheap thrills, but fundamentally unequipped for the profound things of life, like pain and grief.'

'Oh, is that all? What that makes you is a normal male human being.'

It's my turn to snort. ' Nobody thinks I'm feeling this and part of my problem as I've just said is that I don't have the emotional equipment for suffering. But all the pain is really happening, whatever anyone thinks.'

'And you can't deal with it?'

'No. I can't.'

What they're listening to on
The Wang Dang Doodle this week:
'I'm Gonna Be A Wheel Some Day' (Fats Domino)
'Get A Job' (The Silhouettes)
'King Of The Whole Wide World' (Elvis Presley)

Willie from MainFrame has an attractively sculpted American face and good, white teeth. But she is, I suspect as I shake her slim, dry hand, a space cadet.

'Great to meet you,' she is going. 'Beautiful piece of writing, really – we love it.'

'That's right,' Julian says. 'Sit down, sit down. Let me get you both a drink.'

We're in a bar near the Bullring, all limed oak and halogen lights. Julian looks like Fletcher off *Porridge* – a young Fletcher: he's maybe thirty. But he speaks standard Mick Jagger Estuary.

'We love this,' Willie is saying, nodding her head, so that her ash-blonde ponytail bobs behind her. It makes me think of a friendly Shetland pony. 'We love it so much. This is the kind of script we always dreamed of getting.'

'Really?' I'm half-buying what she says.

Vince isn't. 'Have you done a lot of sitcoms, then?'

'Not exactly,' Willie says. 'But we've had plans to for a real long time.'

'What sort of things do you normally work on, then?' Vince asks.

'Oh gosh. Well – we made a stand-up gameshow with Phil Jupitus. *All Stand*? Maybe you saw that?'

We didn't.

'And we've worked with Jarvis Cocker. We did a video for the single Pulp put out, oh, maybe three singles before 'Common People'?'

'I love Pulp,' Vince says, which I never knew. Maybe he really will try to be diplomatic.

'But not everything we've done has been that kind of, quality, I guess you'd say. We made a Friday night pubs-out show for cable here in Birmingham. You wouldn't have seen that, I guess. Like *Eurotrash*, without the budget. It's done real well.'

Julian has arrived back with a tray of drinks. When he has re-installed himself in our booth, he produces cigarettes and offers them to Vince and me. Vince can't stand being around cigarette smoke; this won't help his Be Diplomatic campaign. Julian grips a king-size between his teeth. My heart sinks. In my experience, it takes a special kind of thruster to hold a cigarette that way.

Willie doesn't so much drop names as spill them. Brix Smith from The Fall is a good friend of hers. She started out working for Michael Winner. She and Anthea Turner share a trainer at their health club.

```
[ INT: LARGE HALL, LAID OUT FOR CD FAIR. THERE ARE
DOZENS OF STALLS AND A FEW HUNDRED PEOPLE. ZOOM IN
ON BORIS & DRAGON IN THE MIDDLE OF THIS SCENE. THEY
ARE FLIPPING THROUGH LPs AT ONE OF THE STALLS.]
```

BORIS: I think we are on a very difficult
quest. Here, people don't even like Bob Dylan.
Beatles, yes. Pink Floyd, yes. Cure, yes. Bob
Dylan, only every blue moon. More Bob Dylan
records in Belgrade than in England.
      DRAGON: What is it you are saying, Boris?
      BORIS: Only that it may take us some time to
find *Freewheelin'*, original track-listing for
Egon. But that's okay. Better to travel then
arrive.

Willie tells us that Armando Ianucci is perfect for Boris. And she thinks they can get him.

I say, 'He has a pretty strong Scottish accent, though.'

'Oh sure, sure. But he's a professional, guys. He can do a, what is it, Hungarian accent –'

'Serbian,' Vince corrects. 'And not only is Armando Ianucci Scottish, he's also not funny.'

What, I wonder, has become of the Be Diplomatic campaign?

'Oh really?' Willie goes, sounding as if Vince has suggested that Bill Clinton is a transvestite.

'He's not funny to Vince,' I say. 'To a lot of people, though, he's very funny.'

'Yeah?' Vince says. 'When was the last time somebody said to you, "Did you see *The Friday Night Armistice*? What a riot!"?'

'What about Dragon?' I ask, to get off the subject of Armando Ianucci. 'Who did you have in mind for Dragon?'

'Oh, oh, this one is purr-fect. This you will love – and I think we can pull it off: John Candy!'

'Who is funny,' Vince says. 'But dead.'

'He is?' Willie says. 'He's dead? But that's awful.'

We part from the MainFrame team on good terms, although Vince and I don't hold out much hope of these two ever talking up a budget for *Boris & Dragon,* which is what they are assuring us they will do.

It's late afternoon when I drop Vince in Stoke, from where he will catch a train home.

Completing the final leg of the journey alone, I keep thinking about Sarah and me in terms of a storm that won't break. I know it doesn't take much in the way of stress to upset the equilibrium of a relationship, and we have been going through higher than average stress levels. All the same, understanding the dynamics of our situation doesn't seem to help. I mean, if a lion bites your arm off, you can understand the reasons for having no arm until you're blue in the face, but it doesn't alter the fact that blood is pumping out of you by the gallon and the place where your arm used to be hurts like hell. And so on, and so on; up, down and all around these heartaches.

Of course, Vince and I scarcely touched on the subject, but when we did once, somewhere in the Watford Junction ballpark, he suggested that my faith must help me a lot. I suppose I must have just agreed and changed the subject – or, more likely, he changed the subject. But his comment comes back to me now, when I'm driving alone: *your faith must help a lot.* And a little voice inside says, *It would if you exercised it more.* Which is when it occurs to me that the things which make us need God the most are the ones most likely to drive us away from him.

In the kitchen at home, Batman is sitting on a chair with his chin resting on the edge of the table. Close by him is a note from Sarah, telling me that she and Molly have moved out.

Crikey

The first thing I think is, Well screw you then.

I throw the note back on the kitchen table and go over to the letter rack by the window to see if anything interesting has come in the post. Nothing has. Turning back, I'm suddenly annoyed with Batman and swipe him off the table. He gives me a hurt look.

'Just clear off, Batman,' I snap. 'You've no chance with me today.'

He pads to the cat-dishes on the floor next to the fridge. 'Mip.'

'No way.'

He shoots me the expression Gromit, in *The Wrong Trousers,* gives to camera when Feathers McGraw goes upstairs for the first time at Wallaby Terrace: hard done by, to say the least.

'Go and find Robin,' I order. Batman stares back, reluctant to do anything I say.

I stomp into the front room and play back the messages. One of them is Dorothy Wood informing us that home group is at their place tomorrow night.

'Hah!' I scoff.

Derek's distorted, distant voice: *Hello, Sarah and Joe. Nothing important.*

Somebody reminding Sarah there's no Mums and Toddlers next week because of a jumble sale. I punch the skip key. The final three messages aren't messages, just irksome beeps – probably the same person being persistent. Curious, I do a 1471. We were called today at 17.43. The caller withheld their number.

While I'm at the phone, I have an idea and press redial to see who Sarah phoned last. My chest is stiff with tension as I wait to see who will answer.

– Hello, 4450, a familiar voice says.

'Hi.' A voice I know straightaway. 'William?'

– Who did you expect, Joe?

'Sorry, William. I'm trying to find Sarah – it's just I've been out all day, come home and there's nobody here. I'm a bit anxious about them, that's all.'

– What made you think she'd be here?

'I did a redial on the last call she made.'

– She mustn't have got through.

'Okay. Well, I'm sure she hasn't gone far.' I'm conscious of the strain of being civil when civil is the last thing I feel. 'I'll get on then.'

Back in the kitchen, I read Sarah's note for the fourth or fifth time:

> I'm not making any progress like this, Joe.
> I need to try living elsewhere for a little.
> Will phone.
> Love,
>
> S.
>
> P.S. Molly's with me.

What does she mean by progress, I fret for the umpteenth time. And where is elsewhere, for heaven's sake? And why wouldn't Molly be with her? Where else would she be?

'Bloody woman,' I shout.

I pull out the drawer where I happen to have a stash of Villigers and, in the absence of a match, light one off the gas ring. I want a drink to go with it, but there's no beer in the fridge and I can't get very excited about the bottle of 'Californian Red' Sarah bought at Safeway earlier in the week. Besides, I feel the need of a stiffer drink. From the shelf where olive oil, balsamic vinegar, soy sauce and things of that ilk live, I extract a half bottle of brandy Sarah uses for baking and fill a Paris goblet from it.

When I'm plumped down on the sofa in the TV room I can think of nothing I want to do except smoke this cigar and drink this big, big brandy. It's an idea and one that I plan to go through with, but really I know all I am going to do this evening is be angry.

She'll be back, I argue, because, inadequate as she may find me, I am the only person really in the same boat as her. Her family won't talk about what we're going through, and none of her friends understands what it means to have a child missing. She'll be back because we are bound together in this, as if we were running a three-legged race at Martha's school sports day.

I can't sit still, so I leave the brandy and go out to the back garden with the cigar. Not much remains of the day: light in which you can see the end of the garden, but not sit out and read a newspaper. It's warm, close, even. Everything out here annoys me: the swing, Molly's tricycle, the slide, the sandpit and – especially – Sarah's herb garden.

For what seems like a long time, I stand and stare at the mint, rosemary, basil and the fennel, the bloody fennel. The tall, misshapen stalks and the gossamer haze of their upper foliage have always seemed pointless and ugly to me. When I have fumed at them for long enough, I grip the Villiger between my lips, grab one of the fennels half way down its stalk, yank it out and fling it behind me, in the process scattering soil over the lawn. I repeat this with each of the fennel plants until there are four of them lying slain on the lawn. It looks like a low-budget production of *Day of the Triffids*. Triffids, 0; Humankind, 4.

Less than satisfied, I turn my attention to the plastic sand-pit, which I grab from beneath and flip over, so that stagnant rain-water and slimy sand spill over Sarah's little rockery. I grunt, grab the frame of the swing and pull and push until the spikes at its four corners clear the turf. When I shove the whole structure over on its side, it bounces awkwardly and bangs my shin.

'Stupid,' I scream, and kick the frame and then the plastic seat. 'Ya *stupid*.' And I kick it again, and finding I am out of breath now, turn to go in and see Colin, my neighbour, leaning on the staff of a garden implement regarding me much as David Attenborough might a rampaging gorilla.

'All right, Joe,' he says in his non-committal way.

The raucous sounds of *The Big Breakfast* drag me back to consciousness. My watch says it's ten to nine, which is bad, and I'm stiff from spending the night on the sofa.

As I stand and try to push my back into shape, I absorb last night's debris. The brandy bottle stands empty on the TV cupboard. My head hurts, although I do feel quite pleasantly hollow. The chattering sounds from *The Big Breakfast* draw my attention for a moment or two, but the rolling, swooping camerawork gets right to me and I bash the TV off.

As I move in the vaguest way, my foot catches on something and I look down to see a splay of videotapes and boxes. I pick them up one by one and piece together my evening on the sofa: my home recordings of The Beatles *Anthology* TV series and *The Best of The Tube*; boxes for sell-through videos of The Stones' *Rock'n'Roll Circus* and REM's *Tourfilm*. Signs of increasing desperation, which remind me of what happened yesterday.

'Sarah!' I shout in vain through the house.

I return to the answer machine, so emphatically unhelpful last night. A couple more anonymous beeps, and, when I do a 1471, another caller-withheld-their-number message. Last night's persistent unknown, presumably. 'Shitbags,' I mutter and hang up before the frigidly literal voice completes. It doesn't matter, is what I think, and register an urgent need for coffee. I'm no more than in the kitchen when the phone rings and I'm back in the front room before you can say 'Alexander Graham Bell.'

'Sarah,' I go, breathless as Jerry Lee Lewis or Jean-Paul Belmondo, depending on how you wasted your youth.

– Sorry, wrong girl.

'Gill!'

– Are you all right?

'Fine, why?'

– You sound like you've been on something.

'Nope.'

– It's Thursday again...and you haven't rung me.

'Oh, right.' I say when I get her drift. 'Sorry about that.'

– I've been trying to get you.

At the thought of Sarah picking up the phone to Gill, alarm bells go off in my head. 'You have? Was that you who kept withholding your number?'

– It's a useful trick.

I imagine all the surreptitious calls she will have made to her married man. 'It's good to hear from you.'

– I know. I want you to come with me to Blackpool. I have an overwhelming desire to see the Illuminations, and they finish next week.

'What? Go now?'

– This afternoon.

My heart sinks. I'm running late with a couple of jobs. 'Will you be able to see them in the afternoon? I thought the lights were kind of a night-time thing.'

– Yes, but if we went this afternoon, I'm sure we could find some way of distracting ourselves until it gets dark.

'Really?'

Can you swing it to come, then?

'I can,' I say. I can swing anything I want now; I have lost my entire family, surely a fantasy most married men must have harboured every once in a while. I have lost my family and I am free to be everything I used to be: my own man, master of my own time. Free to regress to some *Loaded* nirvana, a little voice inside me adds.

Pick you up at one.

'Whoa – I've got a lot of work on at the moment. How about two?'

Half-past one or I'm going on my own.

'It's a deal.'

During the morning, I don't clear as much of my backlog as I need to, but, despite the fact that my brain isn't firing on all cylinders, I break the back of it.

I would get on better if I didn't wonder about Sarah and Molly, if I didn't debate the pros and cons of the course of action I seem to be pursuing. My curiosity about where Sarah may have got to is intense, and as the morning passes, I am surprised to find myself missing her.

I also consider how weary of her I have been for months. Her leaving feels to an extent like something falling into place. I'm not sure how much longer I could have survived living with somebody who has given up on me, who doesn't care what happens to me.

On the other hand, I can't help feeling that her note – which I think I can recite word for word – isn't as negative as it might have been. She doesn't sound angry. Her saying she isn't making any progress suggests that there is progress to be made, even that she wants to make it. She says she needs to try living somewhere else, which sounds tentative, not terminal – and doesn't she say 'for a little'? It isn't permanent. She isn't cutting me off, as she promises to phone. She signs off with love, which in the circumstances I would guess is conscious rather than inadvertent. The note definitely contains several positive indicators.

Sarah's departure is a blow to my pride. People at Mersey Valley will give me a wide berth for fear that family breakdown could be contagious – *Unclean, unclean.* They will pass me in the school hall during post-service tea and coffee the way I pass those homeless beggars I choose not to give to: guiltily, furtively.

In between times, I concentrate on the mouse and the screen and finish one, then two jobs. Given the amount of concentration I am able to muster for them, these jobs may not be my best efforts, but in some shape or fashion they are completed and will have to do.

While my emotions are ploughed up, down and across by a variety of responses to Sarah leaving me, a low, hard-bitten part of me can't help thinking that her absence presents the perfect opportunity to have a good time with Gill, which I tell myself is acceptable in the circumstances. Sarah has abandoned me, not the other way round, so doesn't that leave me at liberty to do as I please? If things develop between me and Gill on this trip to Blackpool why would it be wrong? I'm not a married man anymore, but a man abandoned by his wife. It sounds morally reasonable to me. And let's not forget that Sarah and I haven't made love since early February – almost ten months ago. (Forget?)

Many times I rehearse Gill's memorable statement on casual sex from all those years ago: *You know how I feel about it.* I rehearse it enough to make me slide toothpaste and my toothbrush into my coat pocket.

'Are you ready?' she says, sweeping into the hall at half-past one.

I take in her bright appearance: a purple and fuchsia Goretex kagoul, custard raglan cardigan, taupe jeans and French-blue suede brothel-creepers. Too much to hope for, but I want to hope.

'Shall we get straight off?'

'Yep.' I reach for my coat off the newel post, one very like the newel post in the hallway of the shared house I was in when Gill and I were having our thing. It transports me back to one night close to the end of that time.

I was having trouble with my conscience and trying to ease off the sex. It had worked – up until the point where she was about to go home. She was standing coat in hand on the bottom step of the stairs. Leaning on the newel post, I gave her a chaste kiss which in seconds turned into a passionate clinch that shot us upstairs to my room with hardly a pause for breath.

I lift my coat off the newel post. 'Do I need to bring anything?'

'As long as you've got your parachute, you'll be all right.'

'Parachute?'

'The jump from the top of the Tower?'

M60, M61, M6, M55, as my father-in-law might say, and, somewhere on the M55 Gill yelps, 'Look! There it is.'

And Blackpool Tower from miles away, isolated in the soft green and brown landscape, looks inviting. Removed from its tinsel-town sur-roundings, the Tower seems almost romantic. From this distance, it could be the Eiffel Tower.

'Haven't you ever been to Blackpool?' I ask.

'Yes. Lot of magicians in Blackpool. Ohh, doesn't it look lovely? It's such an exotic place, right out on its own.' As if to get the full benefit of the vista, Gill winds down her window a couple of inches

Her animated behaviour and her shape as she stretches for another Extra Strong Mint from the storage area in front of the gear lever stirs my mojo and I savour the sheen of her dark, fine hair.

From the motorway, Gill threads her way confidently through residential Blackpool.

'Do you often bunk off work to spend the day with women other than your wife?' she asks.

I look at her face to see if she means to be unkind. My guess is she doesn't. 'Last Thursday was the first time.'

'Don't look so vulnerable!'

'I'm not.' I half-laugh. 'What about you? What was the story with the married man you mentioned?' The light goes out of her face. 'Or don't you want to talk about it?'

'Not a lot, no. The snapshot version is that he was kind of a public figure, which made it difficult. And it had a messy ending.' She gives me an open look, I think an affectionate look. 'He wasn't anything like you.'

'Good. Or should I say bad?'

She raises one quizzical shoulder the way I thought only French starlets did. She describes her travels through the years we were out of touch – back-packing in Nepal, six months in Australia and New Zealand, Eastern Europe in the aftermath of the collapse of communism.

Meanwhile, I'm admiring the distinctive way she shifts the gear lever from second to third, from fourth back to third, palm forwards. I soak up her deft fingers touching the indicator stalk down, flicking it back up.

When she's holding forth on the way technology is distracting people from genuine experience, I study the firm, brisk way she negotiates the traffic. I nod and agree and interview; I notice the zoo passing on one side and, on the other, a park with a boating lake.

As we circle the edge of the town, sometimes I'm not paying much attention at all to what she's saying. I'm puzzling over whom Sarah is staying with. I'm missing Molly and wondering when I will see her again. I'm clenching my molars with irritation at Sarah, somehow growing to believe that everything that has gone wrong for us is more her fault than mine.

What was there that I could have done to prevent Martha's abduction? What happened to me could have happened to the most attentive mother (let alone father) in the world. And the fact of the matter is that it's Sarah's intransigence and awkwardness which has been souring the air we breathe for months, Sarah's bloody-mindedness that has been the barrier to either of us making any of the progress her note referred to.

'Here we are,' Gill says, winding her window down and admitting a briny breeze with the late autumn chill. 'The sea.'

'Bracing,' I say, emerging from my gathering funk.

We turn right at the front and as we drive along parallel to the shore our view of the sea is blocked by Illuminations tableaux: Jack and the Beanstalk, *Noddy*, George and the Dragon, *Dr Who*, The Three Bears, *Star Wars*. A cream and green tram clanks by. Nothing like Manchester's Metrolink, this system must be sixty or seventy years older.

Gill turns right again and reverses in one movement into a space not far from the seafront. She switches the engine off and it's immediately peaceful, still inside the cabin. 'I know it's only Blackpool beach and I know the water is probably foul,' she says, 'but still, the seaside is exciting, don't you think?'

Perhaps I wouldn't go that far, but I can't help feeling perked up by the sight of the water and the taste of fresh sea air. 'Well, I suppose I do like to be beside the seaside.'

'Really?' She doesn't catch my stab at gentle wit.

'I do like to be beside the sea.'

'Oh, I get you.'

'And there's lots of girls besides I should like to be beside –'

'– beside the seaside, beside the sea.'

I give her a patter of ironic applause. She lets out a hungry, feline laugh, wraps her hand around the back of my neck and engages my mouth in a moist, warm kiss I can feel all the way to Auckland. I have time to notice something like gardenia in her perfume, different from last week's, and the apple scent lingering from her shampoo. Too quickly, the kiss is over, Gill is out of the car and I'm left giddy-headed in the passenger seat, beside the sea, no longer beside the girl and a little beside myself. The toothpaste bulges in my coat pocket as my penis bulges in the crotch of my trousers and I am giddy with the idea that I can do this, I can jump off this cliff without a backwards glance, believing as I plummet that it is all that can save me.

Getting out, I look across the car's roof at her and, since we're in Blackpool, adopt my best George Formby to say, 'Crikey!'

I Wouldn't Like Me
If I Were You

When we reach North Pier, its decayed white paint and low-rent stalls don't fill me with anticipation. The sea is grey and murky, flexing its muscles on the pier's infrastructure. It's only late October, yet already it feels wintry, like January somehow. And the belligerent sky holds out as little holiday promise as the sea beneath it. It's strange what desire will cause you to put up with.

'What've you got planned?'

'Come over here.' She slides her arm through the crook of mine to lead me to the railings on our left. 'What about that?' she asks of the view of the Tower, the Golden Mile and Central Pier. Closer to hand, white horses break on the sands between the two piers.

'Your idea of fun would be to get out on the waves in your boat, with me folded in two beneath the boom, right?'

She smiles, a soft, accepting smile. Her nimble fingers are neatly arranged on my forearm, none of them any longer than another, and I place my free hand over them.

She looks at what I've done, and at me. 'I'm not telling you what my idea of fun is.'

Which reminds me that from Day One not telling me anything about anything has pretty much been her first principle.

She detaches from me and moves on down the pier. 'Come with me.'

We pass a woman with a camera and a tiny monkey on her shoulder, a mini-dodgems track and a variety of slot-machine toddler rides, which make me think about Molly, and by extension, Sarah. But I refuse to accept the baggage that comes with that. Our marriage is on its deathbed, and Sarah is the one who's dealt it all the major blows. Plus, as I keep telling myself, she's walked out on me. I'm a free man, and I'm going to enjoy it.

When the end of the pier is in sight, we are facing a small wooden building that has been decorated in the swirling graphics of traditional circus posters. The paintwork has seen better days, but the sign on the front is clear enough and reading it, I can see what brings Gill here:

Buster Bailey's
Museum of Magic

The double doors are open. A beaded curtain runs across the doorway. On either side of the flimsy doors are curling photographs behind cloudy Perspex. A tarpaulin banner strung up between doorway and the museum sign declares:

Visit Buster's Magic Café

'Buster a friend of yours?' I ask.

'Absolutely.'

We're up close to the perspex now and I see that the photographs are of magicians at work. The labels identify them, and I recognise a couple of the names at least: Harry Houdini and David Copperfield. Flashes of coloured paper advertising the museum's highlights – Card Tricks, Illusions, Fire Magic, Children's Magic, Escapology – are tacked up between the photographs. The script has been done by hand, and the calligraphy isn't bad.

I say, 'How about a magic coffee?'

Gill links arms with me, smiles broadly and emanates something short of adoration but on the right side of affection. 'Okay.'

Not sure what to do with this uncharacteristically straightforward behaviour, I smile and nod and feel a bit goofy. I kind of wonder if I am being hoodwinked and if I am I don't know why.

The beads on the curtain are glass and clink as we pass through. Inside are a small, tabled area and a long, higgledy-piggledy poster exhibition on display boards which screen off what I guess is the Museum of Magic. A recent looking poster for a Penn & Teller show in London is right next to a a much older one which reads 'HARRY HOUDINI

KING OF CARDS'. One corner is missing from a dog-eared poster advertising 'Aldini's Magic Mountain' at the 1948 Chicago World's Fair.

'Nobody home,' Gill says, drawing to a halt

I'm close enough to inhale the gardenia again. 'Maybe Buster's done a whatsit, a vanish.'

She shoots me a look that isn't playful, and I wonder what's going on. Since she's just kissed me ten minutes ago, why doesn't she want to banter now?

'Can I get you something?' says a voice I can't see. Gill steps away from me, allowing me a view of the voice's owner – an overweight teenage girl. She's wearing a maroon chenille dress that comes down to her hi-top trainers. Maybe the outfit is meant to lend her a hint of show-biz, but she fills it so completely she looks more like a salami than a magician's assistant.

'I'm having a Coke,' Gill says. 'How about you, Joe?'

Behind the girl is a stainless steel and glass cabinet littered with children's magic items, which I suppose must be for sale, but the packaging is so battered and faded on most of the boxes it seems unlikely that there's a big rush on them. Beyond that is an old sink unit with an electric kettle sitting on the drainer, next to which is a catering tin of Red Mountain and a carton of long-life milk. Chances of a Dodgy Beverage: extraordinarily high.

'Coke sounds great.'

The girl accepts our order with a morose nod. 'Summat to eat?'

'No thanks,' Gill says. 'Is Neville in?'

'He went out.'

'Will he be long?'

The girl shrugs and disappears.

We sit at one of the five available tables, all covered in orange rayon cloths, each with its own mock-Tiffany lamp. Ours has a used blue tin-foil ashtray to boot.

'Do you know this girl?' I ask.

'No, but I haven't been here for a while.'

'Who's Neville then?'

She grins. 'Buster. Buster Bailey was his stage name. It's really Neville Pike.'

'So you've dragged me all the way to Blackpool,' I say, 'to visit a magic museum and meet a man called Neville Pike?'

I intended a little gentle joshing, but she turns sombre on me. 'No. I hadn't really thought about calling on Neville. I was going to take you to Robert's Oyster Bar on the front and then onto the Pleasure Beach.'

The salami girl arrives with our two glasses of Coke. I look at Gill's clothes, her haircut, her low-key make-up and can't connect them with Blackpool. 'Did you work here – in Buster Bailey's Museum of Magic?'

'I came here after the married guy I told you about.'

'Ah.'

She pulls her chair in, folds her arms on the orange tablecloth and leans in towards me. 'Look, if you really want to know I'll tell you, I'll give you the whole story. But you won't like me for it. '

'Yes, I will,' I say, although I'm starting to feel doubtful.

'Okay. But remember, you wanted to be told.' She slides a hand through her hair, tucking it behind her ears. 'Okay. My business has two strands: putting on children's parties and corporate entertainment. Both involve magic, if that's what people want, but the main thing we provide is party fun, party atmosphere. We lay on the splash of colour, we make things go off with a bang – literally.'

'What, like party-poppers?'

'Party-poppers, flash-pans, confetti-bombs – all sorts of stage effects. Anyway, I met Richard through a job I did for Manchester City Council –'

'He was a city councillor?'

'Still is. Richard Kelman? He's got his fingers in a lot of pies.'

'He's the guy that's big on all the city centre redevelopment after the IRA bomb.'

'He's Mr New Manchester – and a hard man. And, for eighteen months, I was his bit on the side. God knows why I bought it, but he always claimed he couldn't leave his wife – said he wanted to maintain a stable family for his children. He's a big-time Catholic, and his wife is so devout, she's practically a nun. So.' She secures hair that's still behind her ear behind her ear. 'The long and the short of it is I got pregnant. And I let him talk me into an abortion.' Her eyes search mine for a second or two. 'And then I found out he had somebody else –'

'Somebody besides you and his wife?'

'Uh huh,' she sighs and takes a mouthful of Coke. She looks glum. 'So what happened?'

'I was feeling worse and worse about the child I had aborted –

although as nothing compared to how I would feel later – and I just *hated* him so much. You know, I would see his picture in the paper, shoulder to shoulder with priests, opening a new Catholic school or whatever, and I would relive my abortion and loathe him for this *incredible* hypocrisy.'

'He does sound pretty hateful.' I can't see why Gill would think any of this would make me not like her – unless she reckons that I will be down on her for the abortion.

'Let me finish. When I found out about this other woman he was seeing, I didn't have to think too long about what to do. I wrote three letters. One to him, telling him what I thought of him. One to the third woman – another councillor, as it happens. And one to Richard's wife. I told her about the affair, about the abortion and about the third woman.'

'What did she do?'

'Kicked him out.' She inhales with a slight moan and blows her nose on a paper hankie she's produced from somewhere.

'So what was the attraction? He sounds like a total prick.'

'I dunno – dark hair, dark eyes. I'm always a sucker for 'em. Plus, I suppose I wouldn't be the first woman to be turned on by a man with power. He would always have people running around after him, attending to his needs. He trailed power like –' She twists her paper hankie.

I don't know what she's feeling just now, but I'm off on my own flight, pondering dark hair, dark eyes and power. Not a description that fits me.

I ask, 'But why would you think that this whole story would make me not like you?'

'Plenty of reasons. I broke up a family. I ruined the wife's life and she was an innocent party. And I aborted a child, *my* child. My child who would have been coming up to two now.'

I look at the tears swelling in her eyes and something in me that has been threatening all afternoon to sink goes into a slump. This isn't foot-loose, this isn't fun, this isn't my great escape. This is not the picture that blossomed in my mind this morning when Gill's voice purred from the receiver: *We could find some way of distracting ourselves until it gets dark.* Whatever this is, it isn't a pleasure-filled sabbatical from my marriage. In fact, it's in the same tonal range.

But because I am a guy who has been hoping to sleep with a woman who is not his wife, because the woman who is not his wife has had a less than wonderful experience of married men, I feel impelled to tap my reserve tank of decency.

'Go easy on yourself, Gill,' I say. 'He got what he deserved and the wife was better off without him, if you ask me.'

'All right. But were his kids better off without their Dad? And was my child better off never being born?'

I'm not sure if the reserve tank has enough juice in it. 'Listen, you were traumatised. You found yourself pregnant in a situation where you knew you would get no support. And look at it: you as good as said yourself that this man bullied you into the abortion. These weren't ordinary circumstances. You can't keep torturing yourself for what you did under duress.'

Her lips tighten into two straight lines and she clenches her teeth and looks away from me. 'Well, I do.'

I glimpse the words 'ESCAPE ARTIST' on one of Buster Bailey's vintage posters and think how that's the last thing I am.

'And now I'm telling the story of the child I destroyed' – drawn back from the poster by her voice, I find she's looking me in the eye again – 'to somebody who's had his child stolen from him. I wouldn't like me if I were you.'

She's being melodramatic now. All the same, I tell her that I do like her, which is only the truth. I set a couple of pound coins on the table. 'What I don't like is this place. All this fossilised glitz is getting me down. Come on,' I say, standing up and taking hold of her wrist. 'Let's go to the Pleasure Beach until Illuminations time. Then, if you're really lucky, I'll buy you a necklace that glows in the dark.'

She lets me pull her to her feet.

'You don't mind missing Buster, do you?' I ask.

'No. There's no knowing when he might come back.'

As we walk out of the Museum of Magic, she takes my hand and we walk a hundred metres like that, sister and brother.

I don't know what her expectations about today have been or how she's feeling about me now, but I am aware of struggling to seem bright myself.

Given the way things might have been and the way they have actually gone, it's not as embarrassing as it might have been when, under the shadow of the Pepsi Big One, we bump into Lee Hutchinson.

He notices me just as I see him. 'Iya, Joe.'

'Hiya, Lee,' I shout. We both have to raise our voices: underneath a giant rollercoaster isn't the ideal place to hold a conversation. Lee still looks starved, unwashed and unloved. 'Fancy seeing you here.'

'I know.'

Yours Truly might sound calm and on top of things, but truth to tell the Rank Films muscle man is banging his gong in my chest. *Don't even think about asking*, I am willing Lee. 'You on your own?'

'Naw. I come over with some mates.' He jerks a thumb at a stall behind him. 'They sent me to get the tickets for the Big One.'

As he speaks, I'm peering at the clump of people around the stall in question, and I soon spot Lee's two skally mates. The shrimp is standing next to a teenaged girl who hasn't enough clothes on, hasn't enough filling for her Wonderbra, hasn't the sense she was born with. If she had, she wouldn't be looking so utterly agog as the shrimp sniggers about something, we'll never know what, although my money would be on the general area of bodily functions. And the fat boy, the driver of the old Honda I saw that time I met Lee in Chorlton Water Park? His features are composed into the best Liam Gallagher scowl his hamster jowls will allow, and he is stroking the long hair of the tall girl next to him. They look like nothing so much as owner and Afghan in a crowd scene at Cruft's.

I don't want to even think about Lee's skally pals, so I change tack. 'How's things at home?'

'Few changes.' Lee shouts. 'Me Mam's got a boyfriend.'

'Eh? So what happened to your Dad?'

'He's inside. Got caught robbing a chippy.'

I can't help feeling glad that Lee's father is where he can no longer lay a finger on Lee. 'So what's your Mum's boyfriend like?'

Lee answers me, but whatever he says is drowned out by the roars and shrieks as the Pepsi Big One makes its vertical descent.

'He's a twat,' Lee shouts when the trainful of screams has passed. He isn't smiling. He ducks his head in Gill's direction and adds, 'Sorry, like.'

I say, 'Does he hit you?'

'Not as regular as me Dad.' His eyes meet mine and hold a touch longer than they might.

What does he want *me* to do about it? If I ever could have, I'm way past that point now.

He looks from me to Gill, then back again. 'Is Sarah all right?'

'She's not bad, thanks. This is an old friend of mine: Gill.'

Gill smiles a greeting and I briefly fill her in about Lee and the minibus run.

'Will you tell her I were asking for her?' Lee says.

I have to think for a second before realising he means Sarah. Something in his manner suggests that he feels for us and our missing daughter, but I know it won't be anything he can express.

'I will, Lee. She'll be sorry to have missed you.'

A smile flickers on his small mouth.

'Hoi! Bugalugs!' It's the skinny skally, coming our way. 'Get your short arse to the fookin ticket booth, right.' As he approaches, he recognises me. 'Aright, pal,' he sneers.

I look at Lee, whose face seems to have clenched. What I ought to say is, *I'm not your pal*. What I ought to do is grab Lee and get him as far from this little scumbag as I can, as far as I can and as fast as I can. While I'm thinking, the Big One swoops back down with another tidal wave of screams.

I bite my tongue and shout to Lee, 'Are you okay for a lift back to Manchester?'

The skally flashes an unconvincing smile. 'He don't need one. We've all got a B & B up North Shore. We're staying the night, aren't we, Shortarse?'

'Yeah,' Lee says, and then appears to get with the party line. 'It's okay, Joe. Waz 'n' Vaughan are looking after me. Really.'

What? The way Pinky looked after his mates in *Brighton Rock*. But faster than you could say 'juvenile delinquent', Waz dismisses me with a nod, wraps an arm round Lee's shoulders and escorts him away from us, presumably in the direction of the ticket booth.

Gill catches my eye and, both hands held palm-upwards, gives me a quizzical look.

I sigh like a bastard. 'A long story.'

As we head for a rollercoaster less terrifying than the Big One, I dig deep and muster my bright face one more time for Gill. And in my head a little voice is asking me if it's possible that somebody is trying to tell me something.

But when it's dark, Gill and I walk hand in hand through the electric wonderland of the Illuminations. Sometimes we run and once, in the gloom of a tram shelter, we kiss. The signals my dull antennae are receiving aren't clear. Every time my hands slide into my pockets, my fingers touch the tube of toothpaste and I wonder if I could slip into bed with Gill as easily as I did a decade ago.

The last brown and yellow leaves are twisting, like hanged men, on bare boughs and gusts of rain are sprinkling Gill's windscreen as she steers us through the quiet streets of midnight Chorlton. Normally, I like autumn. It's change and change is full of promise, but change is also full of uncertainty. I shove the car-door closed on our day out, closed on the adolescent fantasy of the two of us checking into a guesthouse on the sea front. And I turn for home and set the teeth-grinding misery of life with Sarah against the mysteries and possibilities of a new start with Gill Forsythe and her magic fingers and wonder.

My Lose/Lose Scenario

After my Blackpool trip I'm hoping that the following evening will be a quiet one. For tea I get the other side of a can of tomato soup without particularly noticing it and the phone rings.

– Joe Bob! A familiar voice greets me.

'Vince.'

– Everything all right? You don't sound too cheerful.

'Things have been better,' I say and explain why that is. On the other end of the line, Vince blows out air. He wants to know if Sarah and I had a big falling-out. I tell him that we haven't been getting on for a while. He wonders what it is we have not been getting on about. I am incredulous. Hasn't he any imagination, any empathy at all? I sigh hard and spell out what I thought was so obvious.

– Oh.

And then I am listening to all the dead air of telephonic space. I try to put a little bounce into my tone and ask what he was phoning about. I hear Vince take a breath before saying:

– Anyway…maybe this will cheer you up: Willie from MainFrame was on the blower this morning.

'Oh yeah? I suppose she wants us to rewrite *Boris & Dragon* as a day-time soap.'

– No. Better than that. She said that she's had a positive response from Granada and they want to see some scripts.

'How come she didn't mention anything about having approached Granada when we saw her the other day?'

– Apparently she and Julian didn't want to get our hopes up.

I'm thinking it would take NASA's biggest rocket to get my hopes up.

★

I go from room to room in search of a sign that Sarah has come back, or just called in to pick up something. Nothing doing, though. Still, I stalk the house – for what I don't know.

In our bedroom, I turn over the clothes in her chest of drawers and in her wardrobe. My impression is that not many of them are missing. This has to be a good sign: either she isn't intending to be away long or she plans to come back soon for more clothes. One item in the wardrobe, a cream silk blouse, takes me back to when I first knew her and a sense of longing as strong as an electric shock goes right through me. I close the wardrobe door on the past, and once again fight the feeling that I won't get through this.

I sit on the edge of our bed and contemplate the significance of my surroundings. On Sarah's bedside table: *How To Really Love Your Child*, *Men Are From Mars, Women Are From Venus* and *Further Along The Road Less-Travelled* – reading to improve the quality of her engagement with other people. On my side of the bed: *Watchmen, The Shawshank Redemption, Right Ho, Jeeves* and a Robert Harris – reading to help me escape from other people.

And I think as I'm sitting there that everything which has been wrong with us is also everything that is good about us: Sarah isn't me and she isn't like me. She sees life differently and she lives differently. First and foremost, she wants to relate to others and fit achievements in around that. Me, I want to get things done above all else and I suppose I need a few hours a week engagement with other people. That's the way I see the difference between us, not necessarily the way she sees it. A conversation we had when Kat Fuller was round a few weeks ago comes back to me now.

We were sitting around in the kitchen over mugs of tea and chunks of McVittie's ginger cake. I don't know what led up to it, but somehow we began to talk about the differences between men and women.

'Men,' Sarah said, 'are real experts at seeing to it that their needs are met. I don't know if it's because of the way mothers have pampered boys in the past, or what. But I would say that the one thing that men really excel at is making sure their needs are met.'

Kat laughed in recognition and I suppose I did too. 'So what,' she asked, 'do women excel at?'

'Meeting the needs of others.'

Kat said, 'So a man's forte is making sure his needs are met, and a woman's is meeting the needs of others?'

'Well,' I said. 'You can't help noticing it's a convincingly win-win scenario.'

I slam the cabinet shut and stand up. And as I'm walking away, my foot catches on something on the carpet close to the bed. When I stop to examine the object, it turns out to be a hard-backed notebook. It's something I've noticed Sarah writing in recently. The cover has a naïve painting of a sunflower with a ladybird on it. Tucked inside the front cover is a card I made for Sarah's last birthday – back before the world was changed. I was surprised to find one of my homemade cards here – the rest of them are on display around the house, collecting dust, maybe, but a memento of romantic times. It was a wide-eye lens shot of a cow's head, looking along its nose. She used to call me cow-nose, inspired by the view when we were canoodling.

The unlined art paper between the covers is filled with Sarah's even, rounded hand. After a glance at a page or two, it's clear that this book is a place where she expresses her feelings about Martha's disappearance.

In March, she writes about 'turning a corner to find a gun at my head'. In May, she feels like she is 'under a blanket of darkness'. She speaks of having 'agonised with God,' wanting to know if she 'can still believe in a loving God.' In September she observes that 'God isn't immune to our pain, but there in it with us'. I can't say I believe this myself at the moment, but it's impossible not to be impressed that Sarah does.

I look up and my eyes fasten on the mantelpiece, on a picture in a broad, flat yellow frame. Martha beams out of the head and shoulders shot, four years old, the life just bursting out of her. Tears begin to seep out of me. I sit down on the edge of the bed and find I am crying, but softly – not nearly hard enough to shift the logjam of pain and regret inside me. I don't know what it's going to take to achieve that.

I mop my eyes with a handkerchief and settle to look at Sarah's journal again.

I've spent my entire life seeking your forgiveness. Now I have to forgive you.

Mine begins to appear to me a convincingly lose/lose scenario.

More Things in Heaven And Earth Than Are Dreamed of In Your Blah-di-Blah

I slip on my winter coat, follow Nell Lane to Hardy Lane and the meadows of the Water Park, blue beneath a bright moon in the broad heavens. The fields here feel open and wide, which is good for my sense of constriction. The moon is high in the sky. The only signs of life are the windows lit soft and yellow over to my right on the backs of Chorltonville houses. As I look up to the stars and down to the houses and fields, Chorlton appears small in the silver, blue and grey. The sprinkled lights of the universe seem awesome, seem to go on forever, and I am a speck beneath them. I'm a speck, but so too are Manchester, Europe and the Earth.

It's cold, too cold for standing around contemplating the moon and the stars. As I build up pace, the warm lights of those homes on the edge of Chorltonville catch my attention again. One of them will be Naomi's old house. If I thought about it hard enough, I could work out which one. Before her illness, I would have passed her place on a walk like this, her dapper semi with the trusty Datsun on the driveway.

I end up at the Moores' front porch, ringing their sonorous bell, perusing their MPV, a Renault Dumpling. They have a Mothercare child-seat like Molly's. I'm wondering as I wait for someone to open the door whether half-past nine is too late to be calling unannounced.

'Joe,' William says, conveying both surprise and a little discomfort. Maybe I have called too late.

'Hi, William. Sorry to drop in unannounced.' I can't help but notice that William hasn't opened his PVC door very far. 'Is this a bad time?'

'No, no. Not at all.' He looks over his shoulder – at what, I can't see.

'Right. It's just I needed to talk – I was wondering if you had half an hour to spare at all?'

'Sure.' William nods quite a bit. 'Sure. That's no problem, Joe.'

'Thanks.' I'm still waiting for him to invite me in. He isn't even opening the door much beyond the width of his face. 'Are you sure this isn't a bad time for you?'

He looks over his shoulder again. 'No, honestly. I was just being a couch-potato. Wall-to-wall docu-soaps; I never wished less to be a fly on the wall.'

'Yeah.' I'm beginning to think that we are going to have this entire conversation beneath William's porch light.

'Tell you what, Joe. Why don't we go out for a jar? Y'see, Lesley has a friend in at the moment.'

'That's all right – a drink sounds good.'

When we are seated in Jackson's Boat with pints apiece, I take in the deserted room. There are two other customers: a guy with a shaved head and a goatee and somebody he's talking to, whose back is towards us.

'Cheers,' William says and dips his moustache into the thick head of his Guinness.

'Cheers.' I set my glass down and cut to the chase. 'Sarah and Molly moved out yesterday.'

The man who was sitting with his back to us, whose face I still can't see, is now standing at the jukebox, punching the keys. The chiming grandeur of Television's 'Marquee Moon' fills the room.

I look back to William. It occurs to me that if Sarah's staying with somebody from Mersey Valley, the news may already be doing the rounds. 'Perhaps you've heard?'

'No – I – no. That's awful.' He wipes cream froth off his moustache. 'Golly, I'm really sorry, Joe.' He manipulates the end of his nose between finger and thumb.

I sigh and my chest seems hard and breathless. 'I don't know…Maybe we've just got beyond trying to cope with what's happened to us. I can't cope with it, anyway. Maybe she can, I don't know. But I'm can't. I'm just beginning to realise it's stupid to try. There *is* no coping with something like this. I might just as well try to cope with, with an earthquake. It's like our house has been disrupted by tremors and shock-waves – whatever happens in an earthquake – and I've been going round tidying up after each one.'

'Straightening the deck-chairs on the *Titanic*?'

'Yeah. Trying to act like it isn't happening. Trying to act like I can do something, when I can't.'

'Don't fight your feelings – give them free reign. Your feelings are only natural. They won't kill you.'

I look at the table-top and straighten my beer-mat.

'Do you have any idea *why* Sarah left?' William asks.

All the space around me seems to have gone. The way I feel now, I could be enveloped in cling-film, cling-film that's shrinking tighter and tighter. I don't have to think about William's surprisingly simple, amazingly challenging question too long before the answer comes to me. 'Well – because I want to put what happened behind me,' I conclude. 'I don't want to face it.'

'You don't want to face it.' He has, I notice, gone into counsellor mode, repeating things back at me. 'Don't want to face what?'

'I don't want to face up to the fact that I took my daughter, whom I love, to the park and lost her.'

'Oh I see.' William pauses and the pressure of the silence building up seems to fill all the space between us and I half-expect that he too will condemn me now that I have confessed to what I can't face. Finally his voice emerges from the dense air:

'Were you taking a nap when she disappeared?'

I see where he is going with his prodding irony; he is now being the proactive therapist. 'No, of course I wasn't.'

'Or maybe you ran into a friend and were so deeply engrossed in conversation that you weren't keeping as much of an eye on Martha as you should have been?'

'No. You know, I only looked the other way for seconds. It feels like I must have told most of the population of the North West that. And I only looked away because something was up with Molly.'

'Right. *I* know that. So how come you act like *you* don't?'

I can't find any good response to the question so I take a slightly different tack. 'The other thing I don't want to face is the fact that Martha's probably dead.'

He nods at me and mulls over what I have said, composing his reply, it seems. 'Yes, Martha *may* be dead. But you can't be sure about that.'

'Maybe not.' I know William is trying to help, but I feel more miserable at this point than I have done since Martha disappeared. I don't know what I have left to lose and I don't know where to turn.

'Have you had any thoughts about what can be done?'

His counselling tactics are starting to get on my tits now. Why wouldn't they? I'm in real turmoil here and somebody I suppose I consider a friend is treating me like one of his shrink's case-load. 'Not much I can do if I can't contact her.'

I notice that 'Marquee Moon' on the jukebox has become 'Emotional Rescue'.

'Listen,' William says, 'how are things between you and the Lord at the moment?'

Maybe it's the fact that this is yet another uncommonly direct question, or maybe it's just that my intention was for me to talk and William to listen. Either way, the flash of anger I experience surprises me. 'How would you feel about him if your entire family went down the toilet?'

William concedes with a nod. 'Point taken.'

The anger spreads rapidly through me, igniting a forest fire on all my flammable material. 'I mean, for crying out loud – what am I? *Job*? What did I do to prompt the Almighty to piss on me so persistently?'

William leans forward, wrapping both hands around the base of his Guinness. 'You wouldn't be human if you weren't angry, Joe. You do know that, don't you?'

'I'm not sure I do,' I say, which is a non-answer; what I want to tell him – shout at him – is *What made a patronising fart like you ever think he could do anyone any good as a counsellor?* Jagger is setting his falsetto as high above the disco bass-line as the moon is hanging in the sky above this pub.

'If our relationship with God is the closest one we will ever have,' William says, '– and I believe it is – then don't we have the right to fall out sometimes?'

'Well, yeah.'

'Otherwise it's not a relationship, it's a dictatorship.'

'Maybe.'

'Life's too long a journey not to fall out with him every once in a while. There are plenty of Biblical precedents. You mentioned Job. There's also Elijah, and Jonah was classic for that,' he says.

I look around the pub, at the snack-hatch, the pumps and opticals behind the bar, the sour-faced barman, Shaved Head and his anonymous mate. A question Sarah asked in her journal echoes in my head: *Am I secure in him, stood firm on his rock, or weak and easily blown over?*

Well, I think. Not much debate about that.

A new record whirrs onto the turntable, the needle crackles in the vinyl and I know from the opening notes that it's the Velvet Underground. Lou Reed has been set free, and he's been bound. You and me both, Lou. You and me both.

I wonder what life will be like without Sarah and Molly. I would really like to vanish. I can think of nothing I am wishing for, no hope I harbour. Without a vision, it says somewhere in The Bible, the people perish.

'Look,' William goes, 'let me be blunt again. How much prayer time do you manage to get in on any given day?'

This causes a fearful, defensive reaction in me; it feels like I am losing a tug o'war. 'A fair amount,' I say, but the truth is I don't think I've managed even one prayer time a week, let alone one a day.

'So, what? Forty-five minutes? Half an hour?'

As I sit slumped in the silence William has left between us, that feeling of constriction comes over me again and I come face to face once more with flat, grey despair.

'So: less time than you would normally think appropriate.'

The forest-fire flames up again. 'Bugger appropriate,' I shout.

William presses his palms soothingly at the air between us.

I lower my voice. 'Bugger appropriate,' I repeat.

He pulls his chair in and fixes me in the eye. 'Here's the thing, Joe. Do you know what is meant by the word "repent"?'

First he patronises me. Now he is giving me a lecture on repentance. 'Aw give me a *break*,' I snap.

'It means turning away from sin. But it's also about turning back to face the Lord – yeah?'

I am looking through him, thinking, *What the hell does he know about what I am going through?* The further I advance in the trajectory of this miserable process, the more I hate Christians with pat explanations. Who is to say that all suffering can be explained – or, finally, borne?

'None of us has it in us to deal with life in our own strength – and that's what you're telling me you've been trying to do.'

'Look: I lost my daughter and I don't know if I will ever see her again. I couldn't care less about sin or repenting. If God had looked after Martha, keeping him happy might be a priority. But he didn't and it's not.'

William clenches his mouth and nods. 'I'm sorry,' he says. 'I've spoken out of turn.' He drains his pint and gets to his feet. 'I need to get back now. You finish your beer and I'll give you a ring tomorrow, okay?'

I give him a gruff nod. 'All right.' We spend half our lives telling people what they want to hear.

Some minutes after the door has closed behind William, I spot Shaved Head and his mate approaching the exit, too. The mate's face looks my way just before disappearing and it is in some way a familiar face. I turn it over in my mind, frustrated for seconds or minutes, before recognition hits: the man in the pinstriped suit – the man at the hospice and at Mersey Valley the last Sunday before Martha disappeared. And – of course! – the man with the waxed jacket in Fletcher Moss. All one.

'Hey!' I shout, although the only one who can hear me is the sour-faced barman, who looks up from his word-search magazine. I snatch my coat and rush towards the door. Outside, there is no sign of anybody. Some way down the lane which leads to a roundabout on the M60, an engine turns over and tail-lights flare red. I sprint after the accelerating car, but don't get close enough to glimpse the plate before the driver, Pinstripe or Shaved Head I guess, has turned at the end of the lane and gone.

Defeated and breathless, I trudge to the footbridge and get halfway across it before grinding to a halt. I don't know how much time passes as I loiter there, looking down at the five-metre expanse of river that is all the Mersey amounts to in Chorlton. I set a foot on the lower crossbar of the railings and put it back on the ground, over and over, watching the river flow.

I'm perplexed. My world has been demolished and I don't understand what's happening anymore. The blackbird. Pinstripe's tweaked smile. The hands held out in Fletcher Moss. I begin to think I must be out of my box and dancing on the lid. But, I tell myself, there are more things in heaven and earth than are dreamed of in your blah-di-blah.

Tuning back into the sounds of the Mersey flowing beside me, I fume about William again. What does he know? He lives in a

Snowcemed pebbledash house. He drives a Renault Dumpling. Which is when I twig it: the Dumpling had a car-seat in the back and neither of William and Lesley's children needs a car seat – their boy is sixteen and the girl fourteen.

I stand stiff and straight as a flagpole and say to the Mersey, 'You fat bastard. You fat duplicitous *bastard.*'

His Bluto Beard and His Wile E. Coyote Cunning

The light comes on in the hall and I can make out the distorted outline of William as he clicks and clunks what seems like an awful lot of locks. The door opens enough to reveal the statutory six inches of William's vertical mid-section.

'So where is Lesley's "friend"?' I ask. 'Eh? Has she gone home yet?'

'Look,' he says, squaring up to me, reminding me that, unlikely as it may appear these days, William once played on the England Under-21s rugby team.

'They're here, aren't they?'

He clasps my upper arm with some force and presses me towards the kitchen. 'Just step inside a minute.'

Once we're where he wants us, William tells me, 'If you'd like to take a seat,' and points to the chi-chi breakfast bar, with its metal stools and their dwarf backrests. I must look askance at the idea of sitting down just now because he holds up a cool-it hand and says, 'Look, just wait here, all right?'

So I'm standing alone on the blue-grey carpet-tiles, taking in the soft glow of under-cupboard strip lighting on white melamine work-tops, the amber Le Creuset saucepan set, hooked in descending order on its matching rack, the half-timbered Roberts radio – all the sedate calm of a sensible middle-class British kitchen. I'm standing there absorbing all of this in a disbelieving 360-degree pan and wondering why the nadir of a year not short of troughs should be taking place in such a restrained setting. The pits, taking place right here, right now, as I perch on one of the Moores' rinky-dink chairs. The cushion is still wrapped in protective cellophane, for crying out loud.

On the breakfast bar is a small rack of cassettes. Two are teaching tapes, I see, both from Christian conferences. Further along are a Simply Red, something by Toto and – for heaven's sake – Demis Roussos' greatest hits. Some little voice is asking if I wouldn't make more progress in this Christian life if I didn't have the moral fascinations of a character in *Seinfeld*.

'Whor-or-oar,' something beside me goes and before I have time to jump back in my skin, the Moores' springer spaniel emerges from the other side of the breakfast bar. They call her by a daft name that escapes me at the moment – Edna or Vera or something. She sidles up to me and puts her doe-faced head on my thigh, making a small whimper.

'Any other time, pal,' I say and nudge her muzzle off me.

She pads back a couple of feet, opens her mouth in a smile and wags her tail encouragingly.

'Go on,' I tell her, raising my voice and waving her away with the back of my hand.

'Hello, Joe,' Lesley says, coming into the room. Her pale skin and fair colouring add to the cool of her kitchen.

'What is this?' I say, getting to my feet. 'Some kind of parlour game?'

'Don't be silly, Joe. Why don't you sit down again and we can have a chat? Mh?'

I can't remember ever being in a place where people were so keen to call me by my name and keep me seated. 'Okay,' I say, complying. 'Now is there any chance I could have a word with my wife?'

Lesley sweeps her cordless electric kettle off its base, under the mixer taps for a fill and back onto the base without splashing any of the immaculate work-tops – something I've never seen achieved in our kitchen. 'Camomile or Typhoo?'

'Nothing, thanks.' The situation here is increasingly making me seem like the redneck husband in *Thelma and Louise* and, consequently, I feel the need of being politer than polite. 'Could you please answer my question?'

Lesley flicks off the switch on the kettle. I notice her hands as they work, fine and tapered – bony, really – and I think of monkey fingers and feel blue in several keys at once.

'I know you'll have been worried about Sarah, and Molly,' Lesley says, leaning the small of her back against the worktop. 'And obviously these must feel like very charged circumstances to you. But the truth is nobody's ganging up on you, Joe. Nobody's taking sides here. Sarah's our friend and you're our friend, too.'

'Well I know –'

'Sarah just rang up yesterday and asked if we could put her up for a short while. And of course we said yes.' She shrugs, then folds her arms.

I remember my last number redial yesterday: what an expedient shit William has turned out to be. 'Could I just please *talk* to her?'

Lesley blinks and rests her hands on the worktop against which she is leaning. The expression on her face is one of eminent good sense, good sense she appears to regret me not having.

'The thing is, Joe, Sarah went to bed with Molly over an hour ago. Molly had a bad night last night – strange surroundings, I suppose – and by teatime tonight both of them were terribly tired. So, I don't know – do you want to wake Sarah, or do you maybe want to let it keep until the morning? It's up to you, of course.'

Which is as good as saying that it isn't up to me at all.

William walks in from wherever he's been and closes the door into the hall behind him: nothing is up to me and I am outnumbered, counting the dog, three to one.

'Have you been explaining the situation?' William asks Lesley.

Almost anything he could do or say would only confirm the way I feel about him after his deviousness – but this B-movie register strikes me as especially irksome. Pretty soon he's going to be aiming for the melodramatic high ground of Bogart's 'Maybe-not-today-maybe-not-tomorrow-but-someday' speech at the end of *Casablanca*.

'Y'know,' I say, 'I can't be*lieve* you could sit there in the pub knowing the state I was in and not tell me what you knew.'

'I'm sorry, Joe. I just didn't want something like this happening.'

'Like what?'

Lesley interrupts before he can reply. 'Like you barging in here and potentially upsetting Sarah when she's already more than enough upset –'

'Which is not my fault!' I shout. I feel like I am going to combust spontaneously.

William sets a hand on my shoulder. 'You're amongst friends, Joe.'

I shrug him off. 'Am I? I wish it felt like I was.'

Lesley says, 'You also have to bear in mind that it's probably a break from everything at home – not just you.'

'How d'you mean?'

'Well –' she glances off to one side, as though weighing up her next remark. 'Think how much that home of yours is tied up with Martha: can't you see how Sarah might need some time away from everything that reminds her of Martha?'

This takes some of the wind out of my sails. Then the damn dog comes out from wherever she has been hiding and puts her head back on my lap.

Lesley's tone lightens. 'Just shove her out of the way if she's bothering you, Joe. She's always throwing herself at anyone who calls round.'

'Joyce!' William hails the dog. 'You soft old thing. C'mere out of that, will you?'

Joyce, it comes back to me now: the Moores' dog is called after Joyce Huggett, best-selling author of Christian lifestyle books, on everything from courtship to hospitalisation. She is to Christian living what Delia Smith is to cookery. *Joyce Huggett*. Now I am really out of this place.

'Okay then,' I say, standing. 'You're probably right.'

'I'm sure I am,' Lesley says.

By the time I get to the front door, Joyce Huggett is still at my heel, like maybe she wants to go bird shooting, or whatever Springers do, with me.

'Listen,' Lesley says, 'you could do everyone a great favour if you like, Joe?'

I look at William with his Bluto beard and his Wile E. Coyote cunning, this new facet of his personality that's emerged tonight, and back at Lesley and I say, 'I could?'

'Would you mind looking after Joyce for a day or two? You see, Molly's petrified of her, and there's no need to be, no need at all. But I'm sure you know what Molly is like with dogs.'

'Uh-huh.' I'm not trying particularly hard to disguise my lack of enthusiasm for dog-sitting, but I can see Lesley has me over a barrel with Molly's dog-phobia.

'Here we go,' William says, chirpy now as he returns with a lime-green plastic dog-bowl. I'm beginning to think that there's something wrong with this pooch.

So now, as so often in Bonnards and Hockneys, a dog has appeared in the frame.

'All right,' I say to her as she canters along at the end of her old-fashioned leather lead. 'All right. But there's no way I'm calling you Joyce.'

We tramp through the big open space that leads to the end of Hardy
Lane.

'How about Jerry?' I say. 'Jerry Springer.'

Johnny Suede's For and Against

When we get home, the dog and I, she shoots through the hall and into the kitchen. By the time I catch her up, and switch on some lights, trouble-in-the-jungle noises are going off. Batman and Robin are on top of the fridge with their hair on end and their teeth set like a sabre-tooth tiger's. Down on the floor, the dog is standing on four calm legs, tail wagging, dopey smile out again.

'Great,' I tell my animal pals. 'A *Jerry Springer Show* pets' special.'

Removing the dog from the kitchen is difficult, even once I get hold of her lead again, because she's Hoovering every last chunk of Whiskas from both cat-dishes. While she's distracted, Batman and Robin make heroic, synchronised leaps off the fridge onto the lino and crash hell for leather, one after the other, through the cat-flap. The cat-flap's plastic frame collapses in pieces on the floor behind them.

I tug on the lead irritably, but have to concede the rest of the Whiskas to her. The cats won't touch it now, that's for sure.

'How big a pain are you going to be, Jerry?'

She's up to her velvet ears in jellied rabbit cubes, and impervious to anything I say, even when I revert to calling her Joyce Huggett. Either the Moores don't feed her, or this dog is a hog.

Joyce or Jerry spends the night shut up with a bowl of water in the study, which is as far away from the kitchen as I can get her. When I close the door on her, she breaks into a value-added whimpering frenzy, but I tell her she can like it or lump it. Batman and Robin may feel the coast is clear by sometime tomorrow.

I don't remember seeing our bed as I was getting into it the night before last, too far gone, and last night I was too tired, but tonight it

141

strikes me hard as a big and empty place, and, when I crawl under the duvet, a cold one.

For what seems like longer than I will be able to put up with, the whimpering offensive persists. Given the crucial information William withheld earlier tonight, it's hard for me not to conclude that the Moores have been sparing with the truth about their dog. Maybe they don't even like the beast; maybe they are opportunists who've been waiting for a mug like me to come along.

It's been a long, long day, and when the hound eventually shuts up, I slide, like a hand into a sheepskin mitt, into deep, woolly sleep.

Buster Bailey beckons me with his magic wand and I approach him and the little girl beside him. I'm incapable of resisting.

'Face me,' Buster calls, his voice rich and leathery from years of stage-work. 'Face me, face me, face me. I need your help with this trick.'

And I do and as I get close, I know the girl is Martha, and I think to myself, *This has to be her, because she's wearing Martha's glitter jelly sandals.* It's Martha, and her skin is a good colour, like she's been for a holiday in the sun. She doesn't seem to see me, but her features are composed and her hair blows gentle and free in the sea breeze. I keep walking forward, the people on either side continue to smile and wave and I wake up.

Which is why I land on the shores of consciousness gasping like a drowning man. My dream was in 70mm Technicolor, realer than reality, and I feel cut to the core by the experience of being so close to Martha. I feel like the broken pieces of my little heart are going to disintegrate.

I imagine I won't be able to get back to sleep and for a long time I don't. When I eventually go over, it can't be more than fifteen minutes before I am yanked back to the grey morning by Joyce Huggett yelping and skraking up above my head. With all the losses, fatalities and skin diseases in *Job*, its author probably thought he would be stretching readers' credulity if he included the part about Job's pain-in-the-ass dog.

My plan was to feed Joyce in the study – to keep her there a much as possible, in fact – but downstairs Batman and Robin are nowhere to be found. Batman and Robin, it seems, have packed up the Batcaravan and abandoned Gotham City.

The postman has been and among the bills and mailshots is a letter from the Mersey Valley eldership, signed by Geoff Simpson. It summarises Tom Beattie's vision for a student church and includes some guff about Manchester having more students than any other city in Europe. So that's why they won't be able to use the minibus for Kids' Church, I tell myself. *Rethinking the use of the minibus,* was Geoff's phrase when the announcement about children's work was made at Mersey Valley my last Sunday there, a phrase which comes back to haunt me now. The letter explains Tom's vision in a little detail and says that the elders are backing him in it. Towards the end of the page, Geoff wonders if we – copies have gone to the whole Kids' Church team – would like to meet up to discuss this. It doesn't sound to me like there is much to discuss. Lee at the Pleasure Beach, marched off arm-in-arm by Waz. I refuse the thought, just another spinning plate that is crashing to the ground around me. And there ain't a thing I can do about any of them. I make a paper aeroplane of the letter and launch it at the swing-bin.

I know I won't do any work worth talking about until I hear from Sarah. What I do instead is bring the dog down and fill her dish with chunky dogfood, which looks suspiciously like chunky catfood. Then I settle down at the kitchen table with a pot of coffee and some toast and marmalade and see what good thinking may do.

I ponder what I will say to Sarah when she rings. Also, my thoughts turn to Gill Forsythe and once more we're wandering the Golden Mile, electric wonderland, hand-in-hand. The reservoir car park. Her lacy white bra-straps and bare back. The kiss I can feel all the way to Auckland. We haven't spoken since she dropped me home after Blackpool. I wonder whether I should check that she's all right. She could have contacted me, though. Maybe checking on Gill would not be so clever.

Something brings to mind that scene in *Johnny Suede* where Johnny does the For and Against list on his girlfriend, and before you can say 'arrested development' I'm doing one of my own.

I do contemplate the odd more serious matter. For instance, I rehearse more things to say to Sarah – I think about what she might want to hear me say. But for half an hour or so, while I am waiting for the phone-call, on a sheet of Molly's sugar-paper I make a chart on life with Sarah.

For	Against
• Good to talk to – normally	• Wants to 'relate' more than I do
• Always positive – normally	• Seems to have recently given up on everything else – except maybe Molly
• Very loving - normally	• Mostly like a wet week now – maybe always?

Joyce Huggett, doyenne of Christian lifestyle books, sits on the chair at the end of the table, her tongue hanging out and what I take to be an encouraging expression on her face. Although I began the exercise tongue-in-cheek, when the coffee and toast are gone I find myself working pretty hard at my For & Against chart.

For	Against
• Good in bed - normally	• Irritating habits (list too long, but including toothpaste tops, dripping taps, putting things where they don't go)
• Been through a lot together	• Put each other through a lot
• We fell in love	• The sea is full of fish
• We have made a family	• I wouldn't join anyclub that would have me as an etc.

And so on.

What stops me going further is Johnny Suede's chart made me laugh and my list is achieving just about the opposite.

I keep on thinking when I take Joyce Huggett for a walk in Chorlton Park.

If you could only get over yourself, some voice inside me is saying, think how far you could see. If you could only get over yourself, you'd be home and dry.

Joyce and I wander across a football pitch, and, just to be dutiful, I throw a stick for her to catch – quite a few times. Stupid game. Cats wouldn't be bothered with chasing the stick more than once, but a dog seems to forget each time that you just threw the stick and she just fetched it back to you.

While Joyce sniffs every tree, every dog's bottom and a great many spots on paths and on the grass that have no visible significance, I reflect on where I stand with the Most High.

From somewhere, I remember the image of the seed falling into the ground and dying to give birth to a new plant, with new fruit and many new seeds. I think, as I have done before, of the caterpillar that dies in its chrysalis to become something both more beautiful and more able. The butterfly isn't just better looking by far than the caterpillar, it also flies rather than crawls.

I swallow hard as Joyce and I advance up the colonnade of trees in the direction of Chorlton Park Junior School. I forgot about all of this. I forgot the principle of dying into new life. I forgot most of what I know about Christian living and realising that feels bitter.

It wasn't my fault, I protest. I wanted to run a mile from losing Martha. It wasn't my fault I wanted to bury myself.

You did a pretty good job of that, the small voice observes.

Joyce and I are plodding along, nearing home, both heads hung low, when I hear Molly.

'Will Daddy have a peasant for me?'

'I shouldn't think so.'

Lifting my head, I see Sarah trying to pick the right one from her huge bunch of keys. Molly is climbing out of her buggy in an ass-backward fashion.

'I would've done if I'd known you were coming,' I shout. In the cool stakes, Miles Davis has got nothing on me.

'Dadd-ee!' Molly disentangles herself from her McLaren buggy, knocks it over and pelts down the garden path to my waiting arms.

'Heyy!' When she thumps into me, I wrap her up tight, snuggle my face close into her warm neck, which has an airy, washed-clean scent to it. My heart – knocked, scarred and left out to dry – is giving it some Red Arrows-style zippedy-doo-da up in the sky. 'How's my best girl?'

Joyce Huggett jumps against my shoulder as I'm squatting there on the garden path and knocks the two of us over. Before I know it, Molly is shrieking, flapping her arms before her like Joe Cocker fighting off a bee-swarm, and throwing a major paddy.

'She won't hurt you,' I say. 'She's softer than caramel sauce.'

'I don't want the dog!' she warbles and the pandemonium, if anything, increases. Then Molly is snatched from me and Sarah is whisking her through the front door, her keys miraculously sorted.

'You're being very dramatic,' Sarah says.

I'm making us a pot of tea. 'Sorry?'

'Last night, from what I hear.'

'I was worried about you. It wasn't very nice not knowing where the two of you were.'

She has been walking about the kitchen, as though sitting down would signal a concession of some kind. Now she's tidying up things that have been left lying around over the past thirty-six hours – things I can feel her nose turning up at, like wineglasses, ashtrays, burnt toast.

'Sorry,' she says, facing me, not sounding it very. 'I suppose I should have mentioned that in my note.'

Molly has been dispatched to her bedroom to sort through her books and toys and pack some in her *Hundred and One Dalmatians* plastic suitcase.

I set the full teapot and two mugs I've selected on the table – Dennis the Menace for me, The Little Mermaid for her.

Her hair looks nice tied up and I still like the fineness of her features, nothing big, nothing clumsy. What she's doing is looking in the cupboard where biscuit tins stay. I know, as I know almost everything about what she thinks and will say and will do, that she is looking for a Kit-Kat multi-pack to give one to Molly.

'What happened to the Kit-Kats?'

'I ate them.'

'What, all of them?'

'I was distressed.' Pissed. 'So,' I say, being provocative I know, 'are you getting anything out of having a break from me?'

She gives me a very fed-up expression. 'It isn't all about *you*, you know. All I want is a bit of perspective. Some time and space, that's all.' By now she is standing behind the chair at the end of the table opposite me. Her arms run straight down onto the chair back. Her cheeks are flushed. She sighs hard. 'It's not easy for me, Joe. You mean a lot to me.'

I look askance at that; at least I try to.

'You're a big part of my life to walk away from,' she says.

'Don't do it, then.'

'Huh.' She sits down on the chair on which she has been leaning.

'I ate all the Kit-Kats because I was drunk. I got drunk because I came back from this reasonably promising meeting about *Boris & Dragon* to find that the remains of my family had gone.'

'What kind of person distracts himself from his abducted or murdered or God knows what daughter by writing comedy scripts?'

I say nothing. Opening the fridge door, I produce a four-pack of Safeway chocolate mousses. 'Maybe Molly would like one of these?'

Sarah flops back in her chair, looking deflated and listless. 'See when she comes down. Leave her to her sorting.'

'I do miss you, you know,' I tell her. 'I miss you and I miss Molly, and what I'd like most in the world is for the three of us – is for the four of us – to be back under one roof again.' I set my hand down softly on her shoulder. If she flinches, it isn't apparent.

She looks up at me. 'More than selling your Boris and whatsit thing?'

'Oh please.'

She rises and moves away from me. 'I'll just go and see how Molly is getting on.'

The mention of this makes my heart sink all over again. 'No, let me. I'd like to talk to her for a bit, catch up and so on, if you're not in a hurry.'

'No big hurry. Go ahead.'

Ten minutes later, Molly comes back downstairs on my shoulder. Under my arm is the *Hundred and One Dalmatians* suitcase, small, but heavy enough with books, bobbles, teddies and plastic figures from her mantel-piece.

'Whoo!' I go, entering the kitchen and depositing daughter and case on the floor. 'Molly's stripped her room bare.'

When I straighten, Sarah, her back to me, is standing over by the corner where we stack up the mail, flipping though yesterday and today's mail. Something about this scene is ringing alarm bells in my head, but I can't quite put my finger on it.

'What's this?' Sarah says, turning with some raspberry-coloured paper, folded in half.

'Nothing,' I say. I try to sound as nonchalant as I can, but I know I don't. I have remembered in an instant just what it is that's alarming about the pile of post.

She opens the sugar-paper and I can feel my heart begin to pound as she studies my For & Against chart.

'You idiot,' she snarls. She screws the chart up in a ball and throws it at my face. It misses, but I get the point. She snatches Molly's hand and grabs the suitcase and its pantingly happy Dalmatians. 'Come on,' Sarah says and there they go, into the hall and out the front door.

What Do We Get For Our Trouble and Pain

The first thing I do when I catch up with Sarah at the Moores' house is apologise for my wretched For & Against chart.

'Forget about it, Joe. It's not worth mentioning again.'

'So I'm forgiven?'

'You're a fool.'

'That's what I'm saying.'

'I *know* you're a fool.'

'Okay, good. But look,' I add, 'you and Molly come back home and I'll move out.'

Sarah asks, 'Where will you go?'

'Oh, I've got a room in a house-share sorted out,' I lie.

'Okay.'

'You have the car. You need a car with Molly.'

'How will you manage for work?'

'I can get the bicycle going again.'

'That'd be helpful. Thanks.'

'No, no – I insist,' I tease, seeing as she offers so little resistance.

'Don't push your luck, Joe.'

Leaving them is hard, and, before I quit the Moores' house, Lesley adds to my burden by asking if I would like to look after Joyce Huggett for a few more days: she and William have to go to away for the weekend.

'Sure, no problem,' I lie.

'You've hit it off with her, haven't you?'

'We're in love. But Joyce wants us to do a marriage preparation course before she can commit to me.'

'Really,' Lesley says. I can tell by her face and her tone that she is yet another person this morning who is unwilling or unable to go along with

149

my stupid jokes.

'She's a great dog.' I feel myself sobering up. A man whose wife has just left him shouldn't be making jokes about the esteemed author of Christian living books. 'She keeps me going.'

'Are you sure it will be okay with the people in this house you're moving into?'

'Honestly, Lesley. They're the most easy-going people you could imagine.' *I've* imagined them, so they can be as easy-going as I like.

'What about the owner of the house? Will he or she mind?'

'I don't think so. He's in – he's in Brunei.'

'Brunei? Really. All I know about Brunei is that the Sultan is one of the wealthiest people in the world.'

'Funny you should mention the Sultan – that's who the owner of this house is working for, apparently.'

'Oh? What does he do?'

'Actually, he's a financial consultant.'

'To the Sultan of Brunei? Golly. Must be good at his job.'

'He is. The people in the house tell me he owns about a dozen houses round South Manchester. So he's obviously worth a bob or two.' I could get into this lying lark.

I have until bedtime to find a place willing to put up a springer spaniel and me.

Walking home to pack a bag, I'm picturing myself on my bike with a rucksack of belongings on my back and Joyce trotting along in my wake. Heading towards Christmas. No room at the inn, the heavens releasing all their piss in a stiff shower which is six feet wide and centred on Yours Truly.

Back at the house, the second post has arrived: a shock, a card from Gill Forsythe. Relieved that it's me and not Sarah who has found it first, I look at the rounded, arty handwriting on the envelope and think about binning it. I don't fully know how I feel about Gill, but I do know that, ever since Blackpool, I have thought of her often, whatever that means. I do know that I have tender feelings for her and I wish my life were less complicated. If it were, two people with needs and troubles, people like Gill and me, could just do something about sharing them. It could be that simple - if it wasn't complicated.

The card is Lord Leighton's 'Flaming June'. It reminds me of a Malcolm MacLaren album sleeve, which shows you how cultured I am.

> I'm sorry we haven't seen each other again. I did enjoy our day in Blackpool. I'm very fond of you, Joe, but I'm not sure you're in any shape for a relationship. I hope you're coming through the other side of this. It'd be good to have a drink sometime, if you feel up to it? Anyway, I hope you'll be happy again soon.

Me, too.

Then I really do bin the card, thrust it through the kitchen swing-bin's lid. It's only thirty seconds or so – the time it takes to cross the room and flick the kettle on – before I go back to the bin, fish the card out and re-read it. As I'm brewing a mug of tea, I set it on the worktop and study 'Flaming June'. When the tea's made, I hold the hot mug in both hands and alternate between looking at the Lord Leighton and flipping the card open to savour the words again. There is a long moment of hot hands and thinking how good a 'Flaming June' I could have, probably for the asking – and then I rush to the bin, remove the lid and bury Gill's card below a soggy mass of pulpy packaging, tea-bags and plate-scrapings.

I've got as far as packing a bag and making a start on packing up my Mac and attendant clobber when the phone rings. I think about not answering it, but the caller lets it keep ringing and the answer-machine apparently isn't switched on and so I pick up and it's Roy Wood.

'Ah, Joe,' he says. Talking to Roy on the phone, I am reminded, makes the receiver against your head start to feel like the softest of pillows.

'Ah, Roy.'

He chuckles. 'Always a laugh, eh?'

'Practically all the time.'

'Ah, Joe, I hope you won't think I'm meddling, but...'

'No, no. Of course not.'

'Well, William Moore was on the phone earlier. And he, well, I hope you won't mind, but he explained your, ah, circumstances to us. You don't mind?'

I mind him not getting to the point. 'No. Everybody's going to know, aren't they? Word about anything gets round Mersey Valley like a forest fire.'

'Obviously Dorothy and I are very sorry that you and Sarah are having this, ah, problem.'

'Well, thanks.'

'And we want to help if we can.'

'That's very nice of you,' I say, and I am touched. But I can't imagine what Roy and Dorothy can do to help. In fact, I begin to feel bad about their concern when I think of all the negative thoughts I have had about them in the past – turning my nose up at Roy's mullet and half-mast cords, being cynical about almost everything to do with Dorothy. 'That's more than kind of you,' I repeat and my heart stings as though pressure is being applied to a fresh wound.

'The thing is – and I hope I'm not insulting you by mentioning this – I don't know whether or not you're aware that Dorothy and I look after some properties for some of Mersey Valley's mission partners?'

'Yeah, now that you mention it, I did know that.'

'Feel free to say no, but Dorothy and I wondered if you might be interested in renting a flat in Whalley Range? It came vacant last week, a one-bedroom flat off College Road. Not the best area in the world, but the flat itself is tidy enough. Pretty small, I should warn you, but it might suit you in the meantime, eh?'

'I'll take it,' I say. Something about the size of my heart is catching in my throat and I don't know whether to laugh or cry. 'I don't deserve friends like you, Roy, I really don't.'

'Oh now, Joe. Which of us deserves anything? Eh? If we got what we deserved, we'd all be sunk, wouldn't we?' And he chuckles again, his laughter like honey. Roy is so Ned Flanders, it feels like he's bound to say 'Okily-dokily' next. But it would be all right if he did.

'What do we get for our trouble and pain?' I ask Joyce, paraphrasing Morrissey.

'A one-bedroom flat in Whalley Range,' she says.

After closing the door of my new home behind Roy, I'm inclined to think that Whalley Range will do very nicely thanks.

My new nest isn't entirely feathered. I walk from living room to kitchen to bedroom and an inventory of what I'm going to call home doesn't take long. I have a table to eat at, a bed to sleep on and a bath with an improvised shower. The Mac is on the table, so I will eat where I work – probably while I work. For music, I have my Walkman and, laid over my packed clothes, a bunch of tapes. *Blood On The Tracks* is among them, of course, as well as some Billie Holiday and a compilation I have recently made called *Feel So Bad*. Hah!

The walls are magnolia and the woodwork is white, neither painted very recently. It feels like being in a holiday flat, only the kitchen is devoid of anything a kitchen should hold: cutlery, crockery, pans – a kettle even.

'What do we think of it so far?' I ask Joyce.

'*Rubbish!*' she says.

I walk through the flat a second time and check off what I am left with. The Mac means I can work. My bike in the hall means I am mobile, up to a point. Also in the hall is a phone-socket, for which I will need to sort a phone and internet access.

I put my head round the kitchen door: I could refrigerate food and grill it, but I would be eating off the grill-pan with my fingers. In the bedroom, I could lie down, but to keep warm at night I would have to sleep under my overcoat. And that's just inside the flat.

Outside, two minutes' walk takes Joyce and me to Netto, where the things they don't offer include Lavazza coffee, half-decent muesli, anything approaching an interesting range of yoghurts. Otherwise, there is an Asian cornershop (not on a corner), a 50s-throwback electrical shop and a minicab office. Sunny downtown Whalley Range also runs to a handful of skinny girls in skimpy clothes working the drive-time traffic.

Now, as Joyce Huggett and I tramp the depressed streets of Whalley Range, I scroll through a second mental inventory – all the treasures of Chorlton not to be found here for, as somebody says in *The Importance Of being Earnest,* love or money. An Italian deli, a Polish deli, a bookshop, a wine-bar, a café bar, a restaurant, a takeaway above the level of a chippy, a record shop, a florist, a garden centre. You name it – Whalley Range hasn't got it.

These are my thoughts as I head towards the Whalley pub at Brooks Bar, where Whalley Range meets Moss Side. I suppose you would have to say that I am generally feeling more glum than not when I lift my head and see one of the very girls in skimpy clothes I've just been thinking about.

She is no more than twenty metres ahead of me, standing on the kerb, studying the oncoming traffic. As I near her, I am struck by her slight build and inadequate clothing: her skirt no more than what I've heard described as a fanny pelmet, her top a stringy singlet. Closer to, I see her blotchy, botched eye. She's unsteadily balanced on too-high heels. I can imagine the goose bumps on her arms and legs, even if I can't yet see them. She is about as voluptuous as a whippet.

Approaching, I am being overwhelmed by something unknown and unstoppable, a black wave of awe and dread that I know already is going to knock me over. I'm maybe ten paces from her when she turns my way and clocks me, studying my face to see if it's bringing trouble or income. I can't know what she sees, but something deep and awful is rising in me, nothing I can express.

'Look,' I say, producing my wallet and fumbling to fish cash from the jumble of till receipts.

'What?' she interrupts. She takes a step back, her dull, dyed-black hair lifting in a sudden breeze. She has no hips or bust, no more flesh on her than the scrawniest sparrow.

'Take this. It's all I've got. If I had more, I'd give it to you.'

'What you want, mate? I've got rates.'

'Nothing. I don't want anything.' I have burst into tears now and big sobs erupt from me. 'Here,' I say, mangling the word as I thrust some notes at her.

The girl stares at the money and then at me. 'Go on home,' she snaps. 'Get some drink down you.' I grab her by the wrist and she says, 'Get off me, fool.'

She has little strength, though, and I wrap her hand around the cash. 'No,' I cry, releasing her. '*You* go home, okay?'

She shuffles the notes, looks up again, says, 'Whatever,' and scurries across the traffic and down the side-road opposite.

The malnourished form, the skimpy clothing and the low self-esteem that brought this urchin to the streets – she could be Tracy. Who knows what Tracy already has to hate herself for?

I surprise myself with how angry I get thinking about the cancelled minibus run. It's lamentable. It's insufferable. Right this minute Lee is probably out shoplifting in Chorlton for his thug pals Waz and Vaughan. What do I know about juvenile crime? It could be housebreaking or sell-

154

ing, as Waz would no doubt put it, whiz or weed. And screw Tom Beattie's students is what I say. They've arrived in Manchester from Surrey and Solihull with all the advantages money can buy. They have been expensively equipped to look after themselves. Who's looking after Lee or Tracy? And anyway, why should it be a question of either Tom's student church or our minibus? Would it be impossible to buy a second minibus? God, as Bono famously declared, isn't short of money.

What they're listening to on
The Wang Dang Doodle this week:
'Poppa Let Me Borrow The Car'
(Carl Perkins)
'I Ain't Got No Home In This World Anymore'
(Woody Guthrie)
'I'm Gonna Move To The Outskirts Of Town'
(Ray Charles)

Joyce Huggett is nose-down in her plastic dish, which I have filled with half a tin of Pal, when the doorbell rings, the last thing I expect. I open up the door and Roy Wood fills the frame, quite a large cardboard box in his arms.

'Me again,' he says.

'My first visitor!'

Roy beams at me over the top of his cardboard box. His mullet has been blown every which way in the wintry breeze. Even on wind-less days, mullets always seem to me to be the haircut equivalent of the head of Janus: instead of two faces, two haircuts. Sensible and reasonably tidy at the front, the sort of haircut that has a company car, belongs to a health club and reads the *Your Money* pages in its Sunday paper. But round the back – what's going on? The haircut that jacked in its job and went to Amsterdam to live in a houseboat *ménage à trois* and perfect the giant spliff. Today, Roy's rear haircut is shooting out of his head. It is the mullet *supreme*, the rampant mullet.

'Come in,' I tell him. 'Have a glass of water!'

'Funny enough, that's why I'm here. Mind if I step in? I could do with setting this down.'

I apologise and stand back to allow Roy through and follow him into the kitchen, where he dumps the box on the table.

'I'd forgotten how little there was here until I came round with you this morning. So —' Roy says, opening the flaps to reveal the contents of his box: saucepans, plates, and cutlery — even an electric kettle.

'Sorry it's a bit basic,' he continues, 'but it should be enough for the meantime, eh?'

'I don't know what to say, Roy. I'm bowled over by how kind you're being to me. You keep on rescuing me.'

'Oh well, it's really Dorothy you have to thank, you know. It was Dorothy who remembered the old pots and pans we have in the cellar. I'd forgotten all about them. And it was Dorothy who thought of you for this flat, when William told us about you and uh —'

'Dorothy?' I say, taken aback. Most of the thoughts I have ever had about her have been negative. Then I realise how my registering surprise must sound and try to cover my tracks: 'Dorothy! She's incredible, Roy. I can't believe she's gone to so much trouble for me.' And I can't. Yet again, I'm chastened. It seems there's no end to how wrong I have been about people.

'No trouble really, Joe. You'd do the same for us if the boot was on the other foot.'

I sit down, because I suddenly need to. 'I don't know. I hope that's true.'

'So —' Roy says, signalling a change of subject. 'D'you think you'll be all right here? It isn't the most homely place, I know. But this is all temporary, eh?'

To emphasise these comforting words, he places a reassuring hand on my shoulder and I burst into loud, shuddering tears. All kinds of sounds come out of me, from howls to grunts, and they hurt like something is being ripped from my chest. I don't think Roy knows what to do, and I hate him being here. I would hate anyone being here as I fall to pieces.

'It's been a bad year for you, Joe.'

Mopping up my wet face with a handkerchief, I laugh and blurt out, 'You're not bloody kidding!'

Roy doesn't know whether to laugh along with me or not. Instead, he asks, 'Shall I get you that glass of water?'

He probably just wants to get away and give me a chance to recover. If only, I think. When he returns, with a mug, not a glass, I take it and thank him. It feels like the moment has passed and I have lost all the dignity I am going to lose here.

'Sorry about that, Roy. Today has just been too much.' I think I was going to say more, but a second wave of weeping and sobbing overcomes me. 'I can't stand it anymore,' I am eventually able to say. 'I want Martha back. I want her *back*.'

Shooting to my feet, I roar out something incoherent and storm into the bedroom, where I throw myself on the bed.

Time passes, who knows how much, before a timid Roy says from the doorway, 'I'll call back tomorrow, shall I?'

Before I can recover myself enough to reply, I hear Roy leaving.

You Know How I Feel About These Things

The train to Hayfield is old, maybe half a century old, and clanks and rollicks as it makes its unhurried way to my destination. I would be less unhurried if I still had a car. I play with my new mobile, a Christmas present I bought myself while I was sorting out a phone and internet access for the flat in Whalley Range. (About my Christmas? Don't ask.) You need an up-to-date mobile for work, I told myself. And furthermore, you're miserable and a new toy never hurt anyone.

So here I am with my screen on and wondering whom I could phone. Nobody, really. *Hi. Sarah and I split up and I'm on my way to have dinner with another woman. I'm hoping recreational sex is on the menu.* Besides, I would inevitably end up saying, *I'm on the train.*

Out the steamed-up window, it's dead of winter, deep January blues, and I'm still wondering why I'm doing this.

Following the nicely drawn map she sent me, I find myself knocking at an unfamiliar door, a good, strong door with an impressive selection of brass attached to it – but not the door of the house I remember from years ago.

'Hello, stranger,' she says in her walnut voice. Russet patches on her sallow face make her look warm. The black, woollen polo neck she wears curls around her chin. She looks worryingly snuggly. With Sarah, what's left to get back with? The choice between Gill and Sarah isn't on the table, but if it were, how hard would it be to choose?

Gill accepts the tissue-wrapped wine bottle I offer and pushes a spongy kiss onto my lips. 'Oh! You're freezing cold. Come in and cosy up to the fire.'

She puts an arm through mine and leads me in my winter coat through the hall to a big lounge where a log fire is roaring.

'Nice place,' I say, and it is. Nothing like the hippy freedom of her last house, though. This is all 90s, and Habitat or Heals, not IKEA. The walls of the lounge done in different colours, warm and bright. Oak flooring with a large tufted rug, plain orange with a scarlet border.

'Throw your coat anywhere,' Gill tells me over her shoulder as she walks across the room to a limed oak cabinet. I surmise this is where her music system must be, for I can see her handling a jewel case. When she closes the cabinet door, the warm sounds of early Louis Armstrong swell in the room.

'Take a seat,' she says. 'Drink?'

I'm laying my coat over an armchair, trying not to make the place look untidy. 'Great.'

When she returns from somewhere – the kitchen, I suppose – she's carrying two big cylindrical tumblers, ice-cubes clinking.

'Try this.'

The glass is tinted green and the liquid inside is yellowish, although with that tint it's hard to tell. Whatever the drink is, it tastes bittersweet.

'Nice.'

'Good.'

She's so consistently unforthcoming. But I'm beyond resisting it. 'So what am I drinking?'

Gill looks at me over the top of her glass. 'Cinzano and lemonade.' She twinkles; in the giving-nothing-away game, another point won: I had to ask.

A tantalising kitchen aroma comes my way. I'm not even going to ask what it is.

She swallows a mouthful of vermouth. I watch the muscles in her throat work. I notice the lines that encircle her neck, good lines. She stoops by the fire, lifts a poker and breaks up a smouldering log. 'Are you lonely in your flat? Or are you glad to be a free man again?'

I shove my hair off the front of my head and pull an earlobe. 'Both.' I would rather be talking about something else – anything other than me.

She approaches and climbs onto my lap, wraps her arms around my back and says, 'Lonely boy.' A kiss smacks next to my ear, popping, mirroring the explosive surprise I feel.

How has this happened to me? (Have I said that before? It could be my mantra, my motto. It could be the words beneath the Porter coat of arms. And the image on the heraldic shield above it? The Porter head with a three-foot bayonet going in one ear and out the other.) How has this happened to me and what am I doing? What *should* I do? If I had any sense at all, what would I do in this situation?

I hold her, inhale the lemon and apple of her neck and hair. She emits a low growl, somewhere between a tiger and Roy Orbison on 'Pretty Woman'. Through my pullover and her lambswool, I can feel the soft plumpness of her breasts as she stretches her arms around my neck. Down around my coccyx, something is stirring.

'I bet you're hungry,' Gill says, clambering off my lap.

A year without sex, all but; hungry isn't in it. 'I am,' I say. And add, for good measure and nobody's benefit but my own, 'Cha-cha-boom.'

While she's in the kitchen, I kick back on the sloppy sofa and take a look around Gill's living room. Not too many prints on the walls. A couple of Nicholas Moss pots on the mantelpiece. Everything that can be tidy is: books, CDs, the handful of magazines on the coffee table, the dried flower arrangements on either side of the hearth.

'Do you want to come through?' Gill calls.

In the kitchen, in her flawless black polo neck and nubbly, red mini-skirt she looks nothing like a person who has just prepared dinner for two. She's tidier than Delia Smith on TV. Maybe, like Delia, she has enlisted the support of a large team of assistants.

She smiles as I come through the doorway. 'There's beer in the fridge. Dinner is spicy, so I thought beer rather than wine – d'you mind opening a couple of bottles?'

When I swing the fridge door out and see the neat bottles of Amstel lined up in it, I feel even better. Amstel makes me think of hot holidays on Greek islands.

I take a sip of the cold beer and look about me as Gill dishes and serves, setting before me a broad white plate with little coins of lamb done in chilli, couscous and green beans in butter. Her fingers fascinate me as she dips a small stainless steel spoon into the ramekin dish of mint sauce and gives it a freshening stir. Hands that are deft and artful verge on the supernatural to me, beyond my ken, no less magical than conjuring.

The kitchen, like the living room, is distinguished by its tidiness. The burnt orange walls look like they've been both re-plastered and painted recently: all the surfaces uniform, the edges sharp. Three medium-sized black and white photographs are hung to either side of the window above the sink. Two of them mean nothing to me, but I recognise Marcello Mastrioanni, when he was young, in the third. Above where I'm sitting – at a table so old the wood has wrinkles – is a large print of a Georgia O'Keefe painting of a poppy. Must have a thing about orange, I think, recalling the 'Flaming June' card she sent me.

She sets a round breadboard of sliced olive bread on the table, warm bread I can smell. She goes to a micro hi-fi unit on the tiled windowsill next to the O'Keefe print. A music system in every room, it seems. She depresses a touch-sensitive button and jazz plays, a saxophone with swirling strings. She sits down opposite me and shunts the breadboard towards me with her dextrous, stubby fingers. 'Help yourself.'

'Thanks. Looks wonderful.' I am smiling at her. I am full of the rare pleasure of being happy in the moment where I am.

Her dark eyes look cola-coloured tonight, glassy on the surface, opaque just beneath it. She lifts her glass of Amstel and tilts it in my direction. 'Happy days.'

'Mm.'

Holding her fork like a spoon, prongs up, Gill stabs a moist green bean. 'Why did you leave it weeks before you rang me?'

'I was trying to resist you.'

With that, her face, which has been stern, cracks. 'Why would you want to resist me?'

'Well – exactly.'

Nina Simone is telling us that she loves Porgy. It's the sound of the morning after; it could be the sound of a psalm. Next to the bread on my side-plate, Gill places her hand over mine. With her thumb, she caresses the veins on the back of my hand, flattening them.

'If you pinch the flesh on the back of a child's hand, it'll bounce back level in a flash. Pinch a person in their seventies and the skin will settle down again quite slowly.'

'And?' she asks.

'Pinch mine.'

She does. The skin returns to its original position like pastry. 'Feeling old?' she asks.

'Like something that's over in a blink. A vapour.'

'You're not so old.'

'Turned thirty-six.'

'October, isn't it?'

Her hand is still stroking mine. I cover it with my free hand. 'It feels like the start of the slippery slope. The beginning of the end.'

'It's not your age – it's what you've been through recently.'

I retrieve a hand to take another drink. 'I've been thinking that in the small expanse of time I'm allowed – well, I want to be as happy as I can.'

She looks at me from under her eyebrows. 'So you rang me.'

Twinkles in the dark reaches of the Coca-Cola.

'So I rang you.'

Later we lie about on one of Gill's plump sofas. We hold onto each other. She strokes my head. I caress her silky hair. We nibble each other's lips, press our mouths together. When our tongues connect, electricity crackles in my chest, my head dizzies and the first rumblings of a *tsunami* start up in my inner depths. She plays a disc of some opera I've never heard of and I imagine it's the sound of all the angels in heaven singing like larks.

'Joe,' she says out of a drowsy peace.

'Yeah?'

'There's something we need to talk about.'

'Sounds ominous.' I laugh, but she doesn't. She purses her lips, inspecting my face. 'Well?'

'I've been seeing Richard Kelman again.'

'Oh.'

The four walls seem to have collapsed one after the other on top of me. I'm covered in dust and mortar.

'You know: you weren't around much.'

'But I thought he hurt you before.'

'Yes. Yes, he did.'

'And you've gone back for more.'

'I can't explain it, Joe. But I do get something out of it.'

'I don't know what to say.'

'But it doesn't have to affect us. You know how I feel about these things.'

'Yeah.'

She caresses my shoulder and leans in to me. 'Joe?'

'But you know how *I* feel about these things.' And I am up off that fat slob-around sofa and heading for my coat.

'Joe,' she says, following me. 'Lighten up. Come on. I thought we had sorted this all out. I thought you had learned to be more grown-up about these things.'

'What you're talking about isn't being grown-up.' I'm sliding into my winter coat and steaming towards the front door. 'I'm one of the least adult people around, and even *I* know that.'

'Is that it?'

I stop and turn to face her. From somewhere inside me, gentleness bubbles to the surface. 'Look, we *have* sorted it out. You want whatever it is you get from Kelman. End of story.' I search her face, not really knowing what I'm seeking. Maybe if I look at her the right way, she will wave the white flag and come out of her bunker willing to be open, willing to make just a small concession and admit that I have something she needs, something she can't find in keeping her options open. But I don't think it's in her. I reach out and draw her to me, wrap my arms and shoulders around her, caress her silky dark hair and take a final breath of her intoxicating aroma. I plant a small kiss on her smooth, soft cheek and say, 'Don't take this the wrong way.'

'What?' she says as we disentangle.

'I only mean it nicely.'

'What?'

I'm opening the door, admitting cold that I am willing to brave. 'And finally today, boys and girls –' Maybe her Bourneville eyes are expressing need, maybe they're not. Either way, it's too late. 'And finally today, boys and girls, watch this –'

She sighs – she's on to me now – interrupting my flow.

But I complete the sentence: 'A vanish.'

As the train trundles me back to Victoria, I discover one message on my voice-mail. It's from D.I. Clayton. He wants me to ring the station at once – no matter how late.

Martha

As Clayton and Andrea Dobson - yes, Andrea Dobson - lead Sarah and me down a corridor, as I smell the ether and floor polish, as I make a conscious effort to put one foot in front of the other, all I can think of is the fact that hope, even the longest, dumbest shot at hope, has gone. It's a harsh reality, which I'm resisting; this is one corridor I don't want to go down.

'The chapel of rest is just through here,' Andrea Dobson says, one of those futile things people say only for the comfort words spoken may bring. Her name, a name I knew the day I first heard it that I would never forget, sings in my head. Andrea Dobson, it turns out, is a WPC who has trained as a bereavement counsellor.

When we enter the room, all I can see is the small, shrouded figure laid out by the curtained window. Sarah, waxen under the strip lighting, emits a shuddering cry, pulls her hand from mine to cover her mouth. 'Ah,' she goes, once, twice and a third time.

'It's okay, love,' Andrea tells her. She wraps her arm over Sarah's shoulders. 'If you don't want to look, you won't have to.'

'No,' Sarah says, whimpering. 'No.'

Her meaning is unclear, but even I can see that at a moment like this any interpretation will do.

I look to Clayton, who nods us on, and now I see how valuable for his job his social-worker face must be. My feet are failing me. Six or seven paces across this impersonal room is the inevitable terminus of the last twelve months. All our sorrows, from Longford Park to this week, distilled, focused and completed at one point in space and time – over there.

Clayton says, 'Joe, maybe you would look? There's no – there's nothing you need to be afraid of seeing.'

164

At first I don't move. Why should I? How can I? Instead, I look at where the little figure lies, covered in white sheets, sheets draped over her and the bed she lies on, all the way to the floor. Not quite to the floor, and beneath the sheets, I see wheels, and I see that it's no bed, but a trolley disguised.

'All right,' I tell him. 'I'll do it.'

And then I'm beside her and I seem to be torn between panting and not breathing. It feels like the others are behind me, at the lip of the room, but Clayton's hand is suddenly reaching over the expanse of white.

'Okay?'

Some sort of sound emerges from my throat.

He lifts back the top of a white sheet and Martha's head is there, her face tinted blue. Her lips are black – with lipstick, it looks like. I sob and fat tears form and roll down my cheeks. And then I rage. 'Aw *Jesus*.' Somebody somewhere did this. Somebody did this to my baby and I want to obliterate them, wipe them from life. 'Jesus God.' Hot, angry hate burns me up. What kind of world do we live in? Animals don't do to their own kind what humans do to one another every day. 'What kind of –' devil, I think but I hold back from saying it and then I'm not holding back anything, I'm crying like a toddler, wrestling with my own tears, and through this storm I can hear Sarah shrieking behind me, roaring.

I look over my shoulder at her. With Clayton and I standing where we are, she won't be able to see anything. And my reactions won't have calmed any fears. 'It's okay,' I tell her. 'Come over. It's okay.'

She's petrified, frozen in space. For long moments, she seems nailed to the carpet-tiles. The look on her face reminds me of Martha's expression when she was tiny and terrified about being left somewhere without us – nursery or Kids' Church.

'Really. You'll be able to look.'

She comes beside me, then she gasps. She weeps, louder than I would have thought possible. I put my arm around her. I would like my embrace to enfold her pain, to contain her noise, but I might as well try to placate a grizzly with its foot in a bear-trap. One moment she is pressing her fists into her chest, the next she is holding her stomach, and all the time she is howling and keening, repetitive sounds that seem to shake the room.

Eventually, whimpering, she sets a soft hand on Martha's cheek, which she strokes.

With her eyes closed, Martha looks at peace. Examining the length of her beneath this sheet, I can hardly believe that the girl at the centre of such heartbreak is so small. I can't get over her black lips. How can her little raspberry pout have turned black? I lift the side of the sheet and reveal a hand, the fingernails still patchily painted crimson: small but chipped precious stones.

Sarah bends from the waist, laying herself over Martha, holding her and kissing her, burying her face in Martha's neck and hair. 'We've found you,' she murmurs. 'You're safe now, honey.'

Feeling useless and lost, I set a hand on Sarah's shoulder where she stoops. My heart burns as I look over Sarah at my blue Martha and remember the moment she was born, me waiting for her to cry, to live. She was premature and coated in the white wax that waterproofs babies in the womb. She looked like a little snowman.

I want to run. I have wanted to run every day of the past year. I want to run like The Flash, just a red blur streaking across the surface of the planet. I want to light out and I can't. Maybe she's not really dead. Surely she isn't? Maybe she will wake up for us.

In my head, I know that this cold blue and black doll isn't my little girl. My Martha left this world months and months ago and the doll is like a Polaroid or an echo of her. But somehow, though my chest feels like a field that has been scorched to the earth and ploughed to the hedges, somehow a comfort.

Sarah is cradling Martha's head, murmuring close in to her face and the small, shut-eyed, blue, black and white face peers over her mother at me. Inevitable as the curtain falling on the last line of the play, I remove my hand from Sarah and softly touch Martha's cheek, so cold it's shocking.

I wait longer than I want to before suggesting that we go home.

'Not yet,' Sarah says.

Later, I take her elbow and say, 'Come on, Sarah.'

'I don't want to leave her.'

When we finally head on, it's only because, after a further torrent of gut-wrenching crying, Sarah goes into an apathetic slump.

They found Martha in a walk-in freezer in Timperley. On Tuesday, two days after my phone message from Clayton, the *Manchester Evening*

News headline is *HOPE ENDS FOR LITTLE MARTHA'S PARENTS.*
When the nationals pick it up the following morning, some genius at the
Mirror manages to come up with *FROZEN LAMB* for their front page.

The post-mortem reveals that she probably died within a couple of
days of being kidnapped. The cause of death given is strangulation.
There's no evidence that she was sexually abused, which is the only merciful aspect of this grim story, and I would have to say that 'merciful' here
is a relative term.

From that black night in the hospital through to the funeral, Sarah
visits Martha three or four times, but not with me. I find the hard, cold
and motionless little corpse – so much less like my first-born child than a
photograph or a camcorder film – too distressing, which means that
Sarah has to enlist Lesley Moore to accompany her on these visits.

'I'm sorry,' I tell Sarah, looking her straight in the face. I hate not
being able to support her in this way, but visiting something that seems
to have as much in common with a frozen joint of meat as my little girl is
too much like the crowning pinnacle of my agonies. Everything is too
much, but this a little too much too much. 'If I could,' I add, 'I would.'

She locks eyes with me for only a moment, looks away and moves off.

My Mum arrives by train and the three remaining Porters all turn out at
Piccadilly to meet her. As ever, in the shape of her glasses and the style of
her hair, she resembles the Queen, but she is a small woman with no ret-
inue, with just a compact suitcase standing beside her on the platform as
we approach.

'Oh my dears,' she says and cries in Sarah's arms, then in mine. I
have to bend low to meet her embrace, all face powder, Aquascutum and
Estée Lauder, and in seconds everyone is crying. With me, the tears I
think are connected to a foggy notion I have that my mother will make
things better.

'Well now,' she says, signalling the end of the hug. 'It's a terrible
thing, but terrible things happen in this world.'

Mum stays at the house, and Sarah, to be fair to her, does invite me
to stay until after the funeral, too. However, from previous experience
it's clear to me that a wife, a daughter and a mother are more women
than I can cope with at once, even at the best of times, and this isn't one
of them.

Mum needs her Croft sherry and her *Coronation Street*, her coffee made with boiled milk and her crossword, her privacy when she has a migraine – and the rest. When he was alive, Dad waited on Mum as though she really was Her Majesty the Queen and so she is accustomed to sit poised like a Doulton princess on a mantelpiece while the world attends her.

We're having lunch, tomato soup with rolls and cheese. Mum sips the Heinz from the lip of her spoon with scarcely a sound, unlike Molly, who slurps like a dentist's suction hose. Mum isn't happy with Molly's table manners, but doesn't feel able to express herself on the subject. I know she will also be unhappy about the fact that we only have dessert, not soup, spoons. Mum is staring at the plate with cheese on, not because of our failure to provide a cheese-board, but because she would like somebody to pass it to her and, as ever at meal-times, will do anything but ask for what she needs. Anyone who had *real* table manners would of course be telepathically solicitous.

Having my mother around makes it very difficult for Sarah and I to deal with the tensions that are mushrooming around us as the day of the funeral approaches. And then Derek, Sarah's Dad arrives, hot-foot from the motorway, spouting road numbers, wrong turns and his frustrations with the fact that it's impossible to find a nice little National Trust tea-room open at this time of year.

Every night I arrive back at the flat in Whalley Range too late and too tired. I can't sleep and I've lost my appetite. When I'm not raging and ranting at the crummy walls, I'm buried in Joyce Huggett's soft, musty fur, bawling. Sometimes, when more tears have come out of me than I would have thought I contained, I look into the caramel and chocolate of Joyce's kindly eyes and laugh bitterly at the pair of us, two sorry fools.

One of the few times Sarah and I get alone, she rails at me, saying, 'I'd have thought you'd be wanting to spend the little time that's left with your daughter.'

'I just can't touch her, and seeing her is no comfort. The only positive thing about being able to see her is knowing that the ordeal is over.'

'It'll *never* be over.'

Now, with the aggravation between us amounting only to me not visiting Martha, seeing Martha, touching Martha, Sarah takes it up a level.

'I think we should bring Molly to the funeral parlour.'

'What?'

'She needs to see her sister. She needs to understand that Martha's really dead.'

'No way, Sarah. What are you trying to do? Scar her for life?'

It's a fact that Martha is the only one ready for her funeral. Sarah has spent hours preparing her, dressing her as though for a party: hair-clips and baubles, Gap cotton fleecy, denims with flowers embroidered on the back pockets, and not forgetting a bead necklace and a treasured ring that came out of a Christmas cracker.

The day we bury her, the late winter sun is out. Sarah plans to get through the day unassisted by medication. I've already worked out that this is almost exactly a year since Martha disappeared. Behind us in the funeral procession, Derek drives Mum in his Ford Frankenstein. Sarah, Molly and I sit in the back of a gleaming funeral car. There's room for three on the leather bench seat but Sarah and Molly share the yawning space between them while I sit on the jump-seat opposite.

'I put her teddy in the coffin and one of her Stanley Bagshaw books,' Sarah tells me. 'And I put the *Toy Story* soundtrack disc in from you.'

This is charitable of her, but painful charity. It's both a kindness to me and a reminder that, in avoiding Martha's remains, I have slighted both her and Sarah. 'Uh huh,' I say, a neutrally as I can manage.

Molly says, 'But I *want* the *Toy Story* disc.'

'It belonged to Martha, though, didn't it, pet?' I say. 'And she liked it a lot, didn't she?'

'I know.' She turns and looks up into Sarah's face. 'Daddy used to sing the song.'

Sarah hesitates before replying, her face, as it has been for what seems like forever, pretty much collapsed. 'Yes, I know he did.'

'You used to call it "Om Beyond", didn't you?' I tell Molly.

'Will you still sing the song, Daddy?'

'I expect I will at some point, but not today, Moll. Okay?'

Sarah has been looking at me, but looks away now. These past few days, the Sarah-looking-away moment has become familiar. The issue, whatever more profound things lie behind it, is my reluctance to go anywhere near Martha's corpse.

I alternate between looking ahead at the hearse and to the side, through the fogged window, where the rest of the world is going about its business.

It seems to take a long time travelling from our side of Chorlton to Southern Cemetery – ten minutes' walk, I know, at most. One reason is that the funeral procession has been inflated by all the media attention devoted to Martha since her body was found. I know without seeing one that the tabloids will be oozing crocodile compassion all over this story, spreading saccharine sympathy over many, many column inches. Sarah and I have shut ourselves off from television and radio news and if anyone comes near me with a newspaper, I will insert it in their gullet.

When the cortège halts inside Southern Cemetery, the size of the crowd there pulls Sarah and I up short and she starts to cry.

'It's nothing to do with anyone,' she says, hiccupping. 'It's nobody's business.'

I expected a good number – a few hundred, as I knew that, for example, most of Mersey Valley would turn out. Nothing like the actuality, though: droves, as far as the eye can see.

I pull the chrome handle and open the door, but when I turn to her, Sarah shows no sign of budging. I fondle her hand, which is sat on her lap, limp as a dead sparrow. 'Come on, hon.'

'I keep thinking that her killer is out there.'

'What?'

'What if he's in the crowd there – watching, gloating.'

'Don't think that. She's safe now.'

'In a better place?'

'I think you should take that pill,' I tell her.

William Moore, being the adult in our midst, has already volunteered to help me carry the coffin. Sarah refused without hesitation when Lesley Moore asked if she wanted to do this. So it is that William and I carry the pale oak coffin between us, the head to me, the foot to him, for the few small moments it takes to walk from hearse to grave. On the coffin lid between us is the wreath that Sarah has spent hours making, fussing and fiddling.

By the graveside, the eye of the throng is gathered under bare, thorny hawthorn trees, crowded by the hundreds that surround us, and mostly in matching pairs: Sarah's Dad and my Mum, William and Lesley Moore, Vince and Becky Ford, Roy and Dorothy Wood, Scott and Kat Fuller. In his funeral address, Geoff Simpson refers to *Deuteronomy*: "The eternal God is your refuge, and underneath are the everlasting arms." I'd like to find them.

The sun shoots harsh white light through the trees. Joe and Sarah Porter are not a matching pair. Press photographers on steps tower over the heads of those at the back, firing at us with their telephoto lenses. The soft, automated winding mechanisms sound like a rack being ratcheted up, which is when I see Ruby, one of Martha's friends from Reception, with her parents, her stupid, stupid parents who have inflicted their child on us today and the combined effect feels like a machete slashing across my chest.

Afterwards, too many people come back to the house for tea and cake, crowding every ground floor room. Standing in the kitchen, I'm surrounded by an overwhelming array, juggling cup and saucer with wedges of poppy-seed and chocolate and fruit cake: the women of Mersey Valley Church have been doing their supportive business over the past couple of days. The mourners are filling their faces enthusiastically, eating being such a vital feature of a wake, but me, I'm overwhelmed by this oppressive morass.

Joyce Huggett, leashed to the drainpipe at the back door, is giving it the odd 'whor-or-oar'. Batman and Robin shot up the stairs when we all arrived and haven't been seen since.

The south-facing kitchen is cheerful in sunlight and despite the reason we are gathered, against the grain of the many broken-hearted hours that Sarah and I have spent in it, the room is jolly. Not me, and not, I can see, Sarah, whose face looks drained, whose body language is weary and exhausted. A wave of compassion for her passes over me, something not far removed from love, and I imagine for a moment that the room clears like the Red Sea parting, clears and leave us to sit down together at the kitchen table and lick our wounds. But no transcendental channel appears. All we have is this house, too small for the crowd, too smothering for Sarah and me.

Lesley Moore and Kat Fuller are distributing fresh tea and further cakes, and I wind up close to the party wall, talking with Vince and

Becky. I'm asking questions, interviewing them, which is a great defence against everything I need to avoid. This is the sort of conversation you have when you are amongst a social throng – as though this were a party like any other. It isn't raising my spirits, but I can see how it might if I weren't so miserable.

Someone must have opened the back door, because I can see Joyce Huggett by her saucepan of drinking water, imploring me with her golden brown eyes, wiggling her whole body at me.

Lesley Moore appears beside me, beaming. 'It's been a real help for us that you and Joyce have hit it off so well.'

The meaning of what she's saying doesn't matter, for she exudes concern and so, warmed, I gratefully pat her arm. 'I should give Joyce something to eat,' I say, more or less excusing myself.

Snaking through the mourners towards the food, I spot an especially fine chocolate cake on the sink-unit. I shift a couple of bouquets abandoned in their cellophane, cut a slice of the rich, moist cake and put it on a side-plate.

'Joyce,' I call, and whistle as I approach her. 'Joyce.'

People are starting to leave. They all have to give Sarah and me the look, the soft word and the hug or the handshake, and each of us has to show in some way that we appreciate their sympathy, has to indicate that we are bowed but we are not defeated. Moments after I have seen the Woods to the door, Roy returns briskly, muttering apologies and fumbling. He pulls something – a pale blue envelope, it turns out – from inside his Crombie and hands it to me.

'Here you are, Joe. Dorothy particularly wanted to give you this, and of course, we nearly forgot. Ho ho.'

'Thanks,' I say, and slip it in my jacket pocket for later.

By dusk, only the Moores and the Fords remain. My mother is having a lie-down. I don't know what's happened to Derek. Somehow it has transpired that William and Lesley are in the front room with Sarah and Molly and I'm in the kitchen with Vince and Becky. Vince is making himself a cheddar sandwich and Becky and I are drinking coffee at the table. I'm glad the crowd has dispersed, that I'm only left with old friends, with whom I can be myself. Here we are, Vince and I, blokes who like stupid stuff, and Becky, who finds that amusing.

'This is a good point to reach, y'know, Joe,' Becky says, looking at me from under her eyebrows, Princess Diana style. 'You've had a horrendous year, but now you can begin to move forward again.'

'Maybe.'

She is sitting upright, her arms neatly folded, giving me the kindly but scalpel-sharp glance I have seen down many years when the three of us have put the world to rights. 'At least now you and Sarah can grieve for Martha properly, eh?'

'You never know,' Vince says, through a mouthful of sandwich, 'hitting the bottom might pull you and Sarah together again.'

'Mm.' I think of my last evening with Gill Forsythe. Vince and Becky know nothing about all of that, nobody does, and it's gone now and I think I'm content with it being gone. None of which makes me feel like getting back with Sarah. Let's face it, starting over with somebody new would be so much more appealing.

Becky takes a moving-things-forwards breath and sits up even straighter. 'What are you going to do tonight? Will you stay here with Sarah?'

'I hadn't thought that far.' Now that I'm presented with it, I can see that it would be the done thing, but not how to do it. 'I suppose I would if she asked me to, but I don't think I could handle suggesting it and being turned down. Today has been enough of a trial already.'

Becky nods, ducks her head and gives me the Diana look again.

'You've got God to get you through,' Vince says. 'I've always envied that a bit.'

'You have?'

'Yep.'

Becky starts to clear up what little mess there is – people have been clearing up in our kitchen all day. 'Do you want to come home with us, Joe?' she asks over her shoulder from the sink.

'Thanks.' I empty my lungs of heavy air. 'It's good of you, but I think if I left Manchester now I might never come back.'

Sarah has a tension headache and can't cope with Molly's demands, so I do the bath and the bedtime stories and prayers and cuddles. When I come downstairs the house is all ship-shape. Mum and Derek are chatting in the front room and when I push open the door of the lounge, I find Sarah alone with a particularly searing movement of a Mahler symphony. For months the sound of the same discs over and over – a Mahler, Mozart's *Requiem*, the soundtrack of *Lorenzo's Oil* – has been driving me round the twist. There have been times when I would have loved to send *Lorenzo's Oil* flying like a silver discus out into the wild blue yonder. But not now. I take my place on the sofa beside Sarah and put my arm around her. She nestles her head against my chest and as the ranked strings of the Berlin Philharmonic carve into us, we cry, cry, cry.

Later, we are both wrung out like a dishcloth and neither of us thinks to do anything but go our separate ways, so I walk Joyce Huggett home to Whalley Range, with never a sweet word the whole way. Many's the time, travelling between house and flat, when I have longed for a car, but not tonight. Tonight I could tramp the streets forever.

Wearily cleaning my teeth, I straighten and catch my reflection in the cruddy medicine cabinet above the bathroom sink. I study the dark rings under my eyes, the tired crow's feet around them and my pale, dry mouth. The image in the glass seems hardly to register me, nor do I warm to what I see, but something livid bursts out of me and with a furious bellow I swing my fist into the mirror, smashing it and staining it with blood from my lacerated knuckles.

When I've finished with the Savlon and Band-Aids, and there is nothing else to do but get into bed and try to sleep, I kneel to pray, the first time in long months. All I say is, 'I know you're there, Father, and I know I have stonewalled you. But I need your help. Please.'

In a Car Like This You Don't Go Away For Weekends

And then, who knows why, snowdrops come, and daffodils and leaves on trees. I'm buried beneath my duvet in the Whalley Range flat and I'm dreaming. I'm on a game show, *The Leonard Cohen Show*.

A brassy arrangement of 'There's No Business Like Show Business' plays, a cheesy voice proclaims, 'Heeeeeeere's Leonard!!' and applause erupts as Leonard Cohen comes skipping down the steps, grinning. He's wearing a gold lamé jacket with big shoulders and a gambler's bow tie. He holds his hand up, protesting the applause.

'Joe Porter from Manchester, friends. He's nearly there!' He turns from the camera to me. 'Three simple questions, Joe. How do you feel?'

'Good. Better than I thought I would.' I laugh nervously.

Leonard wraps an encouraging hand around my shoulder. 'Joe, you're a caution.'

He steps a little back from me and looks at the uppermost question card. 'Okay, let's do it. What is "san serif"? And it ain't a small town in Southern California, kid!'

The prize for winning tonight is a racing-car. I'm working against the clock, a large timepiece up behind me, which instead of ticking while Leonard waits for my answer to each question, makes a noise like a hammer hitting an anvil: CLANG!!

'It's something to do with typefaces, isn't it? A printer's term.'

'A printer's term. That's good enough for me.'

Over to my right, the floor manager holds up a large cue card and the audience bursts into applause.

'Joe, my man, you can really take the heat. Next up: who was the narrator for the British version of *The Magic Roundabout*? Was it a) Eric

Blair, b) Eric Morecambe, c) Eric Thompson or d) Tony Blair?'

CLANG!! CLANG!!

'Remember, the first answer you give is the only one I can accept.'

'Eric Thompson.'

'Eric Thompson is correctamundo, Joe! On the money again.'

More studio applause. Alongside the relief, I can feel cold moisture sliding between my shoulder blades.

'Take it easy, Joe,' Leonard says, as I face my final question. 'If you get this one right, you will be the overall winner of this episode of *The Leonard Cohen Show*. How does that sound to you?'

'It sounds good.'

'You just wait till you drive that car, son. It'll change your whole life.'

Unprompted so far as I can tell, the audience laughs. I don't know why.

'Okay, here she comes now, all dressed in black, with words of love tattooed down her back. Joe! The question is – and for this, let's not forget, folks, he can win a racing car of his own – the question is: if you were to remove your own heart, how would you return it to its rightful place? If you were to remove your own heart, how would you return it to its rightful place? You have ten seconds Joe.'

CLANG!! CLANG!!

'Could you repeat the question please, Leonard?'

'Of course I could, Joe.' He holds his question cards a little closer, then glances to camera. 'He's feeling the pressure, folks. The truth is, I feel it for him.'

The studio audience laughs.

The second hand inches round the large clock face and each clanging anvil sound goes through me as I panic about the answer. There is no answer to this, I'm telling myself. How can there be? More ringing strikes on the anvil.

'Five seconds, Joe,' Leonard says. CLANG!! 'Four seconds.' CLANG!! 'Three seconds.' CLANG!!

'Hang on, I've got it,' I yelp. 'You'd have to swallow it. That would be the only way.'

'Stop that clock!' Leonard shouts, and the second hand immediately freezes, centimetres from twelve o'clock. 'Joe.'

'Yes,' I squeak. I must sound like a eunuch.

'Joe, will you tell me that answer again, please.'

'You'd have to swallow it. I can't see what else you would do.'

Leonard looks at me. His face is that of the consummate poker player. 'Isn't the human body marvellous? You'd swallow the vital organ and your body – *your body, Joe* – *WOULD SORT IT OUT!!* Your answer is *CORRECT!!*'

An air-raid siren goes off, the studio audience goes apeshit and I am grinning fit to bust. Leonard's gold lamé arm is around my shoulders. 'The Joe has gone and done it, people. The Joe is victorious!'

Some other time, some other place, Leonard Cohen is acting as my consultant while I test-drive the car. It is in the style of a Formula One racing-car, only about the size of a go-cart. As I sit in the driver's seat, Leonard Cohen stands above me in black suit and a white shirt buttoned to the neck. His manner is solicitous. On the dream's soundtrack, 'Would You Like To Swing On A Star?' is playing.

I take the car out for a circuit of the test track we're at.

It is incredibly fast and holds the road as if magnetised to it. I feel like I am flying, and not just in a plane – it is as if I'm flying under my own power.

Up ahead, I see the black shape of Leonard Cohen standing where I left him, only seconds before. I slow and draw to a halt beside him.

'How was that?' he asks.

'Unbelievable.'

I notice that my feet are sticking up in the low nose of the car, stretching the membrane of the bodywork. I look around behind me.

'There isn't much space,' I say.

I seem to be considering whether or not to take the car, although nobody has said that not taking it is an option.

'Where would I put any luggage if I was going away for the weekend?'

'In a car like this,' Leonard Cohen says, 'you don't go away for weekends.'

With these words resonating up the tunnel that leads to the waking world, I'm suddenly sitting bolt upright, sprung up the way I've sometimes seen Martha or Molly shoot up from sleep. I express my sense of being stunned in some incoherent fashion, reach out a hand to steady myself and, when it lands on a hairy hummock, leap out of bed with a startled scream.

'Joyce!' I say when the light is on, 'for crying out loud.'

As I rake the ashes of this dream, it's strangely comforting having Joyce Huggett curled up next to me. I don't know everything there is to know about its meaning straight away. However, by dint of the amazing powers of the unconscious mind, I realise with a gob-smacking shock that the faces of the *Leonard Cohen Show* host and the mystery figure at the hospice, Fletcher Moss and Jackson's Boat, are one and the same.

The Turnaround

Roy is in his garage, pale under the strip lighting as he unfolds himself from beneath the bonnet of Naomi's dirt-encrusted Datsun. He's wearing a boiler-suit, his face is smudged and his hands are blackened with oil and engine gunge. His mullet, tucked beneath the upturned collar of the boiler-suit, resembles a small, fuzzy animal caught in a trap.

'Joe!' he says, spotting me. 'I'm terribly sorry – didn't see you there. And there's Joyce, too. Sorry I can't pet you, Joyce; you wouldn't want Castrol GTX all over those lovely furry ears.'

Joyce wags her tail at this attention. Roy wipes his hands on a rag which must once have been a cotton vest. 'Good to see you. Everything okay in Whalley Range?'

'Hunky dory,' I say. 'They're dancing in the street.'

He looks perturbed at the thought. 'Are they?'

'Only a bit of banter, Roy.'

'Ah.' Roy takes the bonnet off its prop and closes it. The paintwork, when it comes into view, is mottled and cloudy. Not even T-Cut could bring up the metallic in the gunmetal grey again. 'Datsun' it says in orange letters on the black plastic grill. Not much poetry in the word, no discernible aesthetic strategy in the colour or the straight-arrow typeface.

I say, 'I don't suppose you'll ever finish restoring this, Roy, will you?'

'Rome wasn't built in a day.'

'No. But apparently Rome looks quite good.'

Roy smiles his mild, blissful smile. 'This is a great little car. Only forty thousand miles on the clock. I've more or less got the mechanics up to scratch. A little elbow grease here and there on the cosmetic front and she'll be quite a beauty.'

'Then what'll you do?'

'Oh y'know – just look after her. I think that's why Naomi left her to me. She wanted somebody to look after her little car.' Roy looks thoughtful for a moment and then says, 'Anyway, it's good to see you, Joe.'

This is Roy's polite way of asking me why I have called.

'Brought you round the rent cheque.'

'My golly! That was a fast month. Well, thank you.'

Roy insists on getting me a receipt and while he is gone, I give his precious jalopy the once-over. I note the dull, square headlights, which are matched with dull, square taillights – not so much designed as dashed off. All nothing compared to the black leatherette plastered over the roof.

'*Starsky and Hutch,*' I am saying, out loud, 'it's like a dwarf, oriental Starsky-and-Hutch –' until I spot a cardboard box on the garage floor. There's an A5 flyer glued to the lid. The flyer doesn't contain much information beyond what you pick up at first glance:

Planet 9
It's the real thing. Really.

But it does say enough about the where and the when to fill me in about the probable why.

'Ah hah,' Roy says, slipping round in his Polyveldts and giving me a start. 'You'd be interested in that.'

'Would I?'

'Well, I think so. Planet 9 is the way we are not letting Tom Beattie's student church destroy what we had built up with the minibus run for Kids' Church.'

What I notice about Roy's response is its characteristic kindness. He could have said that Planet 9 is the kind of thing I used to be interested in. But he didn't. He gave me credit for being more caring than I am.

'Good,' I say, and force a smile. 'I'm glad somebody didn't give up on those kids.'

'It'd be good to see you there, Joe. Complete the old team, ha-ha.'

'I don't know, Roy. A lot has happened since we were all a team.'

His eyes meet mine, he pulls a feeling grimace and nods sympathetically. 'Well if you ever want to come along and take a peek at what we do, you know you're always welcome.'

The day is fresh and sharp, but bright, with fat white clouds. The leaves are all back on the trees. It's the spring day of your sweetest childhood memories. I should be polishing my *Boris and Dragon* script, but I'm walking Joyce Huggett by the Mersey and thinking about Leonard Cohen, a.k.a. Shaved Head's mate, a.k.a. the man in the Barbour jacket and the pinstripe suit. Here, with the big open skies – not Texas-big, but wide by local standards – it's easy to clear the head and gain some perspective.

As Joyce and I have been making our way through the meadows to the river, a mental picture I once had comes back to me. It concerns that most miniature of Jesus' micro-stories, the one about the fabulous pearl.

A merchant is looking for fine pearls. When he discovers the finest pearl in the whole world, he goes away and sells up, lock stock and barrel, in order to be able to buy the pearl he has found. End of story.

The picture in my head those years ago consisted of the pearl buried under some sort of debris, let's say sand and gravel, and a pair of hands working furiously, fingers digging, palms shovelling, to reveal the treasure beneath.

Joyce is snuffling amongst some clumps of grass, nosing about for the location of her next wee. By the time she has succeeded, I've located a stick and lofted it in the direction of the model aeroplane field. She races off down the incline at a frightening lick, ears flying behind her. I half expect her momentum to tumble her head over heels.

Following Joyce down to the field below, I push myself to come up with something – anything – that might sum up this man's assorted personae. What is the connection between a pinstripe suit, a Barbour jacket and Leonard Cohen? There isn't one. What else connects the times I've seen this man? Well – all I can come up with is that gentle smile. In my abiding mental image of him, the corners of his mouth are tweaked, his facial expression is, if you had to put one word to it, warm.

Joyce and I are making our way towards Sale Water Park and my mind is flitting around like the chattering monkey it often is. The mystery man. Martha. Gill Forsythe. Whalley Range. Sarah and Molly. I go over the turnstile in the hedge and come out by the water. Some Canada geese are hobbling about on the patchy grass as I circle the water's edge, but Joyce sprints towards them and they take to the air, honking.

Angular stones press into the not particularly sturdy soles of my shoes. This is the spot where I ran into Lee that time, when he walked round to the hide with me. Lee with his suspiciously new-looking mountain bike. I haven't seen him since the Pleasure Beach, but I've often thought about what might have become of him and his skally mates.

I whistle Joyce and head for the hide. Why not? Half the point when walking the dog is trying to come up with destinations.

Soon I'm sitting on the bench inside the hide, staring ahead of me. I might look like somebody waiting for a hawk or a heron, but I'm not. I don't know what I'm waiting for. An answer, maybe.

Like Van Morrison telling his band to take it down low when he wants to murmur some improvised phrases, to have a hope of hearing God I have to turn everything way down low. When Elijah wanted to hear from God and waited for his presence, it wasn't in the powerful wind, it wasn't in the earthquake, it wasn't in the fire. It was in the gentle whisper that came after all of them. I have to still the chattering monkey in my head. I have to sweep all the dumb signals that jam my airwaves. I have to settle down to nothing but him and me. It feels like a long time, but it's probably not many minutes, and then it comes.

'As high as the heavens are above the earth, so great is his love for those who fear him.'

It comes and I hear it and somehow the Astonishing Ant-Man has morphed into the Silver Surfer. He's shooting through the clouds and out across the solar systems to the infinite reaches of the universe. That's pretty high, that love is a bit great. Silver tears are falling from the Surfer's impassive eyes.

'Okay,' I say. My voice cracks and my heart is inflating fit to burst. 'So why didn't you look after her? I know you can do anything you want to. So why didn't you look after her?'

I'm thinking of Martha, but what I see is Naomi on what was soon to be her deathbed, parched skin and every sharp bone revealed. And the pearl is revealed, too. I hear.

'In a car like this,' the stillest, smallest voice in creation says, 'you don't go away for weekends. With a pearl like this, you can't have other pearls. In this world, there's something wrong with everything. The racing go-kart is the most exciting drive there could be, but there's no storage. Naomi was one of the most precious women who ever lived, and the life she lived was immersed in me, but cancer ate her up before any of the things she wanted to do for me were ever fully accomplished.'

My spirit is being shaken and my body is shuddering in response. Gasping breathlessness punctuates this whole catharsis.

'In a car like this,' the whisper says, 'you don't go away for weekends.'

And now the Surfer is sobbing like a pro, now the Surfer has reached the highest heavens and his heart, like a supernova, is blowing apart.

'As high as the heavens are above the earth,' the soft, still voice says, 'so great is his love for those who fear him.'

My eyes are burning and my heart is bare as fillet steak. And I see the pearl in all its glory, exploding with light and heat and radiance, bright as a supernova.

I come back from the Water Park and into Chorlton flat-out, rubber-legged, pass Woolworths, spiritual home of Vince Ford, cross Wilbraham Road at the pelican and steam by the racks of cheap fashion in Chorlton precinct, spiritual home of Socialist Worker sales teams, hassled Mums, lonesome buskers and the odd livid-faced wino.

The precinct café is diametrically opposed to all that the person I used to be held dear in the world. It hasn't benefited from the skills of an expensive interior designer. Fried eggs, bacon butties, strong tea and Virgin Radio are on offer; *ciabatta*, blueberry muffins and Massive Attack are not even considerations.

I step inside, go to the counter, buy a can of Coke and settle at a table to wait.

All I have to go on is that when Lee and I were emerging from the Water Park and ran into his two cowboy mates, Waz and Vaughan, one of them had told Lee to meet them in the precinct café. Waz and Vaughan would certainly fit in here. It's Baseball Cap Central.

While half an hour and then an hour passes, I have time to wonder how for-real baseball players feel about every redneck, skally and in-bred serial killer in the known universe sporting the designated headgear of their sport. I also have time to ponder again the source of Lee's expensive looking mountain-bike, to fret over the life of crime I imagine he's leading, to try and imagine what it is Tom Cruise and Nicole Kidman have done to hit the front page of the *Daily Star* that somebody is reading two tables away from me.

What they're listening to on
The Wang Dang Doodle this week:
'A Change Is Gonna Come'
(Neville Brothers)
'The Turnaround'
(Big John Patten)
'Hallelujah'
(Leonard Cohen)

On the way to Lee's house in the Mersey Bank estate, I stop at Chorlton Bookshop's window and cop a poster for Planet 9. Quite an effective poster. Somebody at Mersey Valley has been putting Adobe Photoshop to good use. The image is a close-up of a boy and girl, leaning head on head against each other. Their faces, turned to look at the camera, are happy, but in a mischievous rather than a wholesome way: it's like they're in on a joke that you can't help wishing they would share. The typography is well chosen, too – it's the one from *TFI Friday* on Channel 4: 'Planet 9' as the heading, and the strap-line beneath the image is the one I saw on the box of flyers at Roy Wood's house: 'It's the real thing. Really.' In smaller point-size you get the hard facts: what, where, when, how much.

William and Co. have obviously been, as Elvis would say, taking care of business.

I'm not sure what I am going to do if I find him, but I rap the letterbox on Lee's front-door. The door itself is slightly ajar, so I would guess that somebody is in. Through the gap between door and doorway, I clock a trampled KFC box on the doorstep and one corner of a video-case – *The Crow*, in fact - lying on the filthy hall carpet. With no immediate response, I shout a tentative 'Hello?' into the house, which prompts trudging on the staircase. A fat, dull-skinned bloke opens the door – Lee's Mum's new boyfriend, I would guess. He's wearing boxers and a black, faded Guns'n'Roses T-shirt.

'Aright, mate.'

'Hi. I was looking for Lee.'

He folds his arms and hunches his shoulders. 'Not in, mate.'

'Right. Would you mind telling him I called? It's Joe, Joe Porter, from Mersey Valley church?' Stretching it a bit here, but never mind.

He hasn't been looking at me during this. He kicks the *Crow* box down the hallway. ' 'kay. No worries, pal.'

I thank him, trying to sound like I'm taking what he says at face value, and leave.

Small Repairs Are
Not Beyond Me

How did this happen? Over a year has passed since we lost Martha, and look: I can do a fair impression of an adult, most of the time.

It's Sunday, I'm limbering up to dot the 'i's and cross the 't's on my *Boris and Dragon* script. It's early still but it's hot outside, hot and muggy. I'm shuffling the hillocks of post, work and newspapers amassed on the kitchen table when I stumble across a blue envelope. It takes me a moment to work out what it is – the letter from Dorothy that Roy Wood gave me the day of Martha's funeral – but a second or two later, I am tearing open the Basildon Bond stationery and reading Dorothy's note to me:

Psalm 114:7–8

'Tremble, O earth, at the presence of the Lord, at the presence of the God of Jacob, who turned the rock into a pool, the hard rock into springs of water.'
    A word from the Lord for you, Joe. I know he will reveal to you his meaning for your life at this time.

Yours and His,

Dorothy.

My first inclination is to bin it. Dorothy's imagination working overtime again, not to mention the jargon the letter is couched in. But then I pull myself up. That was the way I used to respond to Dorothy. I feel I've changed lately, so I look again.

The Lord, who turned the hard rock into a pool, into springs of water.

It doesn't take much of a fistfight with myself to get on down to Mersey Valley for the first service.

Even in a light T-shirt, I am slimy with sweat: it's humid in the Mersey Valley building and a couple of hundred of us are present. The moment I know that I have done the right thing in coming back is when we sing a song based on Psalm 103, which is where 'As high as the heavens are above the earth, so great is his love for those who fear him' comes from. These days, it seems to be following me around as devotedly as Joyce Huggett. While we are worshipping, something goes through me like a surge of electricity. Wave after wave of passionate sensation flows as my ragged old heart is ripped raw and teardrops fall. I'm so soaked with joy and relief I don't mind who sees me blubbering.

Afterwards, I go through to the annexe for the social part. By the time I join the queue for tea and coffee, the room is already busy with shifting throngs, and I feel anxious about being here after a gap of several months. I worry that nobody will speak to me and at first, my fears are justified: the best I get is a nod or a glancing hello from slight acquaintances. I keep seeing the Planet 9 poster displayed on doors and walls.

Eventually, I reach the kitchen hatch and accept a mug of tea from somebody I've never seen before. Feeling suitably chastened and prodigal, I round a corner and slam face to face into Sarah.

'Hello?' she says, more question than greeting. 'You didn't tell me you were coming to church.'

Saturday is one of my days with Molly, so it's only hours since Sarah and I last spoke. 'I didn't know myself that I was coming – practically 'til I got here.'

I am lost for words, so I ask her where Molly is. Playing hide and seek upstairs with her friends is the answer, one I could have worked out for myself.

'Seems like business as usual here,' I am saying, floundering somewhat, when Lesley Moore appears beside Sarah.

'Joe!' she greets me, sprinkling the air with laughter, like maybe I am the punch-line of some joke she has started to tell Sarah earlier. 'What happened? Did you get bored with the Sunday papers?'

'Oh well. You know what it's like. There's the lie-in with *The Independent on Sunday*, and then there's the five-mile hike that your hound insists on. You don't want her back, do you?'

She puts on a show of amazement, gasping and widening her eyes. 'Joe Porter, what are you like? Nobody would *dare* try to take that dog off you!'

Lesley must have kick-started something, for soon one person after another is looming up with a grin and a glad hand. I'm so gob-smacked by this wave of welcome that, when Geoff Simpson greets me, I have to resist the urge to congratulate him on his sermon. What I feared might be an ordeal of self-consciousness has turned out to be a social merry-go-round. By the time the room begins to thin out, my head is spinning.

'Joe,' a familiar voice is saying, and Sarah is touching my arm before I realise it is her. 'Why don't you come back with Molly and I,' she says, 'and have some dinner?'

We arrive home together, Sarah and Molly and me. 'Home,' I am aware, is a moot term, but I can't help noticing how novel it is for the three of us to be coming back to the house together. The smell of dinner roasting is warming and familiar. I feel like an actor impersonating the man I used to be, sure, but I can't help wondering if God is somehow shaping up to answer one of my two recurrent prayers.

While Molly makes straight for the kitchen table and some bead-threading, I look around. The breakfast dishes are on the dish-rack, long since dried. Heat rises from the oven behind me. Sarah is opening the door just now and I see a casserole dish inside. She lifts it out with oven gloves and sets it on top of the cooker. A small drum of beef is inside, the meat roasted brown, the fat toasted honey. The Porters have never been daunted by the risk of BSE. While Sarah replaces the roast in the oven and adjusts the temperature, I boil the kettle for a pot of tea. When the tea's brewed, I fill up my old Homer Simpson mug, ("Just Because I Don't Care Doesn't Mean I Don't Understand"), which only adds to my feeling of displacement.

Here I am helping Molly to set the table. She puts the cutlery in the wrong place or back to front; I trail her, putting things right. Here I am plugging the blades into the electric carving knife and slicing brown discs off the silverside. Here I am mixing apple squash and pouring wine. Here we are having Sunday dinner, all three of us, all that remains of our family and we only look like a family.

'Where's da doggy?' Molly asks, when we have begun to eat.

'Locked up in the flat. I thought you were scared of her.'

'No. I like doggies now.'

'That's a shame. I could've brought her.' It is a shame. I didn't like leaving Joyce cooped up for the afternoon. Children are full of conflicting signals. 'How about horses? Are you still scared of horses?'

I'm talking to Molly on auto-pilot, I'm eating and drinking and passing things to Sarah before she asks. I'm putting on a show of bright cheer, but beneath the veneer I'm taking in Sarah's brittle manner.

'You always make the best Yorkshire pudding in the world ever,' I tell her.

'Thank you.' She doesn't sound grateful. 'Come on,' she says to Molly. 'Stop playing about with your dinner. I want that plate cleared up before you get any pudding.'

Sarah's face is pale as untreated pine. Her sadness, her anger, her despair – how much of it is my fault?

'Don't want pudding. I want a *frais*.'

'A *frais* is a pudding.'

'Tisn't.'

'Put it this way: if you don't eat your dinner, you can't have a *frais*.'

I'm looking at the shelves straight ahead of me. The recipe books are still stacked up but falling down. The crockery, herbs, spices, sauces, oils, vinegars, paints, felt-pens, crayons and all the rest of the jumble and rubble. I'm looking at it and not even feeling annoyed by it. What does it matter? What do any of her foibles matter now? I could have put up with them if it hadn't all ended like this. Really, I could have forgiven Sarah for being different from me.

Looking up at the top shelf, I sense that something is missing. It takes a few seconds to dawn on me.

'What happened to all my cards?'

'What?'

I point up at the top shelf. 'What happened to all the cards I made for you down the years?'

'Oh, I threw them out.'

'Aw for crying out loud, Sarah!'

'It wasn't revenge or anything. I was just tidying up.'

'I can't believe you did that.'

She takes a mouthful of air. It looks like she's biting back a riposte, and I can imagine several. 'Look, I'm sorry. Perhaps I shouldn't have done it.'

'"Perhaps"?'

'I wasn't thinking – all right?'

'No, I can see.' Maybe I could never forgive her for not being me. Maybe I could never forgive her for being who she is.

Silence settles on the table between us. Her knife and fork ching on her dinner-plate and I look at her face again, her eyelids lowered, and somewhere in there a definite air of triumph. Foggy with despair, I look at Molly.

'You can make some more cards, Daddy.'

Looking like a family and its dog, for we collected Joyce Huggett on the way, the Porters drive into Manchester in what I used to think of as our car, but now think of as Sarah's. Not for the first time, I note how much easier work would be if I had wheels of my own: I've turned down several jobs because of the difficulty of getting around on public transport. And fetching and returning Molly when I have her to stay in Whalley Range would be a lot less hassle, too.

Sarah is driving, brisk with the accelerator, sparing with the indicator, impatient in the day-tripping traffic. I like her tangerine blouse and her indigo chinos.

By the Atlas café-bar, we turn into Castlefield. Go back two thousand years and this was a fortress where the Romans brought the future to blue-painted Anglo-Saxon tribesmen. Now, here where we park up, it's all happening city-dwellers and offices for high-tech companies. Soon we pass a smattering of warehouse developments, the first sight of the waterways and Barça, Mick Hucknall's bar. The air is close and humid, and I am sweating again, mopping my face with a handkerchief. 'It's going to rain. We'll get soaked on this barge.'

'Give over,' Sarah tells me, and the reproof is so lived-in it's heart-warming. 'You always think it's going to rain.'

'We do live in Manchester, Sarah. It always is going to rain.' We are starting to sound like our old selves here. 'What time does this barge trip leave at, anyway?'

'There'll be lots of them, don't worry.'

'How do you know? Who says there are lots of them? We'll probably have to hang round half the afternoon waiting for one.'

'What's wrong with hanging around? It's a place designed for hanging around. Stop fretting for goodness' sake.'

We pass under a huge railway viaduct, rusting but grand, so mono-
lithic you half expect to see Brunel in front of it in a smokestack hat,
chomping on a cigar. When we come into the centre of the Bridgewater
Canal basin, there's no sign of a barge and it turns out that the next one
isn't until three o'clock – another forty-five minutes.

Sarah says, 'I told you there'd be lots of barges.'

Until sailing-time, we're sitting in Dmitri's on Deansgate, and I've been
admiring the way Sarah's honey hair has been bunched at the middle of
the back of her head. I'm thinking how attractive she looks and this is
something of a shock to me. Not because she isn't a good-looking
woman, but because this past year she has wearied me down to my bones.

But last year is over and though it threatened to kill us, somehow we
aren't dead. Bad things happened to us, but the way I reacted to them
was down to me. This is my life and I am responsible for it. I have to settle for the damage I have done: small repairs are not beyond me.

'Listen,' I say, leaning over the table to be closer to Sarah. 'I'm
sorry.'

She frowns. 'What about?'

'It all. Martha. The way I responded to her disappearance. The way
I responded to you. All of that. And further back – I'm sorry I didn't go
on having counselling with William. Maybe if I had, I would have been
able to handle this year much better. I'm sorry.'

Her face is still and I can't read it. I think she must want more and I
press myself to give it to her:

'Look – I'm not blind to myself. I know I've buried my feelings
about Martha. I've done everything I could to hide from my feelings
about what happened.' Step on the gas and wipe that tear away, I think.
'It's not conscious; I had no choice about it. I wish I could have reacted
differently.'

She looks me in the eye for longer than she has done for months and
I hang with bated breath on her next word. None comes. She mops up
orange from around the base of Molly's glass. She tells Molly to let her

hold the glass while Molly drinks from the straw.

'I don't know what to say to that.' She looks up again. 'It's almost too late for apologies. I feel too damaged.'

'But I haven't done anything to you.'

'I didn't say you had.'

'You make me feel as though I have – all the time.'

'Let's not argue in front of Molly.'

'She'll survive. I think we should argue. I think we should argue for as long as it takes to get this whole thing sorted.'

The skin of her lower cheek creases where care has worn a furrow. 'It can't *be* sorted, Joe.'

'I'm not talking about Martha. I mean you and me.'

'Just leave it. This isn't the right moment.'

'When would be?'

'I said leave it.'

If I could travel in time, I'd return to the first year we were going out. I'd go back and speak to Joe and Sarah. I'd tell them that they would end up living with each other for years and years. I'd say that the kind of love they have can never survive living together and intimate knowledge of each other. I'd tell them that they should make sure they enjoy every moment of their early days as a couple. They should suck every ounce of flavour from those days, because things will never be as good again.

Sarah is getting up to go. 'Come on. Let's not miss this barge.'

I spot a familiar face amongst the throng onboard with us: Richard Kelman, Mr New Manchester, Gill's heartbreaker. The reason I notice him is that his mobile rings before the barge has even set off. My own mobile phone is tangible here in my pocket, but it's switched off. Looking at Kelman, the image of man on mobile during a Sunday outing confirms my prejudices. During the hour-long trip, he spends almost as much time making and taking calls as he does interacting with real people.

As the barge chugs through Castlefield, stinging my nostrils with diesel fumes, I study Kelman. His toad-like features are pallid and flat behind his fine, expensive glasses. It seems fitting that he's here in Castlefield, one of the gems of new Manchester, and I can't help wondering whether a person in his shoes can ever afford to be spotted in the unreconstructed, un-mended parts of the city – in Gorton or Crumpsall.

He's with a woman and two children – his family, I can tell by his body language when he's relating to the kids. Evidently he and Mrs Kelman have patched up their differences. But he's back with Gill. (Maybe one of his calls is from Gill?) Perhaps he's back with the woman councillor too? You have to admire his ability to fool around.

I wonder how hard I would have had to press Gill to finish with Kelman and make a go of it with me. Maybe not that hard. Was it a test that I failed? Maybe she hadn't really gone back to him. Even if she had, was she only telling me about it to get me to lay my claim on her?

Thunder rumbles deep down in the sky, followed by a magnesium flare of lightening. 'You see,' I say, looking at Sarah and pointing to the sky.

'Honestly.' She shoots me her fed-up expression. 'We're having our barge trip and we aren't wet yet. Just keep calm, Joe.'

I look away, because all I can give her in return is my fed-up look, which will not help my case. And I'm not sure I can muster much enthusiasm for my case anyway. Against the murk of the water, Molly's eyes seem a brighter blue.

'Daddy? When I'm a big girl, I want to drive a barge. But I will have to learn to swim first.'

'Why?' I ask.

'In case I crash.'

Each time I look at Kelman, I think how easy it would be to phone Gill.

We have no sooner stepped on dry land again than Sarah has to whisk Molly off to the nearest toilets, in the YMCA building. Standing there, my hand enfolds the mobile phone in my pocket and for a moment or two, I resist taking it out. The arguments for and against have been well rehearsed, but no matter. It's like the choice you had in primary school between correcting the mistakes on your page and turning over a fresh leaf. I always liked to take a new page and, more than that, rip out its error-blemished predecessor, rip it out down to the scraps that snagged on the staples.

I take the mobile out and stare hard at it. My thumb hovers over the ON button. Okay, there are drawbacks with Gill, but we have done no damage to each other and the path ahead is clear, near as damn-it. With

Sarah, no end of damage and nothing less than prolonged and exhausting work to even glimpse a way ahead. I depress the button and the little screen flares green. A few clicks and there it is: Disley code and five familiar digits. I fondle the green telephone symbol so deliberatingly I can practically feel the whorls of my thumb print catching on its texture.

If Sarah and Molly were to emerge from the YMCA now, the choice would be made for me, but they don't. Being a man and stupid, being so much less of an adult than I would like to be, I am thinking of Gill, softly buxom in her black lambswool, I am thinking of her monkey fingers. But I have a choice here, and, even at this late stage, choosing right might be a step towards adult life, which is how my thumb comes to move a couple of millimetres to the left and press down firmly.

'Switching Off,' the little green screen says and movement of some kind makes me look up and here are Sarah and Molly walking towards me.

Our bodies moist in the steamy air, we amble back through the Sunday streets. Maybe an argument would be easier to handle on the move, where there is space and flow. Whatever, the dust-up doesn't come until we are back at the car and Sarah is strapping Molly into her car-seat.

'So when,' I ask, opening the passenger door, 'is a good time for sorting out our differences?'

'I think they have been sorted. You moved out. That seems pretty sorted to me.'

'Only if that's what you want.'

'I thought it was what *you* wanted.' She slams Molly's door shut. 'Close your door. I don't want her to hear.'

Although I'm peeved by this not-in-front-of-the-children crap, I do as I'm told. 'It doesn't solve the problem of all the tension between us. Even living apart, that's difficult to put up with.'

'Hah. *Now* you want to deal with it. You're too late.'

'So put me right for next time.'

'What makes you think there'll be a next time?'

A dagger appears before me and I seize it without thinking and shove it in. 'I didn't mean with you.'

'Oh.' Thunder rolls dark and deep through the heavens. I see I have inflicted damage. Lightning flashes far behind her and silvers Sarah and the roof of the car, which is what the world has come down to.

'Well?'

'Oh, you know it all anyway. What's the point of going through it again? When Martha was taken, I wanted to talk about it and you want-ed to run from it. I had – I have – all these feelings I needed to deal with and you just disappeared into yourself, like a hibernating hedgehog. That's all. And you know that already. But you don't *do* anything about it.'

'Look, Sarah,' I say, 'I'm not sure I can help the way I react. I just can't face profound feelings like these, and I don't think I will ever be able to. But I could have tried to understand your feelings better.'

'Yes.'

The first fat raindrops are falling pell-mell about us. 'I still could.'

She's looking straight ahead. She doesn't say anything. The sound of rain drumming on the car-roof separating us seems to be all that there is.

'You could help me do it,' I prompt. Joyce Huggett is tugging on the lead, sniffing at something on the cobblestones.

Sarah's tangerine blouse is being blotched, no, splattered, and the rain is running through her hair and coursing over the lines of her face. I hear high-pitched shouting and duck to look in through the window at Molly. Before Sarah does anything which might bring this battle to an end, I rip open the back door on my side. 'What is it, Molly?'

'You're getting wet.'

'I know. Look at your book, will you.' Before she can answer, I shove the door to again and emerge, like Punch in a puppet theatre, to face Sarah from my side of the car. Joyce is still stretching my arm, pulling on the lead that is looped round my wrist. The rain is coming down in stair-rods, rat-a-tatting on the car-roof and drilling into my head.

As if inhaling patience, Sarah draws a breath and shouts above the rain's percussion, 'You didn't just run from your feelings – you ran from me. You're talking as if there was just one difference between us: that you wanted to hide your feelings and I wanted to express mine. But here's another difference: I thought we were a couple and I believed we would go through something like this together.'

For a moment, I don't know what to say to this. Sarah looks impas-sively at me, much the way I've seen her look at plants in greenhouses. The rain is shooting down now, drilling into us. My T-shirt is soaked and drips are speeding off the end of my nose. Joyce, whatever it is she smells on the cobblestones, is impervious to the rain.

'Isn't it possible I had no choice about that either?' I bellow back. 'Isn't it all one?'

'No,' she says and marches round the car to deal with me face-to-face. 'I think you had a choice. I think you chose to distance yourself from me.'

We're back at the *impasse* beyond which we have yet to go. Molly's pudgy little face appears pressed up to the rain-flecked glass on my side of the car. Sarah mustn't have got as far as fastening her belt. I ignore the plaintive little face and square up to her mother again. 'And you resent what I did.'

No response.

'For crying out loud, Sarah, what do you want? I've said I'm sorry and I'm trying to tell you that I have no control over my reactions to losing Martha. Have you any control over yours?'

Her hair is flattened wet against her head and her clothes are drenched by now. She looks like the original lost duck. 'No.'

'Yours isn't the only way to grieve, y'know.'

'I know.'

'But you *don't*. You don't act like you know.' I reach out and take her hands and hold them up like a bouquet between us. 'Can't you see? I'm trying to repair the damage here. I want us to get over what happened – together.'

She blinks twice, three times, and although the thunder grumbles again and at my heel Joyce Huggett is whimpering, I swear I can hear Sarah's big eyelashes splashing in brine.

'Are you willing to accept that I don't have to react to Martha the way you do?'

More blinking. Joyce turns up the whimpering.

Sarah is looking right into me. 'You didn't say anything about getting over this together.'

'Well I'm saying it now.' I'm still shouting, still holding her hands up between us, though I'm not sure of the function of this: praying or wrestling. She is luminous in another flash of lightning. 'So are we allowed to react differently?'

'I suppose.'

'And are we going to forgive each other?'

The Holy Roller

After my previous attempts to find him, I walk round to Lee's house one more time. It's the Mum's boyfriend again: blotched skin, pseudo-co-operative.

'Oh aye,' he goes. 'I give him your message, but you know what kids are like – in one ear and out the other, eh?'

I think of Lee often, imagining the kind of City & Guilds hoodlum apprenticeship Waz and Vaughan might be giving him – and the verbal abuse, too. I even remember to pray for him. For weeks now, I have been persisting with the Almighty. Daily, I knock on the doors of heaven, for my family back and for Lee, and I trust in all those verses in scripture that promise a result to the persistent.

What they're listening to on
The Wang Dang Doodle this week:
'Marching Through The Wilderness'
(David Byrne)
'Stand By Me'
(Ben E. King)
'Beginning To See The Light'
(Velvet Underground).

Here I am in the Porter kitchen again, where this story began back at New Year 1997, when we were having a hard time getting out of the house to visit Naomi. That day seems like a snare to me now, a corner I turned and fell off the world.

It's mid-July. This year it has rained all through the spring and this far into the summer. It wouldn't be a huge surprise if a big boat with a whole bunch of exotic animals on board floated by. Even now, a shower taps against the kitchen window.

William Moore is holding forth at one end of the table and several people – Dorothy, Roy, Kat Fuller – are paying earnest attention. After all, William is our new pastor. Recently, at his three-year review, Geoff Simpson stood down. I don't know whether or not Tom Beattie would have been offered the job. It didn't arise: Tom is now full-time with his thriving student church.

He set up a charity to fund the operation and **excellent,** (always lower-case), and has just opened a juice bar in Fallowfield, right opposite Owens Park, the main halls of residence for Manchester University. Incredibly, Tom's juice bar is fashionable.

While William continues his monologue, I wash dishes for what seems like an eternity. Now and then Molly scurries through with the Fuller kids, all of them shrieking. She's at nursery school now, a Big Girl. Much of the time, Joyce Huggett sits at my feet. Unlike others from our home group, she shows no interest in what her former owner is saying. She's with me now – permanently, it appears. Although I wouldn't say so to anyone, I often think that Joyce is a little message from God, somebody for me to look after and hope he's looking after Martha in return.

Sarah's doing well. Things began to improve for her once she knew the worst. She goes to Leeds once a week to see a Christian psychiatrist. Here she is bringing me more plates to wash. 'You're keeping a low profile,' she says.

And Dorothy appears beside Sarah, interrupting: 'Not for much longer!' She holds her hand in the air, long delicate fingers putting all human traffic on hold. 'Where's Roy? It's time for the surprise. Roy! *Roy!*'

Roy is chuckling. 'I'm here, love. Behind you.'

And I'm like, *Would somebody throw me a bone here?*

'Walk this way,' Roy tells me, and laughs at his own joke as he adopts a passable John Cleese funny walk. Roy being funny is so unexpected, I laugh out loud, too.

A be-mulleted Pied Piper, Roy leads everyone out of the house and round the next corner, where – of course – Naomi's Datsun sits, gunmetal grey gleaming moist in the rain. Last time I saw it, this old car looked its age, but now it's in show-room condition.

'Here,' Roy says, holding keys out in my direction.

'What?' I say.

'She's all yours.'

'You're just giving it to me? After all that loving restoration?'

'Naomi would have been glad to see it being used.'

'But I thought you wanted to bring it back to its former glory and then put it under wraps.'

'No, I just like having something to tinker about with. '

Dorothy says, 'Roy and I thought it would make life easier for you and Molly. It must be difficult getting a child back and forth between here and Whalley Range with no car.'

'Whoo,' I go, lost for words, my eyes stinging. 'Thank you, but –'

'Are you going to say it or am I?' Sarah asks. Molly is leaning back against her legs, with Sarah's hands resting on her narrow shoulders.

'You.'

She looks at the members of our home group, from one face to another. 'Well – Joe is moving back in with Molly and me. On Tuesday.'

After the beat of a moment, people cheer and break into applause.

'Well now,' Roy says to Molly, 'that's a bit of good news, isn't it? It'll be nice for you to have your Daddy living with you, won't it?'

Molly is bursting with her own little joke: 'But I don't think Batman and Robin will be very pleased.'

'Oh? Why is that then?' Roy asks.

She is tittering now. 'Because Joyce Huggett'll be coming too.'

'But listen, Roy,' I say. 'What I was trying to tell you a moment ago is that, fantastically kind as it is of you and Dorothy, I won't really need the Datsun.'

'Oh.' Roy seems deflated.

'No, it's yours,' Dorothy says, offering the final word on the subject. 'You *will* need it.'

I laugh. 'What? Is that a prophetic word, Dorothy?'

She smiles and raises her neatly plucked eyebrows.

Sarah asks me, 'What kind of car is this?'

'It's a Datsun. A Datsun Holy Roller, I believe.'

'Cha-cha-boom,' she quips.

'What?' I say, and we both laugh.

I can get a good *cappuccino* almost anywhere in Manchester now. Since the bomb, town is one big building site. Every time you go in, a new shop has opened, a new office block has gone up. On the café front, there's the Seattle Coffee Company near Waterstone's. The Cornerhouse has revamped its *cappuccino* bar. There's even a rumour that Waterstone's are going to open an in-house café. Of course, this is utterly and totally sod's law: now that good cafés are just the eensiest bit less important to me, they are popping up, like daffodils in March, almost everywhere. And why does a good *cappuccino* now matter less than it once did? Maybe it's because before all of this, before I lost my child, my marriage, before I almost lost my faith, trivial things mattered far too much. You probably got there ahead of me.

Marks & Spencer are building a new store to replace the one that was blown up – the biggest Marks in the world, apparently. The Royal Exchange Theatre is back in action, with a new colour scheme. Inside, there are so many paint effects, it looks as though Jocasta Innes has thrown a party. Exchange Square, a novelty the architects have come up with, will become the centre of new Manchester.

The local rags spout unending, smug guff about it. *A city for the new millennium. 21st Century Manchester.* Photographs of Richard Kelman often sit alongside this sort of story. You can tell by the composition and by the spotlights reflected in his eyes that somebody has paid a lot for this picture to be taken. Which still doesn't prevent him looking like a toad.

In a quiet way, as Manchester has been mended, I have too. I put a name to my pain – grief – and that has made it easier to live with.

Knowing what happened to Martha helped Sarah and me. Not knowing was much, much worse. During the summer following Martha's abduction, another little girl was taken – somewhere in the Midlands. During the press coverage of it, one report mentioned a case in Denmark where a paedophile kept an abducted girl in one room for ten years. At least Martha was spared that. I think I would feel better if Martha's killer was found, but my instincts are that he won't be.

My first morning back at home, I wake up slowly in the usual fashion, with John Humphreys and Sue McGregor in the shower, a plate of, (as Molly would say), jammy toast and about a pint of Lavazza – black gold, Turin tea.

I'm getting myself in the groove with the Big G., worshipping, praying and generally taking a jog round the ramparts of Zion to catch an inspirational glimpse of what goes on the other side of the great divide, when the phone rings.

– Boris!

'Ah-hah. Dragon! What's happening?'

– It is original drummer from Human League. We have find *Freewheelin'*, original track-listing.

'We have?'

– We have.

'Have you heard something?'

– I think so! MainFrame has persuaded Granada to make a pilot.

'Weh-hey.'

– And we get paid a bit of money to write it.

'Weh-hey again.'

In some fairy tales, at the start of the journey he or she must undertake, the hero is cursed by an old woman. In others, rather than a curse, the old woman may be the source of a blessing: the Fairy Godmother provides Cinderella with the transport she needs to go to the ball.

On Thursday afternoon, two days after I came back home, Molly and I drive, in the Holy Roller, to Boots in Chorlton Precinct. She has been prescribed an antibiotic for a cough that won't shift. We have the medication safe in its dinky paper bag. Molly grips a *Tellytubbies* magazine we just bought under her little arm.

'Which one do you like best, Daddy,' she asks, 'La-La or Tinky-Winky?'

'The Noo-Noo is my favourite. It's because I'm a boy, probably.'

We reach the Holy Roller, which is in the car park behind the Precinct, and I help Molly into the back and fasten her into her car seat. Because it's muggy, I wind down the windows. I start the engine, I ask her if she wants some music. I'm turning the dial to try and find a good tune when I spot two kids sprinting out of the back entrance to the Precinct. They are running flat out, gripping what looks like bunched up fleecies to their chests and shouting and screaming. No, one of them is shouting and screaming – the shrimp in the baseball cap. The other one isn't. The other one is Lee.

In order to get a closer look, I drive in their direction. Once I am clear of the adjacent cars, I get a better view of the boys. They've stopped at a bike, which is chained to a lamppost.

'Fookin' unlock it now!' the kid in the baseball cap is shrieking, roughly in the tonal range of a hysterical piglet. He keeps looking back towards the Precinct. 'Stupid *shite*!'

Lee is fumbling with a key.

'Fook sake, come *on*,' the other one – Waz, who else? – shouts. 'At this rate, we might as well wander round to the Dibbles and turn ourselves in.'

Lee works away at the padlock. Waz keeps darting glances over his shoulder. I'm nearing them, steadily, steadily.

'What is it, Daddy?' Molly asks.

'Some naughty boys.'

The padlock and chain come off. Lee goes to get on the bike – that expensive-looking mountain bike I saw before – but he's only half way there before Waz flexes the arm that isn't holding on for dear life to fleecies and wrestles him to the ground.

'Hey!' Lee protests.

Waz is pressing down hard on the pedals, heading with his booty in the direction of the Medical Centre and all points beyond this car park. 'See you,' he grunts with a horse-laugh.

'Bastard!' Lee calls after Waz and sprints after him.

In my rear-view mirror, I glimpse two blokes emerging from the Precinct – given the fleecies, it's a fair bet they're from the fashion shop – and scanning the car park. I put my foot down and close the distance between Lee and me in seconds. I'm banking on the clothes shop guys' view of my numberplate being obscured by all the parked cars separating us.

'Lee!' I shout through the open passenger window. 'Lee!'

He turns, slowing. 'Joe?'

I drive ahead of him a few yards, fling open the far-side door. 'Get in, quick.'

A week's worth of conflicting thoughts and feelings collide on Lee's face and he throws himself onto the passenger seat.

'Lee?' I say as we bomb past the Medical Centre and on towards Oswald Road.

'Yeah?'

'D'you want to shut your flipping door?'

We drive by high school kids in their blue polo shirts and I glance at the fascia clock; given that school is finished for the day, there seems only one place to go.

When, two or three minutes later, we turn into the Mersey Valley car park, Lee says, 'What we doing here?'

'Dis is our church,' Molly says.

For a nano-second, Lee is dumbfounded. 'They don't have church on week-days, do they?'

In the main meeting room in the annexe, we are faced with a large, vivid backdrop. 'Planet 9', it says in that *TFI Friday* typeface, and, also familiar from the poster in the bookshop window, 'It's the real thing. Really.' The rest of the backdrop consists of silhouettes in vivid colours, all in action poses, many with interesting hair-styles: a Tintin cow's lick, pig-tails, spiky-tops, pineapple-heads.

Beneath the backdrop, Kat Fuller is setting up a puppet theatre. She happens to look our way and comes straight over. 'Hello, Molly,' she says, getting down on her honkers to Molly's level. 'How are you?'

'Got a little cough, actually.'

'Oh dear,' she says, straightening up. 'Joe. Good to see you. And Lee Hutchinson! Did nobody send you a letter about the start of Planet 9?'

Lee squirms, ducks his head awkwardly. 'Don't think so.'

'I bet they did and you used it for making paper aeroplanes.'

Or rolling spliffs, I think.

'Come here with me, y'little truant,' Kat says, wrapping Lee's skinny frame in a sideways hug. 'You can help me sort out this puppet theatre.'

Mersey Valley's portable PA is already filling the room with Christian dance music – The World Wide Message Tribe, I'm pretty sure. Five or six people in burnt orange Planet 9 T-shirts are looking purposeful in various ways. Roy Wood walks in from the direction of the kitchens, pushing a trolley loaded with squash in plastic cups and several packets of bourbons.

Seeing me, he shouts, 'Joe Porter, back from the dead! It must be a miracle.'

I can't help laughing. 'Rumours of my resurrection have been greatly exaggerated.'

Roy beams. 'Anyway, Joe – what brings you along here today?'

'You! You said to pop in some time and see what your kids' club is like.'

'You know, Dorothy will be so pleased. She's been praying for you for months.'

Life, God, something keeps on wrong-footing me. I probably deserve nothing from anybody. My other shortcomings apart, I have recently failed to look after my daughter and I came close to wrecking my marriage. But if there is one person from whom I'm certain I deserve nothing, it's Dorothy Wood. For as long as I have known her, I have judged Dorothy and, more often than not, been irritated by her. But it was Dorothy who provided the flat in Whalley Range and for all I know, Dorothy has been alone in praying for me during what must be my worst year ever. (I hope it's my worst year ever.)

A gang of excited kids flows through the open doorway. I recognise the uniforms of a couple of the local junior schools. Roy and Kat greet the kids, who look pleased to have reached this point in their day. I recognise two or three from when I did Kids' Church, Tracy among them.

She is taller than when I last saw her and maybe a little better turned out: plaits and a new-looking gold hair-band. Some of the reason she looks smarter is that she's in school uniform and in the days when I saw her regularly she was in threadbare mufti. At one point I catch her eye, smile and raise a hand in greeting. She smiles back uninhibitedly. No sign that she remembers how often I used to tell her off for being unpleasant to other kids. Sometimes you can't help thinking that kids are more gracious to adults than we deserve.

A hooter sounds loud over the P.A. – not any old hooter, but the kind you get on trains in old Mickey Mouse cartoons – and Kat Fuller is at the front, criss-crossing two chequered flags.

'Okay, guys,' she says. She has a lapel-mic and her voice fills the room. 'Time you lot started enjoying yourselves.'

Evening in the Porters' kitchen. Early days still for the mended Porter family. Molly is in bed, just, and her Mum and Dad are clearing up. As I stack dishes away in cupboards, Sarah makes a pot of tea.

'You remember what Naomi prayed for us that last time we went to the hospice?' she asks.

'About being living sacrifices – being poured out. I remember.' Of course I remember: the old woman's curse at the start of the fairy tale. By the end, it might just turn out to be a blessing. The Witch and the Fairy God-mother? What do you know, maybe they were the same person.

'But there was more, something about seeing how great God's love for us is.'

I stop what I'm doing, which leaves me turned to stone with a handful of clean mugs. 'I'd forgotten about that.'

Sarah sets the teapot on the table, we sit down and she pours.

The notion of seeing how great God's love for us is stirs up a few other things that have been on my mind. For instance, Dorothy's verses about the hard rock turning into springs of water. For instance, where God is when bad things happen to good people.

'I'm thinking of getting involved with Planet 9,' I say.

She looks at me, not exactly happy; it's still a long way from here to happy. She nods, looking away again.

I don't know that I've arrived as an adult just yet, but I can say I'm travelling. My priorities, once askew, are now in flux.

I took my two girls to the park and I only came back with one. I miss my other girl. I don't say God would cause a bad thing to happen so that a good thing could come out of it. No. However, I'm starting to suspect that when bad things happen to good people, somehow, in ways I don't begin to understand, God can bring good things out of them.

Acknowledgements

Very great thanks to Sue Little, Judith Murdoch and Jenny Newman. Warm thanks also to the writer's group we called Rosebuds (Julie Armstrong, Heather Leach and Helen Newall); Jeremy Thompson; Sarah Jones and Harold Thompson; Andy Butler, Gill Davies, John Simons, Julia Hedley and Alistair McCulloch at Edge Hill, where the Research Development Fund kindly released me from some teaching while I was writing this book; Edge Hill Creative Writing students; Roger Webster at Liverpool John Moores University; Harold Graham; Rachel, Poppy and Noah Graham. And, like the singer at the Grammies in the Loudon Wainwright song (who cited his producer and Jesus Christ), I'm thanking the Lord, the closest friend a boy can have.